I0692790

Threads of Fate

A STEP TOO FAR

TOM CRAMPTON

ENTWINED PUBLISHING

A Step Too Far
ISBN # 978-1-80250-247-3
©Copyright Tom Crampton 2025
Cover Art by Kelly Martin ©Copyright April 2025
Interior text design by Entwined Publishing
Published by Echoes, an Entwined Publishing imprint

Published in 2025 by Entwined Publishing, United Kingdom.

Entwined Publishing is a division of Totally Entwined Group Limited.

A STEP TOO FAR

Dedication

For Tim Mahoney.

There isn't enough room here to list all the reasons why this book is for you, but it must be said that this series of books wouldn't exist if you hadn't taken me on that glorious trip to Laguna Beach all those years ago.

Entwined Publishing books by Tom Crampton

Threads of Fate
A Different Corner
A Step Too Far

Acknowledgements

I wanted to extend my sincere thanks to the following people for all of their help, advice and support during the writing of this book—Jack Walters, Hannah Shearer, Paul Thrussell, and Bill Portlock.

Special thanks to Gabe Gane and my editor Anna Olson for steering me back onto the right path when the original draft veered off in another direction.

Thank you to everyone at Entwined Publishing for their continued support and encouragement.

Finally, my love and gratitude go to my husband Charlie Gitura Yates for keeping me sane and grounded, whilst always managing to make me laugh and smile.

Chapter One

Alex was disgusted with himself. He'd been living alone in Los Angeles for six years now and he still hadn't learnt to cook. Although he was able to afford to eat out every night, what shamed him the most was the guilt that every evening he'd come home to the new house he'd bought about a year ago, stomach full, and saunter into his gleaming, unused, state-of-the-art kitchen only to leave after retrieving a glass of wine. Last week, one evening after work, resolute to prove to himself that cooking couldn't be that difficult, he'd stopped off at a supermarket and bought ingredients to prepare a basic meal that his secretary at work had assured him *anyone* could cook. The end result wasn't pretty to look at and had a funny smell, but he ate it and congratulated himself on his efforts after each mouthful. Two days later, Alex was well enough to leave the confines of his bedroom with its en-suite bathroom, and return to work. Never one to back down from a challenge, Alex was now even more determined to master even basic culinary skills. After considering the options available to him, he decided on another course of action. Who'd have thought that shame could be such a wonderful motivator?

* * * *

The last time Alex had been this nervous was on his first day starting a new job after finishing university. After scanning the map of the building displayed on a wall in the foyer, he took the stairs two at a time up to the fourth floor, cursing the early evening traffic that had made him late. Once he found the right room, he cracked open the door of the cookery class and peered in. A group of women were inside, spread out along three rows, each one behind an individual cooking station. They were talking animatedly to each other as they unpacked groceries. Having second thoughts, Alex pulled the door closed. Before he could step away, the door was yanked back open by a diminutive skinny lady whose head was crowned with an impressive silver-grey afro.

"Tell me," she said, her grave tone rooting Alex to the spot. "Are you here to cook, or are you one of those types that likes to peep at women without them seeing?"

Alex shook his head and meekly held up his carrier bag of ingredients, his ticket for admission. The woman harrumphed, then waved him inside. Alex stepped into the room and counted eleven women in total. They turned and greeted him with a chorus of friendly hellos. Alex nodded at them in polite acknowledgement and let the skinny lady escort him to a vacant spot at one end of the third and final row. He turned to smile at his neighbour and was astonished to find he'd been mistaken.

"Thank God. I thought I was the only man here." Alex sighed and let his shoulders relax. He laughed weakly, embarrassed by his transparent display of relief.

The man chuckled and leaned closer, extending his right hand. "Don't worry, they don't bite. I'm Luis."

Alex shook his hand, disarmed by the warm welcome and Luis' chestnut-brown eyes, the edges of which crinkled with apparent amusement. "My name's Alex. It's a pleasure to meet you."

Luis cocked his head. "Do I detect an English accent?"

Alex grinned sheepishly. "Is it that obvious?"

Luis opened his mouth to reply, but the skinny lady standing at the front of the room clapped her hands together to get everyone's attention. The room fell silent under her glare.

Throughout the class, Alex sneaked occasional furtive glances at Luis. Besides being tall and slim, Luis carried himself with a fluid elegance. Each movement flowed into the next. There was no stiffness or awkward pauses. Alex suspected he might be a dancer, although he looked too old to still be in that profession. It soon became apparent that this was not Luis' first lesson. Alex shifted his eyes up from the knife that Luis was using with practiced ease to concentrate on the man himself. The olive-copper tones of Luis' skin glowed under the fluorescent lights overhead, hinting at Latin American descent. His tightly curled black hair was cropped short and clung closely to his scalp. Distinguished smears of grey gathered at his temples, complemented by a dusting of salt and pepper stubble that covered his jaw. A sharp tap on Alex's shoulder demanded his attention. He turned to find the instructor standing next to him. She pointed at Alex's saucepan on top of the stove. Something was burning.

* * * *

At the end of his first lesson, Alex was surprised that the instructor hadn't taken him to one side and suggested that it would be best if he didn't come back. Not only had he ruined a perfectly good saucepan, but he'd added far too much salt to his dish, rendering it inedible. Not even Luis' covertly whispered instructions and advice, offered only when the teacher's back was turned, could save the day. Afterwards, Luis tried to be encouraging, for which Alex was grateful. He had even been brave enough to taste the ruined meal. Moments later though, Alex had caught him discreetly spitting the mouthful of food into a bin.

* * * *

Alex couldn't really say that he was surprised at himself for turning up undeterred at the following week's lesson. He'd been intrigued by Luis and his friendly nature, and had plucked up the courage to attend once more in the hope that he was there again. The second class had ended with them both sharing a bowl of Alex's Italian tomato soup. Alex had flushed when Luis loudly declared that it was a culinary triumph. By the end of the first month, it was evident how well they got on, and the two of them lingered in the corridor after each lesson, chatting back and forth before they made their way down and out of the building. Two months later, after a lesson that culminated in Alex burning one of his fingers, Luis suggested that they go for a quick drink — something to deaden the pain. They picked the first bar that they came to, a few doors down the street. Inside, it was gloomy, anonymous and devoid of character. For Alex, it was a far cry from the British pubs he'd visited whilst a student. They approached the bar.

"Let me guess," said Luis, turning to Alex. "Are you a whiskey man?"

Alex smiled and shook his head. "Sorry. The last time I drank whiskey was in England." An unpleasant memory surfaced unbidden. "It left a bad taste in my mouth," he added.

"How about a beer then?"

"Sure."

Luis turned to the barman and ordered. Alex walked over to a corner table away from the bar. The place was empty, but he didn't want to sit where they could be overheard. While he waited, Alex carefully unwrapped the damp paper towel from around his burnt finger. He couldn't believe that he'd accidentally pressed it against the inside of the oven whilst putting a dish inside to warm. The skin was blistered down one side. He flexed it experimentally and winced.

Luis arrived with the beers. He sat down and reached out across the table. "Let's have a look." He carefully took Alex's hand in his own and turned it back and forth in the dim light. "That looks painful, but at least the skin isn't broken. There's a pharmacy further down the block. Shall I go and see if they have any bandages?"

"I'm fine, really," Alex replied, pulling his hand free. "I've got some at home. Besides, this will help." He picked up one of the bottles of beer and pressed it against his finger. The cold beads of condensation reduced the pain to a dull throb.

"Well, okay," said Luis, looking doubtful. He glanced around then leaned forward towards Alex. "I don't think much of this place," he added in a hoarse whisper.

Alex took a long swig from the bottle. "At least the beer's good." He stifled a sudden belch. "Excuse me." Alex leant back in his chair and grinned at Luis. He held up his injured hand. "I wonder what will go wrong next week? Maybe I'll inadvertently give everyone food poisoning?"

Luis smiled briefly. "Yeah, about that..." He shifted in his chair. "There's something I need to tell you."

Alex's grin faded.

"I'm moving away from Pasadena soon and won't be able to attend the classes anymore. I've bought a place further down the coast. Have you ever visited Laguna Beach?"

"No, I haven't," replied Alex. He tried to maintain a neutral expression. "How long have you been planning this?" Luis didn't answer and looked away. Alex apologised. "I'm sorry, that's none of my business."

"It's okay." Luis fiddled with the label on his bottle of beer. "I'm sorry, too. I should have told you sooner."

Alex shook his head and took another swig of beer before replying. "No, you weren't under any obligation to." He smiled at Luis, hoping that it didn't appear too forced. "Congratulations. I'm pleased for you."

Luis looked relieved. "We can still hang out, you know." He nodded enthusiastically, as if the idea had just occurred to him. "Once I've moved in, why don't you drive down and visit? Come for supper. We could cook it together."

Alex burst out laughing. "What, and risk me burning your new house down?"

"I mean it," said Luis softly.

Alex was silent for a moment before replying. "I know. Thank you. I will, I promise."

* * * *

September 1987

Alex ambled along the curving wooden boardwalk until he found an empty bench facing the ocean. He'd arrived early this morning so he could sit here for a bit. Luis would be along soon and they would go to the food market to buy ingredients for lunch and dinner. It was a warm, balmy day which was a respite from the recent long hot summer. This was only his second time here visiting Luis since he'd moved to Laguna Beach in early August. Even though it was a two-hour drive down, it was nice to get out of LA. Alex's favourite part was turning off the freeway and driving down the long winding Laguna Canyon Road, which ended at a junction, where — without warning — the sea was damn well straight in front. Once Alex had discovered that Luis was in fact an artist and not a dancer, he could appreciate why Luis had moved from Pasadena to the more bohemian Laguna Beach. Having grown up by the sea in Hastings, back in England, Alex understood all too well the call of the ocean, even though both places were worlds apart. In front of him, the waves rolled in and the surf thundered up the glittering yellow beach.

Alex couldn't ignore that there was now a sadness attached to being close to the ocean once more. In the six years he'd lived in Los Angeles, Alex had never visited the coast. He occasionally tried to convince himself that it hadn't been intentional, but in retrospect, it was pointless trying to pretend otherwise. The prospect of seeing Luis again after he had moved to Laguna Beach had reunited him with the sea after so long apart. On his first visit, they had walked for what seemed like hours along the beautiful golden beach that stretched away into the haze. Alex had revealed to Luis that he had grown up in the coastal town of Hastings. He never liked to talk about his old life and had only told Luis fragments, mentioning briefly that he was divorced and had a son back in England. Spending time with Luis was calming. In his presence there was a natural equilibrium in the space around him, which invited Alex to open up. Luis had asked him to describe Hastings. Alex could remember pointing down at Luis' feet and the battered sandals he liked to wear.

"Living in Hastings was like wearing a favourite old pair of shoes. Still comfortable to walk around in, although to look at they're now faded, scuffed and tired." Luis had turned to him and smiled, but reflected in his eyes had been an element of sadness. Alex had never forgotten what Luis said next.

"Why do you always seem a little lost and alone? I think you're carrying a lot of baggage on your shoulders. I can see it weighing you down. I hope that maybe one day you'll trust me enough to let me in."

A voice called his name, breaking his train of thought. Alex turned around and looked back towards the road where Luis was waving at him from the pavement. He waved and stood. The ocean could wait. It would always be there if he ever needed it. Right now though, there was someone he wanted to be with. Someone he hoped over time would give him so much more.

* * * *

"What do you think?" asked Luis as they paused on the pavement outside his new house.

"You've had it painted," exclaimed Alex, setting down the bags of groceries at his feet. "It's very blue," he said, admiring the wooden façade. "But I love it."

Luis grinned at him and pointed at the China-blue-painted exterior. "Well, over the years all the wood had been bleached by the sun. I thought it needed some love."

"It looks fantastic," Alex assured him, wishing that he were bold enough to make such a colourful statement inside his home back in Calabasas, where the decor was muted and tasteful, yet bland. "I can't wait to see what you do with the front garden."

Luis opened the gate set into the white picket fence that bordered the front of the property. They walked up the short path that bisected the small overgrown lawn—the front garden was currently a blank canvas requiring attention. Inside, chaos reigned supreme. All along the hallway, different-sized artworks were stacked on the floor, leaning against the walls. A few pieces had been hung, seemingly at random. Alex followed Luis through to the kitchen, being mindful not to let the shopping bags brush up against the fragile pictures. As they entered, the bleached wooden floorboards creaked pleasingly underfoot.

"Still unpacking, I see?" said Alex, stating the obvious. Around him, piles of boxes covered the floor and occupied every available kitchen surface.

Luis looked sheepish and shrugged. "I try to do a box or two every day. You know how it is."

Alex chuckled but didn't say anything. If this was his house, he wouldn't have been able to have a restful first night's sleep here until everything had been unpacked and put away.

"I suppose if we're going to make some lunch, I'd better clear some space," said Luis. He gazed around the room and frowned.

Alex could tell that Luis didn't have a clue where to start. "To be honest, I think that just moving boxes around isn't going to solve the problem. Why don't you let me help you? Let's unpack some of them and put stuff away. Then eventually we might discover a kitchen underneath it all."

Luis laughed good-naturedly. "You're right. I'm a nightmare. I can't believe I've been here for over a month. The problem is that I get easily distracted."

"Well, that's not going to happen today," said Alex, ripping the tape off a sealed box sitting on top of the sink drainer. He peered inside. "Saucepans. Where would you like these to live?" One glance at the panicked expression on Luis' face told him everything he needed to know. It was going to be a long morning.

* * * *

Luis hung the ticking wooden clock on the hook above the kitchen door and stepped back. "I think that's level."

"Where the hell did you buy that?" asked Alex, eyeing the ugly clock that resembled a birdhouse.

"Oh, I forget now, but as soon as I saw it I had to have it." Luis turned to Alex and held his hand up. "Listen, it's about to chime the hour."

They both fell silent and stared at the clock. After a long pause, the minute and hour hands struck midday. A tiny door opened above the clock face revealing a miniature, crudely carved wooden bird. The call of a

18

cuckoo sounded twelve times. Luis clapped his hands together once in delight. Alex raised his eyebrows at him and shook his head.

"Oh, I know, it's incredibly kitsch, but that's part of its charm," explained Luis.

"And there I was thinking that you were a man of taste," Alex said in a deadpan voice.

Luis grabbed a nearby tea towel and swatted him with it. "I'm sure that when you finally get around to inviting me to your house, I'll find something on display there that is offensive to the eye."

"Well good luck searching, but you'll be hard pressed to find anything as awful as that clock," teased Alex, moving back out of striking distance.

Luis tossed the tea towel onto the empty kitchen countertop. "You're probably right." He turned in a full circle. "I can't believe you unpacked everything and found space for it all."

Alex folded the last empty cardboard box flat and stacked it with the others in the small walk-in larder. "Hey, it was a two-man job. Plus I was getting hungry."

Luis walked over to the kitchen table, its surface now clear except for the shopping bags from earlier. "Me, too. I'll make us a quick salad to go with the cheese and cold cuts." He paused in exploring the contents of the shopping bags and looked over at Alex. "I really do appreciate your help. You didn't have to. You've been working all week."

"I wanted to," replied Alex. "In fact, in some perverse sort of way, I actually enjoyed it." There was something that he liked about the warmth in Luis' gaze.

"You're a strange man, Alex Spencer," Luis remarked. "I guess that's why we get on so well."

* * * *

Lunch was served outside in the back garden, beneath an ancient eucalyptus tree which was the centrepiece of the space. The ground beneath it was laid with square tiles that radiated out in concentric circles from around the base of the tree. Weeds and yellowing grass grew out of the cracks where the tiles joined one another. The old, rusted garden furniture they had unearthed from inside the dusty garage bore their weight, and a clean paper tablecloth added to the sense of occasion.

Alex spooned salad leaves onto his plate. "This is nice." He gestured to the gnarled branches overhead that cast gently moving shadows across the table. "I like it out here. Would you agree that it's more of a courtyard than a garden?"

"I guess so," replied Luis as he poured them both some homemade lemonade. "It's a bit too minimalist for me at the moment," he added, handing Alex a glass. "I'll buy some large pots and fill them with plants. That'll soften the edges."

Luis sat down and helped himself to a wafer-thin slice of pastrami. "Alex, there's something I wanted to ask you. We've known each other for a while now, so I didn't think you'd be offended if I told you that as a rule, I don't tend to invite strangers into my home. Seeing that you're also going to be staying for dinner, I was wondering if you'd indulge me and tell the story about how you came to be here. In the past six months, all I really know about you is that you grew up by the sea in England. You were married, then divorced and you have a son. Somehow you ended up living in LA and working in, what did you say, aviation?"

"I actually used to specialise in aeronautical research, but I now work more in the field of astronautics." Judging by Luis' glazed expression, Alex decided that now was not the time for specifics. "I suppose aviation will do." He put down his cutlery and patted the sides of his mouth with a napkin.

"Please don't think I'm trying to pry," interrupted Luis hastily. "I respect your privacy. It's just that I'd like to get to know you better."

"Of course I don't think that," said Alex, waving the suggestion away. "I do have to say that there's also a lot about you that I don't know. You were born in Mexico City, although you had to move around a lot due to your dad's work." Alex extended one finger of his right hand up in the air. "You discovered you were gay when you were a teenager." Two fingers. "Then you graduated from the California College of Arts and haven't looked back since." Three fingers. "That's pretty much all I know, except that you're also a far better cook than I am."

Luis grinned and looked abashed. "Touché. Is that really all I've told you? So what on earth have we been talking about over the last six months?" He let loose a loud burst of laughter.

"I've no idea," replied Alex, unable to hide his smile. Luis' laughter was infectious, and he couldn't help but join him.

Luis wiped his eyes with the back of his hand. "Well, maybe it's about time we stopped being strangers and filled in the gaps by elaborating a bit? You tell me about growing up in Hastings, and I'll tell you about moving to LA." He picked up his glass of lemonade and held it out in front of him. "Deal?"

Alex clinked his own glass against Alex's. "Deal, although I have to warn you that most of it was incredibly boring and you'll soon regret having asked me."

Luis picked up his fork and speared a cherry tomato on his plate. He examined it critically before popping it in his mouth. "Let me be the judge of that," he said, in between chewing. "Tell me a bit about your parents and what it was like living by the sea."

Alex sat still for a moment as he considered what to say. "Actually, I was raised for the most part by my aunt," he began slowly. "It's funny, but whilst I was growing up in Hastings, I never gave the town a second thought. It was only after I left for college that I would look forward to returning there."

Chapter Two

December 1959

Although the remains of a coal fire glowed in the small grate, the single-paned window was brutally inefficient at keeping the cold out. Alex shivered and stirred the embers with a poker. He hated English winters. The off-white net curtain swayed slightly as eddies of cold air blew through tiny gaps in the window frame. *I mustn't complain – I'm one of the lucky ones*, Alex reminded himself. Horror stories abounded from other students complaining about having no heating at all in their lodgings or sub-standard cooking facilities. The room was functional. That was the only word that had come to mind when Alex had first been shown it by his landlady Mrs Ellis. There was a single bed pressed up against a corner of the room, with overly starched bed linen, the colours bleached and pale from countless washes. To the right of the window stood a thin tall wardrobe made of dark wood, and against another wall was a chest of drawers, its wooden surface pitted and scarred with watermarks and stains. It was the small fireplace that had swayed Alex. Being slight in frame, he was prone to the cold. The thought of studying in here whilst the shadows of the flames in the grate danced as they were cast onto the bare walls of the room, had entranced him. As a child, he'd been forbidden from wandering too close to the fire on the rare occasion his mother lit one, so to have his own would be a novelty. He'd said yes to the room and moved in that day.

Alex returned to his desk, which was a recent addition. When he wasn't attending the College of Aeronautics in the nearby village of Cranfield, he'd needed somewhere to study. Spending his free time holed up in a local library hadn't appealed to him. There were too many distractions, so buying a desk had been the next logical step. He looked at the piles of textbooks and sheets of paper filled with calculations and his familiar, small, neat handwriting. His eyes hurt. It was time for a break. He'd been studying all evening. Alex's stomach rumbled loudly. He hadn't eaten since lunchtime. The alarm clock by his bed read nine-thirty. Mrs Ellis had prepared him something to eat earlier. Although it cost a bit extra each week when he paid his rent, Alex was glad that he had accepted his landlady's offer of an evening meal each night.

Out on the landing, Alex paused and listened. There was no sound or movement coming from the floor above. That wasn't unusual. The only other lodger had the room on the second floor and was barely ever there. Alex had once politely said good evening to the stranger after walking into the gloomy kitchen downstairs and finding him sitting at the table, eating. He had immediately retreated back upstairs to his room, not wanting to engage in pleasantries. Since then, they had passed occasionally on the stairwell, both murmuring apologies for blocking each other's path. Alex had no idea what the man did, and when questioned, Mrs Ellis was none the wiser.

"As long as I get me rent, his business is none of mine," Mrs Ellis had said. "That's a lesson you'd be wise to learn from, don't you think?"

Alex had apologised. He hadn't meant to pry. It was just mildly disconcerting sharing a house with a stranger. The man was older, probably in his mid-thirties, guessed Alex, who was only nineteen. As for Mrs Ellis, her age was a complete conundrum. Further along the landing, Alex passed the bathroom and stopped at the top of the stairs. Behind him was the door to Mrs Ellis's bedroom which was at the front of the house, the door always firmly shut. The muted sound of the television downstairs drifted up the stairwell. His landlady spent every evening in the front room glued to her favourite shows. Alex descended the carpeted staircase and went back down the hall to the kitchen. It was immaculate, with everything in its place. Mrs Ellis was very house proud, and there was always a duster tucked into her apron.

Inside the now cool oven was a plate with a couple of sausages and a grey mound of mashed potato marooned in a thin sea of gravy. It had gone cold. Alex didn't mind. Food was food. He'd never really had any interest in it apart from using it to fuel his body. He grabbed some cutlery from a drawer, sat down at the small table and began to mechanically shovel food into his mouth. He'd eaten far worse, and sometimes had gone without. When he was growing up, after his father had died, his mother's funny little episodes increased in frequency. Sometimes she would forget to cook, and he would be forced to feed himself. Looking back, he couldn't remember the number of times he had ended up eating small portions of dried breakfast cereal or a couple of crackers as he sat on the floor of the mostly bare larder whilst his mother lay in a darkened room overhead.

Back upstairs, Alex decided against another hour of study. There was always tomorrow evening. He crossed to the window and lifted the net curtain. There was condensation on the glass which he wiped with the heel of his hand. Outside, the street was wet and uninviting. The glass shivered in its frame as a gust of wind beat upon it. Alex had been lodging here for three months, but he had yet to venture outside and explore Milton Keynes properly. So far, he had only wandered as far as the local shops, and to walk daily to the bus stop that ferried him on the nine-mile journey from here to Cranfield College and back. What he'd seen so far hadn't excited him, and he preferred to spend his evenings and weekends in his room studying. He liked his own company, and Mrs Ellis let him be.

Alex decided on an early night. He scooped up his wash bag and walked down the hall to the communal bathroom. Once finished, he returned to his room and undressed. Lying in bed staring at the ceiling, Alex cast himself back to when he was younger, and recalled a moment when he was only nine years old, realising that for the first time, he couldn't remember what his father looked like anymore. Like yesterday, he could remember the younger version of himself lying in bed, concentrating hard, his face scrunching up with the effort. The military uniform came to mind easily enough. The brown-green woollen fabric had always felt thick and coarse against his small fingers when he was little and his father had picked him up. He was tall in stature, and Alex used to have to crane his head back to look up at him. Now though, his father's face remained hidden in shadow beneath the brim of his military hat, with no defining features visible.

"You look so much like your father," his mother had been fond of saying.

Alex found this comforting, and always recalled her words when he looked at his reflection and saw his own blue eyes regarding himself. Blond hair crowned his head, styled with a meticulously neat side parting. The sides and back were trimmed short. Although his unlined skin was pale, a rosebud of red always stood out on each cheek, whatever the weather. He drew his left hand out from under the covers and ran it over the dusting of fine stubble that covered his chin and just above his upper lip. It was too fair to be noticeable, but he shaved it off every morning, as he hated the feel of it on his face. Alex's eyelids grew heavy. In his mind's eye, he could still see his reflection. He smiled. Seeing himself always reminded him that somewhere deep inside, a little part of his father remained.

The bedside alarm was shrill, and always woke Alex with a start. He lay there for a moment, allowing the last vestiges of sleep to fade away. Leaving the warm confines of the bed was always a struggle on these cold dark winter mornings. Alex sighed and threw back the covers. It was always better to get his morning bathroom routine out of the way as quickly as possible. He gazed at the fireplace longingly. The small mound of ash sat forlornly in the bottom of the grate. Tonight, Alex promised himself, he would stop off on the way home and buy some more coal. If he didn't keep warm, then he was likely to catch a cold, which was the last thing he needed. His mother had always told him that he was a sickly child, prone to illness. Alex grabbed his towel that was hanging on the back of the door. It still felt slightly damp from yesterday. He hurried down the hall in his pyjamas to the freezing bathroom where he showered quickly and efficiently. Once dressed, Alex gathered up his study papers from his desk and stuffed them inside his leather satchel. He removed his scarf and overcoat from the wardrobe. It was time to go. As he descended the stairs, Mrs Ellis came out of the kitchen, the sound of the radio audible behind her.

"Mr Spencer? There's some tea left in the pot. Have you got time for a cuppa?"

Alex looked at his watch and resisted the urge to smile. He could spare five minutes. This was one of Mrs Ellis's little tricks, used to corner him whenever she needed a word.

"Thank you, Mrs Ellis. That would be lovely."

He followed her into the kitchen where she gestured at one of the kitchen chairs. Following her cue, Alex sat down and picked up the brimming teacup in front of him. Mrs Ellis looked on with apparent satisfaction as he sipped from it.

"I wish you'd consider me providing you with a breakfast each morning, Mr Spencer," Mrs Ellis complained. "A young man like you can't go off to college every day with no food in his stomach. I doubt you would notice the few extra pennies it would cost."

Alex had heard this before. He wasn't sure if she was just being motherly, or just trying to bleed some extra money out of him. Since lodging here, he had always found Mrs Ellis to be a bit of an enigma.

"Honestly, Mrs Ellis, I'm fine. I never feel hungry in the morning. I prefer to wait till lunchtime."

She shook her head, clearly exasperated with his obstinacy. "My husband, God rest his soul, never went a day without breakfast."

Well, look where that got him, Alex wanted to reply, but didn't. She meant well, but sometimes he found their battle of wills to be exhausting. He imagined that her husband must have been a quiet man who allowed her to rule the roost. Anything for a quiet life.

"Maybe after the Christmas holidays, we could come to some new arrangement for weekends?" he conceded. "I would have more time on Saturday and Sunday mornings to eat something then."

Mrs Ellis brightened considerably and unfolded her crossed arms. Alex didn't begrudge her trying to eke out a living, and she was certainly no battle axe. Although she looked formidable, he suspected otherwise. Squat and rotund, she lacked any feminine curves in her barrel-like form, but Alex would never have described her as fat. Apparently, she and her husband had owned a bakery together, and her meaty forearms were testament to years of kneading dough. Her face was plain and fleshy, but Alex admired the way she always wore a little bit of makeup around her eyes and a different dress each day, revealing her short legs covered by brown stockings and upon her feet the same battered pair of house slippers.

"Ah yes, when will you be heading off home then?" she asked.

"I was hoping to travel around the twentieth. I'll be gone about two weeks. Are you sure you're still happy to keep my room for me?"

"Don't you worry yourself, Mr Spencer. As I said before, as a long-term lodger, I'll always hold your room for you." She picked up his empty teacup and crossed to the sink.

"Thank you, Mrs Ellis. That's good to know." Alex reached down for his satchel which was leaning against the chair and stood up. "I'd best be on my way. I'll see you this evening, and thanks for the tea."

Mrs Ellis looked around and nodded at him before returning to the other dishes in the sink. Alex opened the front door and stepped out onto the pavement. It was another grey, grim, featureless day. At least it wasn't raining. *One must always consider the positives in life*, he told himself as he set off at a brisk pace towards the bus stop.

As the bus wound through the back roads towards the college, Alex rested his forehead against the cold window, his breath fogging the glass. His thoughts strayed towards his mother. Although she had passed away five years ago, it was as if she had never left him. At times he resented her intrusion inside his head, but usually it was a source of comfort. Although he had been too young to have received any paternal advice from his father, his mother had more than made up for it with her relentless pursuit of his well-being. At times though, he'd felt suffocated and cosseted by her good intentions. It was as if she wanted to hide him away from the dangers rife in the outside world. Following the death of his father, Alex remembered experiencing bewilderment at the sudden change in his mother. Her dark fugue states were infrequent at first, but over time they increased in regularity. Alex had to wait till he was much older to finally understand what had happened and the dreadful toll it had wrought upon his mother.

Aunt Edith, who he would be travelling to spend the Christmas holidays with, had intervened when he was nine years old and turned up at their home, insisting, quite vehemently, that her sister and nephew come and live with her by the coast in Hastings where they would be properly cared for. Alex drew the outline of a tall thin house in the condensation on the window. It was four storeys high, grand and imposing to the young boy who'd stood on the street outside the front garden gate, looking up at its façade for the first time. The transition to the town of Hastings had never bothered the younger Alex. He'd had no real friends at his old school that he would miss and kept very much to himself at the new one. He was with his mother. That was all that mattered. Alex stepped off the bus after murmuring his thanks to the driver. He watched it depart before crossing the road and hurrying through the entrance to Cranfield College. He was home. This was where he was happiest, content to lose himself in the study of the laws of maths and physics, and the complexities of flight.

* * * *

The next ten days passed quickly in a haze of completing end of term papers. He'd walked out of the college on the last day, surrounded by his fellow students who were all jubilant at the prospect of going home. Alex was always in two minds whenever he travelled back to Hastings. The town would remind him of the tragedy of his mother's final years and the fear and helpless trust he had for Aunt Edith who'd taken on the mantle of his upbringing. But then again, it was his true home – a place where he was safe and had a sense of belonging. He settled back in his seat, getting comfortable. The journey was going to take well over three hours. The station guard's whistle sounded, and the train juddered forward. Leaving the college behind always pained him. Not only had he found a subject that he was good at, but it was also something he actively enjoyed. The first year had not been without its trials. Alex had found it disconcerting living on campus in the halls of residence, thrown together with a lot of young men from all corners of the country. He had politely declined invitations to socialise with his different study groups, and after the first term they had stopped asking. Now he had the best of both worlds, lodging with Mrs Ellis and taking the bus to and from college. Privately he was dreading the end of his course. After three years of study, not knowing what followed next terrified him. The future was unknown, and Alex feared what was hidden on the road ahead. It had happened to him before. He and his mother had been living in Aunt Edith's house for about a year when his world changed overnight. He found it strange that now, years later, he could remember the conversation almost word for word, yet he still could not recall his father's face.

* * * *

November 1949

It had been stormy that day, and once home from school, Alex peeled off his damp blazer and walked through the empty kitchen to the large adjoining conservatory where he perched on the edge of a rattan chair and listened to the rain hammering against the glass roof. He'd always found it comforting to sit in there when it was raining, warm and dry, sheltered from the elements. Aunt Edith suddenly appeared, standing in the doorway.

"Do you know what you remind me of, sitting in here so quietly?"

Alex shook his head. She walked closer towards him.

"You remind me of the eye of a hurricane. Do you know why?"

Again, Alex remained silent. Aunt Edith was now standing over him. She bent forward and placed her hands on her knees.

"Because the eye is always at the centre of a hurricane, and there it is always calm. Just like you, sitting here, whilst the storm rages outside." She reached a hand towards him. "Come with me, Alex. Let's go into the back parlour where it's quieter. I want to have a little talk with you."

Dutifully he took her hand and allowed her to lead him out of the conservatory and down a short hallway. The back parlour was a room that he was not allowed into. His mother had told him that Aunt Edith used it as her quiet space reserved for reading, knitting and listening to the wireless. It was a small room without much furniture. Two armchairs were arranged at angles to each other in front of a fireplace. She guided him to one of the chairs and he sat down, enjoying the heat from the coal fire on his bare legs. Aunt Edith sat down in the other chair. Beside her, on the floor, Alex noticed a sewing box perched on stubby looking legs. Next to that was a small round wicker basket that overflowed with balls of wool. Above the mantelpiece was a large oil painting of two black horses racing along a moonlit beach, their hooves churning up the surf. The picture scared him a little, but he didn't know why. Maybe it was the horses. They both had foam flecks gathered at the corners of their mouths and a crazed wide-eyed stare that seemed to follow him around the room.

He turned his attention back to Aunt Edith, who was regarding him strangely. She looked sad. He could now see why she was his mother's sister. His mother wore a similar expression most of the time. Aunt Edith was taller though, wore makeup and dressed in fancy clothes. She scared him, and Alex made sure to keep out of her way and spent most of his time in his attic room at the top of the house. He was certain that she had put him up there because she didn't like little boys, even though she had told him that the reason was that his mother needed peace and quiet in her bedroom on the first floor.

"Do you know what is wrong with your mother?" asked Aunt Edith.

"She's still sad that Daddy died in the war," replied Alex, looking away and into the flames in the grate.

Aunt Edith was quiet for a moment. "Yes, you're right. The thing is..." She paused, then shuffled forward in her seat and reached over to take one of Alex's hands in hers. "The thing is, your mother is not getting any better. In fact, she's been getting worse for a while now. I've been speaking to some doctors—"

"Do they know how to make Mummy happy again?" Alex interrupted, then looked down at his lap, alarmed, as a flash of irritation crossed Aunt Edith's face. "Sorry," he whispered.

His aunt patted his hand and let it drop away. She sat back in her chair. "Listen Alex, sometimes people who are very sad end up hurting themselves. The doctors think your mother is in danger of hurting herself, too."

Alex frowned, not understanding. "You mean she could fall down the stairs or burn herself on the cooker?"

Aunt Edith sighed. "It's more serious than that, Alex. The doctors need to watch over your mother, just like she did when you were a baby sleeping in your cot, and they also need to give her medicine."

Alex sat quietly, absorbing this information. The doctors wanted to help his mummy. That was good. He liked it when she laughed and smiled. Instead, since moving here, she would spend most of her day in her room alone. Every day after school he would knock on her door and see if she was awake. Sometimes there was no answer. Other days she would send him away, pleading tiredness, and not feeling strong enough for visitors. Occasionally, if she was having a better day, she would invite him in, and he would kick his shoes off and scoot up onto the bed, where he would curl up next to her and she would stroke his hair as he told her about his day at school. Once he'd turned round to look at her as they both were lying there, and he saw tears on her cheeks. When he wiped them away and asked why she was crying, she had told him that they were happy tears and for him only. She had let him help her to sit up after that, plumping an extra pillow behind her back so that he could gently brush her long hair with the ornate hairbrush that rested on top of the dresser and that had once belonged to her mother.

"Can I see her?" he asked hopefully.

"Oh, Alex, listen. If the doctors are going to be able to help your mother, then they need her to be in a place where they can look after her night and day. They took her to a hospital nearby this afternoon where she will get the best help possible."

Alex looked around wildly. His mother was gone? He was all alone in this house with only his aunt to look after him. The heat from the fire was suddenly unbearably hot. A wave of nausea flooded his stomach. Alex stood up and abruptly bolted from the room. His aunt called out for him to come back, but he ignored her. He had to see for himself. Alex raced through the conservatory and kitchen, then along the wooden panelled front hall, his shoes squeaking on the polished parquet floor. Without stopping, he flung out a hand to grab the bottom of the banister and swung himself round and took the stairs two at a time. On the first-floor landing, he skidded to a halt outside his mother's bedroom. Alex reached out a tentative hand to the doorknob and turned it. He pushed, and the door swung soundlessly open. The bed was empty and freshly made. Alex stepped into the room and looked around. Everything seemed as it should be. He walked over to the chest of drawers and pulled the top drawer out. It was empty. Alex checked the others. All they contained was some floral scented lining paper. No clothes. He yanked open the wardrobe and stared at the naked wooden hangers. There was no sign that this was his mother's bedroom anymore. He sat on the side of the bed and glanced at the bedside table. Resting there was his mother's hairbrush. Alex picked it up and burst into tears. He slumped back onto the bed and curled himself into a ball, cradling the hairbrush to his chest. Keeping his voice as quiet as a whisper, Alex sang to himself the lullaby his mother used to sing to him when he was younger. His voice trembled and wavered until he finished the song. Once he was calmer, his breathing slowed as he imagined his mother murmuring his name whilst slowly stroking his soft blond hair. His eyes closed.

* * * *

September 1987

Luis remained silent after Alex stopped speaking. "That must've been tough," he said finally.

"It was a long time ago," replied Alex. "Things were different then."

"Even so…" began Luis, his voice trailing off.

Alex picked up his empty glass. "Do you have anything stronger? A beer would taste really good right now."

Luis nodded and pushed back his seat, wincing at the screeching of the chair legs scraping against the tiles. "One beer coming right up." He stacked up their plates and the wooden serving platter, now picked clean. "I'll be right back."

Alex waited until Luis walked back inside through the kitchen door. He exhaled loudly, as if he'd been holding his breath. Although it was a tired old cliché, the act of retelling a small, yet important part of his past to someone else, was a relief. Had he revealed too much? Luis quickly reappeared clutching two brown bottles of beer and set them down in front of Alex. He sat down and rested his hands on the table, his fingers interlaced together. "I want to apologise. I had no right asking you to reveal such painful memories." Luis bit his bottom lip and looked everywhere but at Alex.

Alex leaned forward and briefly gripped Luis' shoulder. "It's okay. Honestly. There's actually something quite cathartic about speaking about it." Luis didn't look convinced. Alex took a swig from his bottle. "I've started now, so let me finish telling you about that journey home for Christmas and the one time I visited my mother."

Luis raised a hand, palm out, towards Alex. "Really, you don't have to. I shouldn't have opened my stupid mouth. Let's just enjoy our beers."

Alex shook his head. "I've never talked about the past with anyone before, but you seem a good listener.

To be honest, it's strange that somehow, certain parts of my childhood remain as clear to me as yesterday."

Chapter Three

December 1959

The train pulled into Hastings Station, and Alex lifted his two suitcases from the luggage rack and disembarked with the other passengers. It was a bitterly cold day, yet outside the station, Alex paused to deliberate. He could take the quick route to the house, following a direct path through the back lanes, or succumb to the call of the sea, which was proving too irresistible to ignore. Whilst at college, the ocean was the only thing he pined for. It calmed him. When his mother had first been committed to hospital, Alex had sought solace in the sea, and with his aunt's permission, would sit for hours on the beach gazing at the undulating waves. It was a short walk down to the front where he sat on the low wall that separated the shingle beach from the pavement and road. The sound of the surf pounding the shore was music to his ears. Here and there, shafts of golden sunlight punched holes through the wispy clouds above him, creating pools of brilliance that sparkled and danced on the surface of the sea. He could feel his spirits lifting. Christmas was meant to be a time for families, coming together, so for Alex it was only natural that his spirits were at a low ebb around this time of year. He even suspected that his aunt was grateful for some company instead of rattling around inside her big old house alone. Apparently there were still some distant relatives dotted around, their link tenuous at best. The indifference and lack of communication from them didn't bother Alex. They had their own lives to lead.

It was time to head home. Alex picked up his cases and headed left along the beach front towards Hastings Old Town. Seagulls screeched and whirled overhead. People hurried past him, their heads down. Alex took his time, despite the chilly wind. Up ahead, set back on the beach, were the old familiar tall black timber storage sheds used by the local fishermen to hang their nets. As he drew closer, the wind carried on it the pungent aroma of fresh fish. Set amongst the wooden huts were fishmongers, hawking today's catch. Alex crossed over the road towards a gloomy narrow passage between two buildings. He glanced at the street sign on the wall which read 'Tamarisk Steps' and walked through the passage and up a small series of steps. Further on, more steps branched off to the right, leading him up higher and higher, until he emerged out onto a road. On his right was a set of railings that looked down over the black netting sheds and the beached fishing boats behind them. Up here in the old town, this high vantage point afforded him a view of the rest of Hastings, with the beach receding away into the distance on his right, the pier clearly visible, jutting out into the water. Alex walked up the road. On his left, in between the houses, he could glimpse the main town down below him, sat in a depression between two hills. He turned into a small cul-de-sac, and there at the end, was his aunt's house. The tall thin four-storey building looked strange standing alone.

Aunt Edith had told Alex how lucky she'd been as the house used to be part of a small terrace, but the other houses had been bombed during the war and never rebuilt. Only hers had been spared. The rubble had long been cleared, and nature had reclaimed the spaces, and Aunt Edith had scattered wildflower seeds and introduced other plants and shrubs over time, so the house now stood proud surrounded by a sea of colour for most of the year. Outside the front gate, Alex inspected the black iron railings that were his responsibility to paint every year once his aunt had trusted him with a paintbrush, because they were prone to rust from the salt in the sea air. The small front garden and surrounding foliage looked muted in December. Most of the plants were clipped back and hunkered down waiting for spring. To the right of the front door was a wooden veranda, currently empty of furniture.

For Alex, spring always officially became summer when Aunt Edith gravitated out here to sit and enjoy the balmy evenings. He opened the gate and struggled up the short path with his suitcases. The house key was in his pocket, but he thought it best to announce his arrival. He hadn't set foot inside for four months. It would be rude to just breeze in. Alex rapped the door knocker a couple of times, then stood back and waited. Eventually he heard movement in the hallway, and a bolt on the door was thrown back. It opened, revealing Aunt Edith looking resplendent and equally demure in a dark grey wool skirt and jacket. All she needed was a hat, and she was ready for a night at the theatre. Alex smiled, bemused that she always dressed so immaculately.

"Ah, you made it then. Good, good. Come on in. Don't let any of the heat out." Aunt Edith held the door open for him.

Alex let himself be ushered in and deposited his bags at the foot of the stairs. He'd learnt a long time ago that his aunt was not given to displays of affection, but it would've been nice to have had some physical acknowledgement that she was pleased to see him, even if it was just a brief pat on the shoulder. The last person to have hugged him had been his mother, and that was years ago now. He couldn't understand why most people were so repressed but had to admit that he was no different when the idea of cuddling a stranger filled him with such horror. Alex didn't need a psychiatrist to tell him that he still missed the reassuring touch of his mother. His aunt, though, was a closed book to him and always had been. Alex was certain that she loved him in her own unique way, and he guessed he loved her, too. After all, she was the only real family he had left.

"How have you been, Auntie?"

She batted away his question with a dismissive wave of her hand. "Take your bags up to your room, and then come through to the kitchen. I'll make us a nice pot of tea."

Alex did as he was told, and a few minutes later he descended the staircase back down to the front hall. He walked past the grandfather clock that still ticked sonorously. Nothing had changed since he was last here. In fact, nothing had changed since he'd first moved into this house with his mother, nearly a decade ago. The house, although narrow, was surprisingly deep, and to this day, Alex never understood why there were so many rooms that were disused, including the entire second floor, their doors shut for years on end.

Apart from Alex's bedroom in the attic, the bathroom and his aunt's bedroom on the first, the only other rooms used were on the ground floor. He slowed his pace as he passed a closed locked door. The room within housed a long wide dining table and chairs, all covered in dust sheets. On the other side of the hall was another door, behind which was an oak panelled formal sitting room, several walls covered with ceiling to floor shelving that housed assorted leather-bound hardback books, dictionaries and encyclopaedias. Empty comfortable wingback chairs waited in each corner.

A twinge of guilt prompted him to remember a time when he was younger. His aunt had gone out shopping, and his mother was sleeping. His curiosity about the locked doors had got the better of him, and he had crept into his aunt's bedroom and found a set of keys in a drawer of her dressing table. Emboldened with his discovery, he'd decided it was time to explore the locked rooms. Alex could remember the thrill of fear running through his body each time the key turned with a satisfying click and the door opened, allowing him to step into the past. The whistle of the kettle cut through his reverie and he hurried along to the kitchen where his aunt was waiting.

* * * *

Over the next few days Alex fell back into the old familiar routine he was used to. During the day he studied, only stopping to have a sandwich or soup for lunch. He would eat dinner with his aunt, who would then retire to her parlour afterwards. Sometimes he would spend the evening reading and taking notes from his copious collection of textbooks, or, depending on the weather, he would take an evening stroll along the seafront. Usually to the pier and back. Alex swore that a dose of sea air before bed helped him to sleep better. Some of his fellow students at college had been aghast when they asked him how many hours studying he did on average each week. It far exceeded their own, and Alex was amused by their reaction. Since he had moved into this house with his mother, Aunt Edith had started to become very attentive regarding his education. She would oversee his homework and attend parents evening at his new junior school, in place of his mother. After his mother was admitted to hospital—which Alex found out later in his teens was really an asylum—his aunt had informed him that she was going to send him to a private senior school when he was eleven, provided he passed the entrance exam. Alex was keenly aware that he wouldn't have gotten this far in life without her intervention. She never raised her voice at him or made threatening demands. Instead, all she possessed was a quiet, grim, steely insistence that he should maximise his potential in life, and Alex dutifully complied.

The call of the seagulls woke Alex on Christmas morning. He pulled back the curtains revealing a sun filled blue sky. It could've been mistaken for a summer's day if Alex hadn't pressed his fingers against the intensely cold pane of glass. Downstairs he walked into the kitchen where his aunt was busy making what looked like stuffing. She was dressed all in black. Her sombre blouse, cardigan and skirt looked out of place here, and for a second, Alex imagined her standing next to a coffin. Carols could be heard emanating from the wireless in the parlour.

"Merry Christmas, Auntie."

"Merry Christmas to you, Alex." She wiped her hands on a tea towel. "Now be a dear and help me by peeling the potatoes. I'll make us some tea and something for breakfast once we've prepared lunch."

Alex selected a peeler from the utensils drawer and took a saucepan and bag of potatoes over to the small kitchen table and sat down. Apart from the carols, there was no other indication that it was Christmas Day. His aunt never allowed a Christmas tree to be put up, citing an allergy to the needles. No Christmas cards were ever put on display. No wreath was hung on the front door. Any carol singers that visited were left outside, the front door unanswered. Alex didn't think it was an aversion to Christmas, but rather complete indifference.

* * * *

They ate in the conservatory with the sunlight pouring in overhead. Turkeys were still scarce, but Alex was happy to have chicken. Mrs Ellis never provided him with a roast dinner, so this was a treat indeed. There were no Christmas crackers on the table, and the only thing that marked the meal as a cause for celebration was a bottle of white wine which Aunt Edith asked Alex to open. Alex couldn't remember the last time he'd had any alcohol, and the couple of glasses he drank went straight to his head. For dessert, they each had a thin slice of spiced rum fruitcake. Although not much was said throughout the meal, Alex did not consider that the conversation was stilted. It was just that they were both not prone to small talk. After they'd finished, Alex cleared the table, whilst Aunt Edith washed up. Once the kitchen was sparkling and everything had been put away, he ran upstairs to his room to get something for his aunt, before she disappeared into the parlour. Back in the kitchen, breathing hard, Alex handed her a badly wrapped package.

"Merry Christmas, Auntie. I know we normally don't give each other presents, but I wanted to give you something to say thank you for all the help you've given me over the years." He glanced at the package held together with tape. "I'm sorry about my attempt to wrap it. It's much harder than it looks."

His aunt looked dismayed. "Oh, Alex, this is very naughty of you. In future, don't waste your money on me, understand?"

"Sorry, Auntie," he said, chastised.

Aunt Edith pulled at the wrapping with difficulty. "I think you were a little bit over-zealous with the tape." After a moment, the paper fell open revealing the contents. "Oh my…" she said softly.

Alex looked on, pleased at her reaction. "I hope you like them, Auntie. I know you like knitting and sewing, so I bought you some patterns so you can make yourself some new clothes. Seeing it's so cold at the moment, I thought warmer clothing would be better, so there's a whole selection, including shawls and cardigans."

Aunt Edith thumbed slowly though the assorted sewing and knitting patterns then looked up at Alex. "I don't know what to say, except thank you. This is an extremely thoughtful present."

Alex found her face difficult to read as she looked back down at the patterns, breaking eye contact. Her left hand reached under the right wrist of her cardigan sleeve and removed a concealed hanky. "If you don't mind, Alex, I have a couple of matters that I must attend to. Will you please excuse me?"

"Of course, Auntie."

She abruptly turned on her heels and walked quickly to the parlour, with the hand clutching the hanky brought up close to her face. Alex stood there alone. Her clipped footsteps stopped as the parlour door closed. Had he just inadvertently upset her? Alex let out a groan. He found women inexplicably complicated, especially emotionally, and was invariably intimidated in their company. It wasn't that they emasculated him, but rather it was because all the women he had met apart from his mother exuded a quiet confidence and strength of character that he was not sure he possessed.

* * * *

Alex woke with a start, breathing hard. It had been another bad dream about his mother. He lay there, his heart hammering in his chest. After his aunt's rather odd reaction to his present, he'd come back upstairs to his room and laid on the bed. He hadn't meant to fall asleep. Maybe it was because of the wine he'd drunk with lunch. Outside the bedroom window it was dark. His alarm clock read ten past seven. It was early evening. He must have been asleep for a few hours.

Alex had no problem recalling the details of the dream. It was always the same one—a variation on the theme of visiting his mother for the first time after she'd been admitted to hospital. He couldn't remember exactly how old he'd been. Maybe nine or nearly ten. In his eyes, still far too young to have been allowed admittance to such a place. At the time, his young mind had not feared hospitals, as they were a place where doctors and nurses made people feel better. His dogged insistence on seeing his mother must have worn Aunt Edith down enough for her to have arranged a visit. Alex was certain now that back then she had known that the place where his mother had resided was no place for a child to enter, but maybe she had her reasons for taking him.

* * * *

January 1950

It was a Saturday morning, a few months after Alex's mother had been admitted to hospital, when Aunt Edith unexpectedly announced that they were going to take a trip to see her. Alex was so surprised and excited that he threw his arms around his aunt's waist and hugged her. She gently pushed him away and told him to go and get ready as they would be leaving in five minutes. Alex had only one item he wanted to take — his mother's hairbrush. Upstairs in his bedroom, he removed it reverently from its place on his bedside table, and placed it in his school satchel, then slung the long strap over a shoulder before heading back downstairs. Aunt Edith was waiting for him in the hallway, and ushered him out of the front door and onto the street where her large, elegant car was parked.

It was a rare thrill to be allowed to sit in the front passenger seat. His legs only just touched the floor of the footwell, and he had to crane his neck to see fully out of the windscreen. The inside of the car was immaculate and smelled of polish and the leather seats. Aunt Edith handed him her handbag, then adjusted the rear-view mirror. She started the engine and manoeuvred the car smoothly out and onto the main road. The journey didn't take too long, and Alex stared out of the window in interest as the car turned down a driveway. Ahead he could see glimpses of a building hidden behind dense trees and shrubbery. As they approached the end of the drive, Aunt Edith slowed the car as it followed a graceful bend around to the right, opening up to reveal the frontage of a large ivy-clad country house.

"Here we are, Alex. Welcome to Horfield House."

In the centre of the turning circle in front of the house was an ornate water fountain. A stone nymph stood balanced on one foot, holding a jug outstretched in its arms, from which a constant stream of water poured into the wide basin below. Alex was confused. It didn't look like a hospital. He looked at his aunt in way of an explanation, but none was forthcoming. After she parked, he dutifully followed her towards the front entrance which was flanked by large stone pillars. The front door was wide open, and inside was a large wooden-panelled entrance hall. Aunt Edith guided Alex to a nearby bench and prompted him to sit. She then approached a long desk behind which a woman wearing a nurse's uniform sat and the two conferred in low voices.

"The doctor will be with us shortly," Aunt Edith said, joining Alex on the bench.

They sat patiently until finally a barrel-chested man, wearing a white doctor's laboratory coat over his checked shirt and tie, came bustling through a set of double doors behind the receptionist. He had a flaming orange beard that reminded Alex of the pirates on the front cover of the book *Treasure Island* that he had found recently in one of the bookcases in his aunt's seldom-used drawing room.

"I'm sorry to have kept you, madam and young sir. I'm Dr Campbell. You're here to visit Mrs Spencer, yes?"

Aunt Edith stood up and gestured for Alex to follow suit. "Yes, I'm her sister Edith and this is her son Alex. I phoned a few days ago." She clutched her handbag primly to her chest. "I trust that everything is in order?"

"Of course, allow me to take you to her," he replied smoothly.

They followed him though another set of doors that led along a quiet corridor, the silence broken by their footsteps on the wooden parquet floor.

"We like to keep our more pliant patients here in the old house," the doctor explained. "We have newer custom-built facilities in the grounds for our patients that require more attention." The doctor turned to Alex and reached out and ruffled his hair. "Your mother has been good as gold, laddie."

"So when can she come home?" Alex asked.

The doctor gave his aunt a dark glance and didn't answer. They walked on, turning corners and following the doctor down more corridors until he stopped abruptly outside a door.

"Shall the young man wait out here?" asked the doctor, indicating towards a couple of wooden chairs placed either side of the door to the room.

"No. He needs to see this."

Alex could tell that the doctor wanted to say something more as his eyes flicked between Alex and Aunt Edith's faces.

"Very well, although I have to warn you that with the medication that she's on, you will find her mildly unresponsive."

Alex wasn't sure what that meant and looked to his aunt for reassurance and an explanation, but she ignored him and followed the doctor who had opened the door to the room and walked inside. Alex gazed around the room taking everything in. Apart from the large hospital bed, the room looked like it could have belonged behind one of the locked doors in Aunt Edith's house. A couple of nautical oil paintings of ships at sea graced the walls. A dusty arrangement of dried flowers sat in place of glowing coals in the Victorian tiled fireplace. The usual dark wooden furniture cluttered the corners, including a wardrobe, a chest of drawers and a shelving unit upon which some random bric-a-brac was displayed. A yellowing lace doily sat on top of a low round table which was placed next to a high wing-back chair, currently occupied by his mother. She was oblivious to her visitors as she stared out of the small bay window that overlooked the fountain and the front of the house. Alex asked himself if she had seen them arrive in the car.

Aunt Edith fingered something attached to the side of the hospital bed. "Leather restraints? Really?" She arched one of her eyebrows at the doctor who gazed dispassionately back at her.

"They are used on the rare occasion when our patients are a danger to themselves and our staff."

Alex moved away from his aunt and the doctor who were now murmuring in low voices. He took tentative steps towards the chair in which his mother sat.

"Mummy?"

He shuffled sideways past the table so he could look at his mother's profile. Once by her side, he reached out and picked up a limp hand from her lap. Her frame was gaunt and waif like. The skin on her face was sallow and sunken. Hooded eyes gazed blankly out of the window. Here resided a shadow. Alex wasn't sure he would be able to stifle a cry if she turned and looked at him. The doctor and his aunt were still conferring quietly together. He ignored them and reached in his bag for his mother's hairbrush.

Without asking anyone's approval, Alex started to slowly brush his mother's hair which was now devoid of colour and hung in dry shreds, like straw. As he settled into a rhythm, she began to make some barely audible, yet appreciative noises. He studied her face, hoping for a reaction, but there was no sign of his mother in that glassy-eyed stare. Her body sitting there reminded him of a time when he came across a rag doll that one of the girls in his class had left abandoned in the playground. It just lay on the ground, inert, with its head cocked to one side and limbs stiffly splayed. He had gone to bed later that same day, and listened to the rain outside, wondering if the doll was still lying there, wet and bedraggled, its dark eyes beaded with raindrops, forever open.

The journey home in the car was conducted in silence. It was only as Aunt Edith parked outside her house and turned the engine off, that she turned and solemnly asked him to tell her when he next wanted to see his mother, and she would be happy to arrange it. Alex just nodded, having already decided that he would never visit that hospital again.

* * * *

September 1987

"I'm not sure how to react to that," said Luis, frowning. A soft rasping sound filled the air as he rubbed his thumbnail repeatedly against the stubble on his chin. "That was a harsh thing for your aunt to do, taking you to see your mom when she was in that state."

Alex shrugged. "It had the desired effect, that's for sure. I never asked again. My aunt was always a practical woman."

"She sounds a bit forbidding, if you don't mind me saying. Like one of those strict English school mistresses you see in old films."

Alex laughed and nodded in agreement. "I get that. I suppose she would seem that way to an outsider. My aunt always had my best interests at heart though." He picked up his beer bottle and held it up to the light. There was about an inch left inside. Alex drained the contents and set it back down on the table. "Right, enough of the 'woe is me' trip down memory lane. I'll tell you some more another time. Why don't we spend this afternoon doing something that doesn't involve sitting around?"

Luis brightened at the suggestion. "Sure, what do you have in mind? Shall we go for a walk on the beach?"

Alex shook his head. "I have a better idea." He pointed at a glass-panelled door set into the back wall on the house which led into the old dining room.

Luis looked at him, his face clouded with confusion. Alex smiled and waited. Through the glass, more cardboard boxes were visible, neatly stacked in piles in the middle of the room.

Luis groaned and raised his hands to his face. "Please tell me you're not serious?" he said, his voice muffled.

"Why not? You told me that the carpenters finished putting up the shelving in there last week. I thought you said that you always wanted your very own library. What are you waiting for?"

Luis dropped his hands into his lap. "This is ridiculous. I don't want you thinking that while you're here, you have to help me unpack everything. That's not fair."

"I don't think that." Alex ignored Luis' exasperated expression and pushed back his chair. He stood up and moved across to the door where he peered in, cupping his hand over his eyes to shield out the sun. "I'm actually interested to see what books you own. I've got nothing to read at the moment." He turned and grinned at Luis. "Maybe you'll lend me a couple? As long as they're not bodice rippers."

"Bodice rippers?" Luis said, incredulous. "Bodice rippers?" he repeated. "What do you take me for?" He started laughing and shaking his head. "You're really something else, you know that?"

"I wouldn't be at all surprised to find a worn-out Jackie Collins novel or an old much-loved book by Barbara Cartland lurking at the bottom of one of those boxes," Alex teased.

"I'm more surprised that you know the names of those writers," countered Luis.

"What can I say? I'm an educated man," replied Alex, turning back to the door. He pushed down on the handle. It was unlocked and the door opened outwards. The smell of newly cut wood and fresh paint drifted out of the room. "May I?" he asked Luis, who had left his seat at the table and was walking towards him.

"Be my guest," offered Luis, gesturing for Alex to step inside.

"Wow," Alex said. "The carpenters did a good job." Apart from two internal doors, three of the walls had been fitted from floor to ceiling with row after row of shelving, all painted gleaming white. Underfoot, wooden floorboards, the colour of walnuts, glowed as sunlight spilt through the door, illuminating them. "Are you sure you have enough books?" he asked, patting the top of one of the many stacks of boxes.

Luis pointed at one of the connecting doors. "There's more through there. Once it's cleared, that room's going to be my studio."

Alex ran the fingers of one hand through his short blond hair. He privately thought that Luis had his work cut out for him, but wasn't going to say anything. He didn't mind helping. It was just nice to be spending time with someone he really liked. "Well, there's no time like the present. Let's get started."

* * * *

Alex shifted uncomfortably in the driver's seat. He was looking forward to a long hot shower once he arrived back home, followed by a well-deserved large glass of red wine. That afternoon, between the two of them they'd managed to unpack all the boxes and fill the shelves with Luis' vast and extensive collection of books that covered an exhaustive array of subjects. Afterwards, despite their aching backs and arms, Luis had insisted that they carry the garden table into the library so that they could eat dinner in there and christen the room. The candlelight had reflected off the spines of the books as they ate. The dinner conversation had been light and free flowing, leading Alex to suspect that Luis was regretting asking him about his childhood earlier and was now avoiding the topic.

Alex checked his rear-view mirror and eased the car down the freeway off-ramp. He would've liked to have been able to say that he had nothing to hide, but that just wasn't true. There was a reason why that specific

Christmas Day, one of many spent with his aunt, had sprung so readily to mind, and he had deliberately chosen not to tell Luis. Something else had unfolded later that evening that had made that Christmas Day more memorable than all the others put together.

Chapter Four

December 1959

Alex stored the dream about his mother away with the other ones. He didn't like to examine them at length anymore. They just made him melancholic and sad. It was too early to go to bed, especially as he had just slept for a couple of hours. He looked at his study materials, and decided he deserved at least one day of the year without his head buried in textbooks. Although it was dark out, it would be nice to get out of the house for a bit and go for a walk, having been cooped up inside all Christmas Day. Downstairs he was about to open the front door when he paused, turned around and headed back towards the kitchen. Alex was thirsty. In the kitchen, he fetched a water glass down from one of the cupboards and carried it over to the sink. Sitting on the kitchen countertop was the unfinished bottle of white wine from lunch. Alex bit his lip. There was something about the gentle way the effect of the wine had softened the edges of his thoughts, when after lunch he had decided to lie down on his bed. He wanted to try it again. Alex poured the remaining third of the bottle into his glass and drank it down in three greedy gulps. He rinsed the glass and put the bottle in the bin. Hopefully Aunt Edith wouldn't notice. Alex stopped outside the closed parlour door. Muffled Christmas music could be heard from inside. He tapped softly on the door.

"Auntie? I'm just heading out for a quick walk. Did you want to come along, too?"

The volume on the radio was turned down, and from within there was the sound of movement. The door opened a couple of feet, and Aunt Edith peered around the edge of the door. "Thank you for the offer, dear boy, but I think the last time I took a moonlit stroll was when I was being courted in my youth." She laughed. It was an unusual sound. More of a soft titter. Alex had only heard it a couple of times before. One of the first things he'd found strange about her when he was younger was that she seemed curiously devoid of emotion. Her voice was more suited to that of a radio announcer, calm and measured, never once betraying a trace of humour or anger. "I think I'll stay here in the warm with the radio and my memories. Make sure you wear a coat. The last thing you need is to go catching a chill."

"I will do, Auntie, thanks," said Alex, turning to go.

"That was a sweet thing you did for me," she added.

He turned back around to face his aunt, who had opened the door wider to stand in the doorway. Behind her, the glow of the fire was throwing shadows over her armchair. Next to the seat was a small side table, upon which stood a bottle of gin and a full glass that glinted with ice. An open photo album was propped up against a leg of the chair, the black and white images blurred and indistinct from this distance. Alex flicked his eyes back up to Aunt Edith.

"The present," she prompted. "I wanted to say thank you again."

"I'm just glad you like it," he said, and smiled at her.

"I might have gone to bed when you get back, so can you make sure all the lights are turned off?"

"Of course. Goodnight."

As Alex stepped away from the door, his aunt leaned out and put a hand on his arm.

"You're a good boy, Alex. You always have been." She patted his arm then, without another word, withdrew back into the room and closed the door.

Alex stood still, momentarily disconcerted. Not only had his aunt paid him a compliment, but she had also displayed a gesture of affection, albeit a small one. He smiled to himself, pleased that just for a second, she had let her guard down. Maybe she was human after all, he mused, walking back up the hall to the front door. After grabbing his coat from the hook on the wall, he stepped out into the inky black evening. Alex retraced the route he had walked on the day he had arrived, back down the Tamarisk Steps to the street level, where opposite, the hulking black shadowy outlines of the tall fishing net sheds stood silently like sentinels. The roads were completely deserted. No people or cars. Just the glow from the front windows of houses, where families were still gathered, celebrating the last remaining hours of Christmas day. A light drizzle blown on the wind dampened Alex's face, and for a brief second he considered turning back. Why wasn't he inside like all these people he could see as he passed by their houses? A voice spoke inside him, its tone self-pitying. *Maybe it's because you don't have a family anymore?* Alex angrily shook his head and turned up the collar of his jacket. He strode on along the pavement, increasing his pace, determined not to answer the part of him that sometimes demanded to be heard. Further on, Alex crossed over the road. Partly to distance himself from the residential houses, but mostly so he could be closer to the sea. The few streetlights dotted along the promenade cast a bluish white glow that illuminated the shingle beach on his left, but didn't stretch down as far as the surf, which he could hear crashing onto the shore, now invisible in the darkness.

Alex breathed in deeply, relishing the sea air and the exercise. He spent far too long sat at his desk studying, so it was important to take some time out and clear his muddied mind and separate his thoughts. There was something surreal about having the promenade completely to himself. Alex checked behind him and saw no movement stretching all the way back to the fishing huts. Up ahead he could see the entrance to the pier, the gates closed and locked. The pier was a black oblong, darker than the evening itself, its immense mass disappearing out into the sea. From underneath, the waves could be heard hitting the pilings that supported it. Alex's step faltered, as with a start, he realised he was not alone. Next to the pier entrance a man was sitting on the low wall that separated the promenade from the beach below. He walked on, trying to appear nonchalant. As he drew level with him, Alex slowed down and nodded at the man, who when viewed up close, was actually much younger and probably around the same age as Alex.

"All right?" said the young man, by way of greeting. "Merry Christmas. Do you have a light?"

Alex looked down at the packet of cigarettes the youth held in his hand. "I'm sorry, I don't smoke." It struck him as strange that he would have cigarettes, but no way of lighting them.

The young man shrugged. "I should give up anyway. I've heard that they're not good for you."

Alex didn't know how to answer, and turned to walk on.

"What brings you out tonight?" the young man said quickly. "Shouldn't you be with your family whilst your gran gets tipsy on the sherry?"

Alex chuckled and stopped in his tracks. There was no harm in having a quick chat. The wine had relaxed him. There was a nice glow in his stomach. In fact, another glass would be good right now. "Actually it's just me and my aunt. She's the one getting tipsy on gin. I just wanted a bit of fresh air after being cooped up all day. What about you?"

"The same." The lad smiled shyly. "It's just been me and my folks, but my dad's had a skinful, and I don't like being around him when he's like that. He gets a bit handy with his fists, if you know what I mean."

Alex understood. "I'm sorry to hear that." A twinge of sympathy ran through him, coupled with the sudden realisation that the youth in front of him was also very handsome. He resisted the urge to reach out and push back the floppy fringe of brown hair that threatened to fall over the boy's eyes. A squall buffeted them both, and big fat raindrops started to fall in abundance. Alex looked around for shelter but there was none nearby. The young man pointed to a set of steps located in the low wall that led down onto the beach.

"Here, quick. We can go under the pier."

Being careful not to slip on the steps, Alex followed him. The wind was blowing the rain sideways and under the pier, so they both climbed up onto the lip of a concrete shelf that was directly below the pier entrance, and took shelter there. Alex clenched his hands into loose fists to stop them trembling. He was aware that it wasn't the chilly winter evening that was to blame. His stomach flip-flopped, and on his tongue he could discern the tang of something metallic. Dulled by the alcohol, his senses blurred between nervousness and excitement as he surrendered himself to the strange certainty that something was about to happen. Something he had desired and dreamed of, yet buried a long time ago.

The young man reached into a pocket and removed a handkerchief. "It's clean," he whispered, as he reached up and used it to wipe the water droplets that clung to Alex's face. "What's your name? You can call me Johnny."

Alex didn't answer. A calmness descended. No longer buffeted by the wind and rain, Alex pictured himself as the eye of the hurricane that his aunt had once told him he reminded her of. There was no need to question what they were doing or why they were here. It all seemed so perfectly right. Johnny moved closer and pulled Alex against him. As he surrendered his mouth to Johnny's probing tongue, his ears were teased by the clink of his belt buckle being opened and the rasp of the zipper on his trousers being slowly lowered. Johnny pulled Alex's trousers down and over his buttocks, the cold air deliciously thrilling against his exposed skin. He then crouched down and his warm wet mouth enveloped Alex's penis. Alex threw his head back and gasped. All rational thought left him, and instead he concentrated on the pulse of pleasure centred at his groin, which grew and grew. Alex reached out a hand to steady himself against the damp concrete wall as the crescendo steadily increased until the point of no return. He cried out and thrust his hips forward, his eyes tightly closed, as wave after wave of pleasure threatened to drown him. Johnny stood up and kissed Alex, forcing his tongue deep inside his mouth. Alex could taste himself, and moaned, his knees close to buckling. Johnny held the back of Alex's head with one hand, not allowing their mouths to part, whilst with the other, he masturbated until, shuddering, he came with a muffled cry. They parted, still standing close. Johnny's laboured breath blew hot against Alex's cheek. Alex busied himself with fastening his trousers and belt and turned to go, jumping down off the low concrete lip, his feet unsteady on the loose shingle.

Johnny snaked out his hand and grasped Alex's arm. "Can we meet here again soon?"

Alex realised that the squall had passed and that the moon had revealed itself, sliding out from its hiding place behind the clouds. The moonlight reflecting off the sea gave just enough illumination for Alex to register the hope shining in Johnny's eyes. He pulled his arm free, and without a reply, hurried away towards the nearby steps that led back up to the promenade. The seafront was empty, but Alex did not want to be followed, so he sprinted across the road and followed a convoluted longer route back home, casting quick glances over his shoulder as he went.

His cheeks burned hot with the shame of what he had just done. He was going to hell. This was not how he had been brought up. A rush of nausea flooded Alex's mouth with saliva. He spat it out, eager to get rid of the taste of himself and the other boy that coated his lips and tongue. The house was dark and silent when Alex quietly let himself in. He took off his shoes and crept up the stairs to his room in his socks. There, Alex undressed and with a cry of disgust realised that the long damp stain down his right trouser leg must have come from Johnny when he ejaculated. He balled up the trousers and shoved them under his bed. In the morning he would have to scrub them with soap and water. He wished it was that easy to get rid of the shame and guilt that clung to him, but deep down, Alex was certain that some stains, especially those on his character, could never be eradicated.

* * * *

In the days that followed, Alex rarely ventured from his room. Even Aunt Edith commented on how withdrawn he was. He blamed his college workload and explained that he might need to travel back to Milton Keynes sooner than planned, so he could avail himself of the college's research materials. She had nodded approvingly. He could always tell how pleased she was to see that he still adhered to the strict work ethic she had instilled in him from a young age. In truth though, Alex was still filled with shame over what had happened under the pier. He blamed the wine for allowing desire to override rational thinking, but deep down inside, a part of him was conscious of the fact that the young man — Alex refused to refer to him by name — had unlocked something within. Something he didn't understand. Something that unnerved him. Was he ill? Possessed of a sickness? Was he going to end up in a special hospital like his mother, an aberration to be hidden away from normal people?

Upstairs in his room, Alex paced restlessly. He didn't dare go out anymore in case he ran into the youth again. In fact, he didn't want to see anybody in case they could tell that he was guilty of unspeakable things. In the bathroom mirror, Alex analysed his features looking for anything that would discern him as different from other men. He found nothing.

Closing his textbook in exasperation, Alex pushed back his chair and turned away from his desk. He couldn't concentrate. His gaze strayed to the shadowy space under his bed where his trousers still lay. He hadn't yet summoned the courage to retrieve and clean them. Out of sight, out of mind. Alex swore loudly, and reached down and yanked the trousers out from their hiding place. He picked them up and laid them out on top of the bed. The stain was still plainly visible. It had become a totem—a mark of another man's pleasure that he had been party to. He was aroused and repelled at the same time. What alarmed Alex most of all was the brief anticipation and thrill that had coursed through his body just by being in close proximity to the young man under the pier the other night. Desire suffused with lust had instantly dispelled any rational logic to consider the danger of what the two of them were doing. Where did these powerful feelings come from?

Alex glanced around at his textbooks with disdain. He was so used to finding the solution to problems in their pages, but knew that algorithms and equations would not help solve the conflicting emotions that coursed through him. Acting on impulse, Alex reached under the bed again and pulled out his two suitcases. It was time to pack. There was nothing to be gained from staying in Hastings. He couldn't concentrate here. Tomorrow was New Year's Eve. There would be a morning train. Parts of the College would still be open, even though the new term hadn't officially begun. He could study there in peace. His mind made up, Alex started to gather his belongings, including the soiled pair of trousers. He would wash them back at Mrs Ellis' and let them dry by the fire in his room.

* * * *

"You seem more like your old self this evening," Aunt Edith commented. "Excited to be going back to college? I expect you miss all your new friends. I keep on forgetting that Hastings must be a bit boring for you."

Alex smiled at his aunt across the kitchen table and rested his spoon in his bowl of soup. "Actually, I like coming back here. I get to see you and walk by the sea. It's my home."

Aunt Edith nodded slowly. "It won't always be, Alex. There will come a time when you'll make your own home. Whilst we are on the subject, have you thought anymore about what you want to do once you graduate?"

Alex suppressed a deep sigh. His aunt's belief that he would never fail was draining. Since his mother became ill, all his aunt had done was map out every stage of his life, and as he was getting older, he suspected she was panicking because she had no choice but to relinquish her control over him. This was one of their many rituals and he always humoured her. She'd done so much for him already.

"I suppose I will have to find myself some sort of job. Maybe in research and development. I haven't thought about it properly as I've still got another couple of years yet."

Aunt Edith dabbed at the corner of her mouth with her napkin and regarded him with her clear intelligent eyes. "That may be, Alex, but those years will fly by. Don't forget your inheritance that you'll receive when you're twenty-one. There's still a little bit of money left from the sale of your parent's house. It should help towards a deposit when you decide to buy your own place."

Alex said nothing. It seemed wrong that he was to benefit from the death of his parents. When his aunt had moved his mother and Alex into her house, ever the practical woman, she had assumed control of the family finances. After his mother was admitted to the hospital, Aunt Edith informed Alex that she'd had to sell his family home to help pay for her treatment, but not to worry. At the time Alex was far too young to understand the complexities of home ownership, his sole focus was the safe and quick return of his mother. Never at any time had Alex not trusted his aunt. Why should he? She'd always had his best interests at heart. In fact, she'd sacrificed a lot for him, and never asked for anything in return except for his devotion to his education. It had been a small price to pay and had come naturally to him. He had nothing else to focus on. In fact, when Alex looked back, it was clear to him that his childhood was over before it had ever really begun.

Even now, listening to her cool, calm, collected voice, Alex could remember coming home from school one day during his fourteenth year to find her waiting for him. In her measured tone, she'd spoken just two words that he never forgot. "*She's gone.*" His reaction at the time, later unsettled him, as his aunt's quiet demeanour was infectious, and he had stoically settled in the same chair that he was sitting in now whilst she made them both a cup of tea. She had kept her back to him as she explained what the doctors had said, which was the same as they had been told many times before. His mother had simply given up the will to live. Her body grew frailer as her spirit dwindled until she was finally granted the release she had craved. A tiny part of Alex was hurt that his mother's knowledge that she still had a son was not enough to lift her from her torpor. Maybe she'd forgotten, his memory lost in the vagaries of her mind?

His aunt had asked him if he had wanted to see her one last time now she was at peace. He had shaken his head vehemently, not needing to think about it even for a second. The last time he had seen her shrunken frame in the wing-backed chair had been enough. To view her now, pale and lifeless, would tip him over the edge. Aunt Edith wanted to know if he was sure. There would never be another opportunity to say goodbye. He'd covered his eyes with his hands in an attempt to block out the image he had of his mother lying motionless on her bed, her chest no longer rising and falling, and whispered "*I'm sure.*"

After they finished their evening meal, his aunt retired to her parlour, and Alex went back upstairs to finish packing. After he'd thrown the last of his clothes into the open suitcases, Alex crossed to the window so he could gaze down upon the familiar sight of Hastings old town spread out below him. He toyed with the idea of one last walk along the seafront, but the look of hope and longing reflected in the young man's eyes under the pier led him to imagine that the promenade was now his hunting ground, and to go there would only invite trouble. Alex turned away from the view. Across the room, the photo frame that graced his bedside table caught his eye. Besides his mother's hairbrush and a few personal items, this was his other treasured possession, and had been given to him by his aunt after his mother had passed away. The silver frame housed a black and white picture of his parents. His father stood behind his mother, wearing his army uniform with his arms wrapped around her waist, both of them looking impossibly young and desperately in love. He moved across to the bed and sat down, picking up the picture frame and cradling it in his hands. Like the hairbrush, it was too precious to take to Milton Keynes. Here both items were always safe and waiting for him every time he returned. Alex studied the smooth skin of his father's face. The only visible lines were gathered at the corners of his eyes and mouth as he smiled at the camera. Having forgotten what his father had looked like in the years after he had died, Alex had had to reacquaint himself with the photo. He found it strange that his mother had not surrounded herself with pictures of her late husband, but maybe it had been too much for her to bear.

A couple of days after his mother had passed away, he'd plucked up the courage to ask his aunt how his father had died. She hadn't been aware that he didn't know, and Alex could still remember the stricken look upon her face before she revealed what her sister had failed to tell her son. It had happened during 1945, after the war was over in Europe. Apparently, his father

George had seen battle abroad, survived and was back in England stationed at his Army base, due to return home within a matter of weeks. It was described as a tragic accident. No one knew exactly what happened, but there was an explosion at a fuel depot, and four men lost their lives, including George.

Alex returned the photo frame to his bedside table, placing it in the exact spot where it had first appeared the day after his aunt told him how his father died. The feeling of melancholy that always pervaded his time in Hastings was draining, both physically and mentally. And dare he admit that it was becoming boring? At times he craved euphoria and excitement—both extremes he knew—but wallowing in the reflective sadness of his childhood was doing him no good. This was why he had to leave. Why did he do this every time he returned home? Was there any reason to keep these memories alive, when in fact some of them should be forgotten? Alex wished he held the answer, but it eluded him. He could live with that, but now was the time to stop. The decision calmed him because he had the inner strength to see it through. His aunt had made sure of that. Alex yawned. It was late. Somehow the rest of the evening had drifted by. He raised the bedroom window a little, before climbing into his small single bed. The air was cold, yet still. The rhythmic pounding of the waves on the shore were barely audible, and as he drifted off to sleep, his breathing slowed until it matched the constant in and out of the surf.

* * * *

The following morning before he left the house, Alex bid farewell to his aunt. He was left bemused by her distracted and uninterested air as she focused on reading the morning newspaper whilst sipping tea at the kitchen table. He might as well have been popping out to the local shops for the way she absently acknowledged his goodbye and told him she would see him later. In fact it would be another three months before he would be journeying back to Hastings for Easter. He'd allowed himself an extra hour before catching his train. There was one final ritual that needed to be completed before he could leave. Struggling with his two suitcases, Alex followed the road down East Hill and into the old town where the local church stood. Once through the main gate, he found his mother's grave easily enough. He'd been here many times before.

The first time Alex had stood here alone, he had sobbed uncontrollably. The harsh reality that both his parents were dead could not have been more apparent. The proximity of her physical body buried only six feet under had taunted him at first. Death was a tease, dangling his mother's corporeal self like a carrot, whilst her spirit was forever lost in the ether. On subsequent visits came acceptance, but at times he questioned the reason for his visits. Of course he wanted to honour his mother and remember her life, but talking to the headstone and only ever receiving silence as a reply was dispiriting. The fact that she was buried alone he also found upsetting. His father was interred in a churchyard near where he had grown up, and Alex had yet to visit it and pay his respects, something he chastised himself for.

When he was ready to leave, Alex bent down and kissed the top of the gravestone. Walking away was always the hardest thing. Leaving his mother dead and alone in the ground was something he would never get used to, and because of this, he never missed a visit to her grave every time he returned from college. There were times when he lay in bed at night in Mrs Ellis's guest house, wracked with guilt as he conjured a picture in his mind of his mother's grave, dark and forgotten in a corner behind the church.

* * * *

The carriage jerked forward with a shudder, and the train slowly rolled out of Hastings Station. As it gathered momentum, Alex stared out of the window wanting to make sure he could gaze upon the sea until the last possible moment. He wouldn't be back here for a while, and maybe that was just as well. Apart from the occasional hesitant times when Alex would tentatively explore the pleasure that his own body could provide him with, the brief moment with the boy under the pier had been his first sexual encounter. He was no fool and would not delude himself by pretending that he hadn't known from around the age of twelve that he found men more attractive than women. The problem was what to do with this information. It was not a subject for discussion.

As Hastings receded behind him and the houses were replaced by countryside, Alex tried to figure out why. He concluded that since the age of eleven when he attended an all-boys senior school, the only women he had spent any time with had been his mother, his aunt, and most recently, Mrs Ellis, although she probably didn't count. There were a couple of girls studying at the college, but his degree was predominantly a male-led field. Alex sat stock still in his seat, stupefied by the simple solution—if he was to meet some young women of a similar age, he would discover that he was normal after all, after being inadvertently surrounded by boys and men most of his life.

A broad grin spread across his face as his spirits lifted. How could he have missed something so obvious? He drummed his fingers on the table in front of him, feeling impatient to return to Milton Keynes. *Relax*, he told himself. *You won't get there any quicker*. He contented himself by watching the countryside slide by, secretly pleased that the answer to this particular problem had been solved without referring to one of his textbooks. Hastings could wait until the next time he returned, as he needed to focus his energy elsewhere. Anyway, the things that he normally missed now seemed tainted. Whenever he imagined himself walking along the beach and looking at the sea which had been his solace for as long as he could remember, he now no longer walked alone. Always a few steps behind, the crunch of his feet audible as each footstep sank into the shingle, the young man from under the pier accompanied him, uninvited.

Chapter Five

October 1987

A knock sounded on Alex's office door. "One second, Larry." Alex held the phone away from his ear. "Come in." He looked up from the notes he was making. The door opened to reveal his colleague Juliette gazing hopefully at him. She was clutching a sheaf of files to her chest. Alex waved her into the room. "Sorry, Larry, as I was saying, the meeting is scheduled for next Wednesday afternoon at two p.m. I'll ask my secretary to send you over a briefing pack. All good? Great. Thanks, Larry. See you then."

"Sorry to interrupt," said Juliette. "I've finally got those reports you wanted."

Alex leaned back in his chair. The black leather upholstery creaked under his weight. "Excellent. Thank you." He gestured at her outfit. "You're looking very smart. Have we got anyone visiting today that I've forgotten about?"

Juliette glanced down at her white shirt and grey wool trousers which fitted her slim frame perfectly. "No, don't worry. If you remember, I'm due in San Francisco on Monday morning for that meeting with Lockheed. I thought I would make a weekend of it and fly up there tonight after work. An old friend from Switzerland lives there. We're going to see a show and maybe find a nice restaurant after." Juliette placed the files down on a corner of Alex's desk.

Alex just nodded. He wasn't about to ask who the friend was. Juliette was famously secretive about her private life. Blessed with intelligence and European beauty, Alex guessed that she must have a long line of potential suitors hounding her. He'd worked closely with Juliette for nearly five years now. When he'd set up this company, she had been instrumental in its success and had become a good friend as well as a trusted colleague. Although Alex considered them to be close and had told her about his friendship with Luis, he didn't take it personally that she didn't share more personal details with him. Being English, he was always guarded about displaying his emotions and revealing too much. Maybe Juliette's Swiss upbringing had instilled the same?

"So have you finally decided what you're going to cook tonight?" asked Juliette, expertly changing the conversation.

"I have," said Alex with triumph. "Rather than try and make something fancy, I thought that it would be good to make something that Luis probably hasn't eaten before."

Juliette crossed her arms and her lips formed into a small smile. "Oh really? And what would that be?"

"An English roast dinner," Alex announced. "Roast chicken with potatoes, stuffing, vegetables and gravy."

"That sounds good," said Juliette, nodding slowly. "Have you made one before?"

"No, but my aunt used to cook them every Sunday when I was growing up, so it'll be fine."

Juliette pushed a few long errant strands of thick chestnut hair back behind her ear. "I know I haven't met him yet, but by the way you've described him, I'm sure he'll appreciate the effort you're going to. I'm glad that you finally have a friend outside of work. I worry about you sometimes."

Alex rolled his eyes causing her to laugh. Although he was over ten years her senior, Alex indulged Juliette's maternal instincts. It was heartening to know someone cared. "I'll tell you how it went when you get back from San Francisco."

Juliette turned towards the door. "Speaking of which, I'd better go. I've got a ton of stuff to do before I head to the airport. Have a good weekend, Alex."

"Thanks. Have a safe flight." As the door closed, Alex glanced at his watch. It was ten past three. His desk was clear apart from the pile of reports. They could wait till Monday. It was Friday afternoon. He had a roast dinner to cook. It wouldn't hurt to finish a bit early for once.

* * * *

Alex stepped out into the garden. The smell of cut grass hung in the air. He nodded with satisfaction. The gardener had done a good job. Even though he'd lived here for six years now, Alex still couldn't get used to the good weather in Los Angeles during the autumn and winter months. Not that he was complaining. Back in England he'd never looked this tanned and healthy. Alex ambled around the perimeter of the garden admiring the pruned shrubs and bushes. Tall trees screened the edges of the property guaranteeing privacy from the neighbouring houses. Alex stopped at the edge of the navy-blue tiled pool and crouched down. He dipped a hand into the sparkling water and was surprised at how warm the water was. Now was not the time for a swim, though. Luis would be arriving soon. Alex stood and walked back towards the main house. He glanced to his left at the guest cottage that was nestled in the corner of the garden. Everything was ready for Luis, who would be sleeping in there tonight. Alex mentally ticked off his list. There were fresh sheets on the bed and clean towels in the bathroom. He had even stocked up the fridge in the kitchenette with orange juice and bottles of water. This was the first time anyone had stayed over and Alex was determined to be the perfect host.

The exterior wall of the lounge was made of glass. Alex grasped the metal handle attached to one of the large panes and pulled it to the right. It effortlessly folded back on itself, opening up the room to the garden. He entered the cavernous lounge with its arched vaulted wooden ceiling and wide unadorned white walls. Although impressive in size, there was something monastic about the space that resonated with him. Then again, some splashes of colour might not go amiss, Alex considered. Maybe he would ask Luis for advice. On the far side of the room a short flight of steps led up to the dining room. Alex resisted the urge to go and check the table settings. He'd been up there twice in the last hour already.

This was not like him. Why was he acting so restless? Maybe it was just a case of nerves. Alex had no idea what Luis would think of the house and that unsettled him. Did he want to impress Luis? Was that it? Alex didn't think so. He liked to think that Luis wasn't shallow enough to be dazzled by displays of affluence. There was far more to him than that. Alex sighed out loud. Who was he fooling? It was the fear of what Luis didn't say that worried him.

Back in England, it had been his ex-wife Joanna who'd made all the decisions about how she wanted the house to be decorated. Would Luis be tactful and keep any negative comments to himself? Alex turned around in a slow circle taking in the furniture and contents of the room. He was well aware of how private a person he was. Did the house reveal aspects of his character that he wanted to remain hidden? The doorbell sounded, startling him. Alex hurried up the short set of stairs that led up into the kitchen and moved quickly through and out into the front hall. He paused in front of a small ornate wall mirror and checked his appearance before opening the front door to find Luis patiently waiting there. He was dressed smartly in a pair of cream chinos and a dark green cotton shirt, complemented by his warm brown eyes and familiar inviting smile.

Alex grinned at him, then stepped forward and the two of them shared a quick hug. "Was the drive up okay? I hope my directions were easy to follow?"

"It was fine, nice and smooth. No rush-hour traffic." Luis glanced back at his car parked on the street beneath a leafy shade tree. "Will the car be all right if I leave it there?"

"It'll be fine," Alex assured him. "Come on in. Welcome to my home."

Luis picked up a leather holdall that rested at his feet. "This is a beautiful neighbourhood. Very quiet." He gestured at the front of Alex's house that was partly shrouded by greenery. "I like all the plants and shrubs."

"Not down to me, I'm afraid," Alex admitted. "They came with the house when I bought it." He led Luis inside and down the white walled hallway. The sound of their footsteps echoed against the wooden parquet floor.

"Wow," Luis exclaimed as they walked into the kitchen. He placed his bag down on the marble topped central island that was the centrepiece of the vast room and turned to Alex. "I can see now why you wanted to learn how to cook." Luis slowly shook his head as he walked around inspecting the gleaming steel and chrome kitchen. "Whoever owned this house before you must have loved food." He pointed at a selection of chopped vegetables piled on a chopping board. "Someone's been busy."

Alex nodded. "I'll cook them in a bit. The food in the oven needs a while longer first. Why don't we go and sit in the garden? Would you like something to drink?"

"Sure. A cold beer would be great."

Alex moved across to the monolithic double refrigerator and removed two bottles from a shelf inside.

"I wanted to say thanks again for letting me stay tonight," said Luis. "I wasn't looking forward to driving up to Los Angeles early Saturday morning and getting caught in all the weekend traffic."

Alex popped the top off one of the frosted bottles and passed it to Luis. "Not at all. In fact it was the perfect excuse to finally invite you up here. You can't risk arriving late to your own exhibition. What would all your adoring fans say?"

Luis laughed. "Scathing art critics, more like." He took a long swig from his beer. "To be honest, it's just a small informal thing. A few paintings on display. For all I know, nobody will turn up."

"I very much doubt that," said Alex as he removed the cap from his bottle. "If you like, I can come with you to provide moral support."

"Thanks, I appreciate the offer, but I'm not sure what I would find worse. You witnessing me hosting an empty room, or watching me having to schmooze with minor luminaries from LA's art world." Luis grimaced. "It's the one part of being an artist that I really dislike."

Alex nodded. "I get that. I know it's not the same, but sometimes my company has to give presentations to secure future contracts, and it always feels like you're whoring yourself a little."

"Exactly!" Luis exclaimed. "Afterwards I always feel like I need a shower."

Alex chuckled. "Well, the alternative is that you could be an unknown painter struggling to sell your work."

Luis nodded. "I lived that life for a number of years until I struck lucky. My mom always used to say that you need to first experience the bad things in life if you are going to truly appreciate the good things that life has to offer."

"Your mother sounds like a wise woman," Alex replied. Luis didn't answer and instead took another swig of beer. "Let's finish these outside," added Alex smoothly, guiding Luis towards the stairs that led down to the lounge and garden.

The next hour passed quickly. Alex gave Luis a tour of the garden and guest cottage, then refreshed their beers. Everything was going to plan. Luis had been very complimentary about both the house and garden. At the appropriate time, Alex excused himself so he could serve dinner. The faint whirr of the oven's fan was audible as Alex walked into the kitchen. Waiting on the countertop was an array of serving dishes that he would carry through once the food was ready. He lit the gas ring under the small saucepan full of gravy that he had prepared earlier. It still looked a bit watery. He added more gravy granules to thicken it. So far, so good.

Alex slipped on a pair of oven gloves and bent down to open the oven door. He leaned back to avoid the inevitable wave of heat, but needn't have bothered. Instead, the fan inside just blew warm air into his face. Frowning, he checked the gas jets lining the bottom of the oven but none of them were alight. Alex inspected the chicken. The skin had crisped somewhat but it was still as grey and anaemic as when he had put it in the oven. Alex prodded one of the potatoes. It was still raw.

"Hey, Alex, do you need a hand?" Luis' voice floated up from the lounge followed by the sound of footsteps on the stairs.

Alex tried to muster up a reply but didn't know what to say. There was no way he could pretend everything was all right. "The gas flame blew out," he finally admitted as behind him Luis approached. "Maybe I shouldn't have turned on the fan." Alex cursed under his breath and lifted the roasting tray out of the oven and slid it onto the marble counter. He plucked a sharp knife from the cutlery drawer. "We can't eat this," Alex stated flatly, as he cut into a chicken breast exposing the pink, barely cooked flesh inside.

Luis peered over Alex's shoulder. "Oh, Alex. I'm so sorry. You went to all this effort."

"I wanted to cook you something nice and instead I've ruined it. I thought I'd got the hang of using this oven."

"We could put it back in and cook it for longer? I don't mind waiting," Luis offered. Alex looked up at the clock on the kitchen wall and shook his head. "It'll be too late by then. You have an early start tomorrow. No one likes going to bed late on a full stomach."

Luis leaned forward and turned off the gas under the saucepan on the hob. The gravy had turned a dark brown-black colour. Alex stirred the gloopy mess and sighed. It was now as thick as honey and clung to the spoon like hot tar.

"I guess the only option now is for us to go out and find a restaurant," said Alex, morosely.

"Maybe," replied Luis. "It's Friday night, though, and we haven't reserved a table. We could just order in a couple of pizzas and relax with a few more beers or some wine?" He moved over to the kitchen island and unzipped his leather holdall. Luis reached inside and fished out a bottle of red wine which he set it down on the countertop. "It's Italian. One of your favourites. What do you say?"

Alex exhaled loudly and turned around. He offered Luis a weak smile. "Actually, that sounds like a great idea."

Luis gestured at the oven. "This could have happened to anyone. It's just bad luck that it happened to you. I'm really touched that you went to all this trouble, but you don't always have to try so hard, you know. Enjoying your company is far more important to me than anything we eat."

"I know," said Alex. "Thank you for saying that. I still should have checked the oven earlier though."

Luis shrugged. "Do you have a phonebook handy? I'll order us a couple of pizzas and then we can clear up the kitchen while we wait for it to be delivered."

Alex rifled in a kitchen drawer and pulled out a sheaf of fast-food flyers. "I keep these in case of an emergency." He handed them to Luis who flicked through them.

"What type of pizza would you like?" asked Luis, as he selected a menu and picked up the kitchen phone.

"Surprise me," said Alex. "Although," he added, "I have to say that if you order pineapple as a topping, you'll be escorted out through that front door faster than you thought possible."

Luis paused whilst dialling and looked gravely over at him. "Point taken."

When Luis had finished ordering the food, Alex set about tidying up. He scraped the congealed gravy into the sink and turned on the tap. "It's funny, but in all the years I was married, Joanna never once had a disaster like tonight in the kitchen."

"Where did she learn to cook?" asked Luis, reaching past him for the wet dish cloth.

"She told me once that she learnt the same way that most daughters do, by helping her mum prepare the family evening meal every day."

"Where did you two first meet?"

Alex turned off the tap and gazed down at the remaining clots of gravy, trying to cast his mind back.

"It was all rather sweet and innocent really, and happened whilst I was studying at college. We met in a pub. Socially there wasn't much else to do back then. I'd never had a girlfriend before. I was one of those awkward teenagers who were a bit of a loner." Alex turned to look at Luis. "Was it very different for you, too?"

Luis glanced over at Alex before resuming wiping down the island countertop. "My mom became quite religious and frowned upon that sort of thing. Girlfriends weren't to be encouraged, according to Father Nestor. My poor dad. My mother was married more to the church than she was to him."

Alex waited for him to elaborate and was about to enquire further when Luis beat him to it and prompted him to continue his story.

* * * *

January 1961

Alex pulled open the pub door and spilled out onto the pavement in a cloud of cigarette smoke and beer fumes. The cold damp air made him instantly lightheaded. He rested a moment, leaning against the side of the pub. He should never have let Roger and Alan buy him that last pint. Of course their girlfriends Linda and Mary had been present, so he couldn't really have said no. His stomach lurched unpleasantly, and he swallowed hard. Alex preferred wine but couldn't be seen ordering himself a glass in a pub. Men drank pints. It had become customary for him to meet his friends down the pub on a Friday evening for about a year now, yet he still couldn't get used to the bitter ale that all the men drank. He supposed it was a small price to pay for the way his social life had changed.

It had taken gritted teeth and a concerted effort on his part, but his fellow students, it seemed, were pleasantly surprised when he approached them in a nervous, yet friendly manner and over a short space of time, he'd cultivated a small collection of friends and acquaintances. Alex still preferred his own company but was astonished by how easily he got on with these people. The fact that they were all studying aeronautics helped, although they had all diversified in their fields of study. It was nice to talk about a subject that other people were passionate about too, and they also did so after college finished for the day, spending evenings huddled round tables in pubs or crowded into a pokey lounge in someone's student housing.

Alex never invited anyone back to his room. Mrs Ellis wouldn't approve, especially if there was a group of them. The pub door squeaked open again and two young women emerged who were whispering to each other before collapsing in giggles. Alex recognised them from where they had been sitting with friends at a neighbouring table. They talked a moment more, then hugged briefly. One of the girls crossed the road and hurried away up the street. The other girl watched her go, then turned and walked in the other direction towards Alex. She gave a small gasp when she realised that he was there, leaning against the wall.

"Sorry, I didn't see you there. You startled me," she said, with a tremor in her voice.

Alex held his hands up. "It's my fault. I shouldn't have been lurking here in the dark. I just needed some fresh air. It's too hot and smoky in there."

The girl smiled uncertainly. "Yes, and it's getting late too. Time to go home."

Alex looked at his watch and nodded. "Are you catching the night bus?" He pointed along the road in front of them.

The girl gave a tiny nod. "Yes, I mustn't miss it as it's the last one."

Alex pushed himself away from the wall. "I'm going that way. I'll walk you to the bus stop if you like? You shouldn't be out alone when it's late." He smiled and held out a hand. "I promise I don't bite. My name's Alex."

The girl stood for a moment, looking indecisive, before leaning forward and clasping the ends of his fingers for the briefest of handshakes. "I'm Joanna. I've seen you and your friends in there before."

"Yes, we like going there. It's a popular pub." Alex fell in alongside her and they ambled slowly up the road.

He had caught Joanna looking at him across the tables a couple of times that evening, and he had to admit that she was very pretty. Her auburn hair was cut in an attractive pleasing bob. She was slim and a couple of inches smaller in height than him. Up close and under the glare from the streetlights, her milky-white skin glowed. Her beauty was natural, and not enhanced by layers of makeup. She turned her head suddenly and caught him staring at her. Dimples appeared in each cheek as she smiled, displaying even white teeth.

"I, I'm sorry," stammered Alex.

"Are you just making sure that I'm real?"

Alex laughed awkwardly, and ran a hand through his blond hair. "You were sat on the table next to mine. I hope we weren't too loud."

"Not at all, although I could tell you were students at Cranfield as soon as you started talking about plane engines." Joanna gave him an amused glance.

"We're that obvious, are we?" he asked, embarrassed. Her knowing smile was answer enough. He liked that she was gently poking fun at him. "So, what about you? Are you a student, too?"

"Oh goodness no. I work in a department store in the city centre. Not very grand, but it puts food on the table. My dad's out of work. He's been ill for a while now."

"I'm sorry to hear that," Alex said.

"It is what it is, I guess. We'll get by."

They walked on in silence. Just up ahead illuminated under a streetlight was a bus stop. "Is this where you catch the bus?"

Joanna nodded. "There should be one along in a couple of minutes. Thank you for walking with me, but you don't have to wait."

"I'm happy to, really," said Alex, as they slowed to a stop on the pavement. "It's not too far for me to walk home, and I have no classes tomorrow."

"You don't live on campus at Cranfield College?" Joanna asked.

Alex shook his head. "Not anymore. I did for my first year. Now I'm renting a room here in Milton Keynes. I like it. I've got my own fireplace," he said, proudly.

Joanna looked at him with amusement. "I didn't realise that was the first thing students looked for when renting a room."

Alex blinked in confusion. "What? Oh no, it wasn't. It was a complete surprise..." He was going to explain further, but her smile stopped him. "You're teasing me."

Joanna nodded. "Mmm-hmm."

Alex let out a relieved laugh and scratched the back of his head with embarrassment.

The low rumble of an engine sounded in the distance, and back down the street, the distant glare of the bus headlights lit up the road and elongated both of their shadows along the pavement.

"Will you be in the pub next Friday?" he blurted out, as the bus drove closer.

Joanna turned to him wearing a half smile. "I might be." The bus pulled up and the double doors folded open with a hiss. "Good night, Alex," said Joanna as she stepped aboard.

The doors closed. Joanna took a seat towards the rear, and the bus pulled away. She hadn't waved goodbye. Instead she'd just sat there, looking straight ahead. Even though she'd given nothing away, Alex sensed that she liked him. Most women did, he was finding, although he was unsure why. Roger and Alan's girlfriends said he was clever and funny. Maybe it was because he was attentive towards them, polite and courteous, including them in their conversations, even when the boys' talk invariably turned to their studies. He pulled his jacket tighter around himself, and increased his pace along the pavement, eager to get home.

* * * *

October 1987

Alex was amazed at how much came flooding back whilst he was recounting the first time he met Joanna.

He was about to tell Luis about the second time they'd arranged to meet and the subsequent invitation to lunch at her house a few months later, when the doorbell rang.

"That'll be the pizzas," he said.

Luis pulled a couple of bills out of his trouser pocket. "Here, take these." He held them out towards Alex, who shook his head and raised a hand in a warding off gesture.

"Absolutely not. I invited you for dinner. I'll pay for these. I insist." Alex patted his back pocket to check that his wallet was there. "I'll be back in a moment. Help yourself to another beer."

Alex left the kitchen before Luis could argue and strode up the hall pulling out his wallet as he went.

"Good evening, sir," said the young man cheerily, as Alex opened the front door wide. "You ordered two pizzas?"

"That's right." Alex withdrew a couple of twenties from his wallet. "Will this cover it?"

The sandy-haired teenager handed over the two oversized pizza boxes he was carrying and took the cash from Alex's hand. As he checked the money, Alex looked him over and winced inwardly. The poor young man's face was covered with a rash of acne. His skin was pockmarked with craters full of angry mini eruptions.

"You've given me too much here." The boy thrust his hands in the pockets of his pizza delivery uniform. "I should be able to break a twenty. Hold on."

"You know what?" interrupted Alex. "Keep it. Consider it your tip."

"Really?" The young man smiled, revealing a dazzling set of bright white teeth. "Thanks." He stuffed the money away and dipped his head towards Alex. "Have a good one, sir. Enjoy the pizzas."

"I will, thanks." Alex gave him a nod in return and took the pizzas inside. As he closed the door, he stood still for a moment. Seeing that poor boy's acne had triggered a memory. That night after he'd walked Joanna to the bus stop, he'd seen an older man whose face was pitted with scarred damaged skin. Alex frowned as he tried to recall where. It had something to do with a playground in a park.

* * * *

January 1961

The sound of Joanna's bus faded in the night air, leaving Alex with only his footsteps for company. There was still about a mile to walk. He crossed over the road. Up ahead was the entrance to a small park. If he cut across to the other side of it, he could easily shave five or ten minutes off his journey. The pathway was uninviting and shrouded in shadows but looked completely deserted. Picturing his warm bed hastened his decision, and he stepped off the lit pavement and into the gloom. It was a short narrow path framed with bushes on either side. All the foliage was shaded a muted grey in the darkness. Alex walked slowly, and waited for his eyes to become accustomed to his dim surroundings. The path opened out onto a huge flat grassy area. Small pathways intersected the lawn, leading off in different directions. Rather than follow one of the meandering paths, Alex fixed his gaze on a tall tree on the other side of the park, behind which were lit streets. It took Alex longer than expected to walk across, but he was nearly there. Up ahead was a children's playground. The swings hung motionless, and the roundabout was still. An abandoned dark-coloured scarf was draped over a bar of the climbing frame. Alex skirted around the seesaw and slide and looked towards the edge of the park where there was a path that he hoped led out to the street beyond.

Next to it was a small one-storey building, the front of which had two illuminated lights hanging above two open doorways. As he walked closer, the signs above each doorway became visible. One read "Ladies," and the other, "Gents." Alex's bladder announced that after the pints he'd drunk in the pub, it was now uncomfortably full. As Alex walked inside, the smell of stale urine and strong disinfectant assaulted his nostrils. Four toilet stalls lined one wall, their doors all open. Opposite were six urinals fixed to the wall. The room was clad in pale green tiles that gleamed in the glow from the ceiling light which was housed in a yellowing plastic casing. A couple of spider webs hung from it. Alex walked towards the urinals, passing two sinks that had seen better days. A mirror was fixed above each sink, and as Alex passed, he grimaced at his reflection. The ceiling light had rendered his skin an unhealthy pallor. He quickly looked away and chose the urinal farthest from the sinks. As he undid the zip of his trousers, Alex gazed down and could see an oversized cake of solid disinfectant nestled amongst the stray pubic hairs gathered around the rusting plug hole. It was a lurid yellow and green in colour. He freed his penis from his underwear, and was about to let loose a torrent of liquid when footsteps echoed on the tiled bathroom floor.

Alex glanced over his shoulder. A man entered through the doorway. He wore a thick long overcoat and was wearing a trilby with the brim pulled down low over his face. Alex's bladder muscles tightened as the man approached the urinal next to his and unzipped his fly. The sound of water hitting the urinal was almost immediate, and Alex gritted his teeth and stared ahead, willing the man to hurry up and leave. He hated using a toilet in public, and especially hated the proximity of others at the urinal.

The man must have noticed that all he was doing was standing there. Heat started to flush Alex's cheeks. The man finished urinating but didn't step back and move away towards the sink. He just stood there. The silent tension in the air was palpable. Alex couldn't bear it any longer. He glanced to his left and met the stare of the man who was wearing the same hopeful look that the boy under the pier had given him. The skin on the man's face was pitted with old scars. Unable to help himself, Alex looked down as the man turned slightly towards him, revealing a stiff, angry cock that jutted out from between his trouser zip. It was long and slightly curved with a purple tip that glistened obscenely under the yellowish light above. The man reached out a hand towards Alex's crotch, but Alex took an involuntary step back and stuffed his own shrunken penis back inside his underwear, then hastily pulled up the zip. He turned quickly on his heel and bolted from the building.

Once outside, he didn't stop. Alex located the nearby path in the gloom and walked quickly along it, listening out for footsteps that would indicate that the man was following him. As he emerged onto a road and the comforting glow of streetlights, Alex tried to calm his trembling body. A tumble of emotions coursed through him. *Why did that man expose himself? Do I look like the type of man who engages in sexual acts with other men in public?* Alex asked himself these questions and more but had no answers.

One thing he was aware of was that the incident under the pier had been fuelled by desire. What just happened in the toilets had resulted in nothing but feelings of disgust and contempt towards the man. Alex wiped his hands on his trousers. His body now seemed soiled and unclean. It was late and he knew that there would be no hot water at home, but even if he had to wash in cold, that would help him scrub away the imaginary dirt clinging to his body. With his bladder still full, Alex scurried along the street, glad that it was deserted. Nobody had seen him. He tried to dismiss the pervading sense of guilt that was irrational, but there, nonetheless. He hadn't done anything wrong, so why did he have to damn well keep on telling himself that?

* * * *

October 1987

Alex shuddered and sagged against the front door, still clutching the warm pizza boxes. He quickly banished the memory away and licked his lips. His mouth was dry. It was time for another beer. "Pull yourself together," he muttered, standing up straight.

"Here we are," Alex announced as he walked into the kitchen. "I don't know about you, but I'm starving." He set the pizza boxes down on the centre island.

Luis lifted the lid of one of the boxes and inhaled deeply. "Damn, that smells good."

Alex snatched up his beer and drank until he'd drained the bottle. He wiped his mouth with the back of his hand. "These pizzas are huge," he remarked. "Do you think you can eat a whole one?"

"I'm going to give it a damn good try," replied Luis, lifting a large wedge of pizza out of the box. Long ropes of mozzarella cheese hung down and stretched out as he pulled the slice free. "I opened the wine I bought and poured us both a glass. Help yourself." Alex's stomach rumbled loudly as Luis bit into the pizza. "You'd better hurry up before I eat it all," added Luis, in-between chews. "I want to hear more about your fairy-tale romance."

"Fairy-tale?" Alex scoffed as he opened up the other box and selected a slice. "It was hardly that."

"Well, what would you call it then?" asked Luis, reaching for his glass of wine.

Alex regarded Luis for a moment. He seemed genuinely interested in hearing about Alex's past, and hadn't been judgemental so far. Then again, he hadn't heard the whole story. That could change depending on how much Alex told him. "Hindsight is a wonderful thing," began Alex, "but some people might say that the night Joanna and I met outside the pub would turn out to be the biggest mistake we'd ever make."

Chapter Six

January 1961

"For God's sake, Alex!" exclaimed Roger. "Will you please stop acting like a startled whippet every time the pub door opens?"

Linda and Mary giggled out loud as Alex's face flushed and he irritably fingered his tight collar.

"It's too hot and smoky in here," he complained, scowling at the tables full of people surrounding them.

Alan jostled through the crowd gathered around the bar, carrying a tray of drinks which he placed down on the table.

"Not much of that left, is there?" remarked Roger, holding up his pint. The top inch was missing.

"Sorry," said Alan. "I nearly dropped the lot trying to get back to the table. We need to find a quieter pub for our next round."

"Maybe," said Alex, taking a sip. "Let's wait here a bit longer."

Alan nudged Roger. "I think someone's in love."

The girls giggled again, and Alex scowled. He had made a mistake telling Roger and Alan about meeting Joanna. They had ribbed him mercilessly all week, and it was the first thing they'd gleefully told Linda and Mary about when they'd all met up here at the pub over an hour ago.

"Well, it doesn't look like she's coming," Alex said darkly. "I haven't seen her friend in here either."

"Well, maybe they're running late," said Roger. He gestured at Linda and Mary. "You know how long these two keep us waiting sometimes."

Alex couldn't help but smile as a flurry of indignant protests erupted from the girls. The door of the pub creaked as it was pushed open, allowing in a gust of cold night air that eddied and swirled in the blue haze of cigarette smoke that hung like mist above the bar. Alex craned his neck and tried to see through the packed, seated crowd that separated him from the door, but his view was blocked. The noise and heat were starting to irritate him, and his eyes were stinging from all the smoke.

Alex regarded the rest of his pint with distaste. He'd finish it, then go. If the others wanted to go elsewhere, then fine, but he was not in the mood. Joanna hadn't shown up, and he was annoyed with himself for his buoyant mood earlier whilst getting ready to go out. It had all been for nothing. He must have misread the signals he had received from her last week when they'd walked to the night bus. Alex sat back, happy to let the others do the talking. His mind was elsewhere. Now that he was in his last year of college, he needed to focus entirely on his studies. Another part of him, though, wanted to quash whatever it was that was buried deep inside that caused him to be attracted to men. This was important, and needed to be addressed if he was going to live a happy life. Joanna seemed nice. He had never had a relationship with a girl before, so logically it made sense that he should at least try to start one.

"Right, I think I'm going to have an early night," said Alex, downing the rest of his pint and standing up.

"But we've only been here for an hour," said Alan, surprised.

"I know. I'm tired."

Alan looked like he wanted to say more, but Roger leaned in close to him and said something in a low voice that Alex couldn't make out above all the noise in the crowded pub.

"We'll see you at college on Monday," said Roger. "Get some rest and make sure you don't study all bloody weekend."

Alex said his goodbyes and shrugged on his overcoat. Guilt followed him to the door, but he was sure they would forget about him before they'd finished their next drink. Outside, he inhaled deeply, clearing his lungs of the smoky pub fog. It tasted good, and he paused to savour it for a moment. Up above, the moon hung brightly. The night sky was mostly clear, and stars twinkled overhead. Alex fastened his coat and walked away from the pub. A car pulled into the kerb behind him. Alex paid it no heed and carried on walking, until a voice called his name. He quickly spun around. Joanna was shutting the back passenger door of the car whilst frantically waving at him, trying to catch his attention. Alex walked back towards her as the car pulled back out onto the road.

"I'm sorry I'm late," said Joanna breathlessly. "Dad had a breathing attack and I had to help Mum calm him down."

"Is he okay? What's wrong with him? Is it asthma?"

Joanna shook her head. "He's got a bad heart. Has done for years. It's got worse recently though, since he became overweight. Mum looks after him, but sometimes I must help, too." Joanna pushed back a few strands of stray hair and tucked them behind her ear. "I knew my friend Susan was going out tonight with her fella, so I managed to get a lift here." Joanna frowned suddenly. "You were walking away from the pub. Are you leaving?"

"I didn't think you were coming," admitted Alex, sheepishly.

"Well, I'm glad I arrived when I did, otherwise I'd have had to go straight home. Without Susan, I wouldn't want to be seen sitting in a pub on my own."

"I'm sorry—I should have waited longer."

"Don't worry," said Joanna brightly, "It was my fault. Shall we go inside?"

"Actually, would you mind if we went somewhere quieter? It's packed in there and hot and smoky. I doubt we would find anywhere to sit."

Joanna didn't reply immediately. It dawned on Alex that she had wanted to return to this pub because it was busy. She had only met him briefly the week before, and he was still a stranger to her. "There's another pub just down the road. We could try there?" Alex gave what he hoped was a winning smile.

Joanna visibly relaxed. "All right, let's see what it's like."

They set off down the road. Alex was aware of her proximity but made sure not to get too close. He wanted her to be comfortable in his presence. Neither of them had gotten off to a good start. "I hope you don't mind me saying this, but you look very pretty tonight. That dress looks really nice on you."

"That's lovely of you to say. You've scrubbed up quite well yourself." Joanna then gave him a bashful smile, revealing the same even white teeth that he had admired last week. In self-conscious movements, she smoothed out the folds in her dark blue dress and pulled her cream cardigan tighter around herself. Alex was pleased that the smile stayed on her face.

"I really am sorry about your dad," he said earnestly.

"Thank you. I worry about him and my mum. My younger sister too. Like me, she left school at sixteen. We both work as my mum spends all day looking after Dad."

Alex wasn't sure how to reply. Even though he'd had a tragic childhood, he'd also been very privileged with regards to his education. It sounded like poor Joanna and her sister had had no choice at all but to go out and earn money for the family. There was always sadness hidden away in many aspects of people's lives. He wasn't alone or special in that regard.

"I think you should both be proud of looking after your parents the way you do," he said finally.

"We try our best," she replied matter-of-factly. "So do you have any brothers or sisters?"

Alex couldn't ignore the not-so-subtle change in conversation. Her situation at home was obviously a sensitive subject, so he would refrain from mentioning it again tonight. "No, I'm an only child." He wanted to tell her more but wasn't sure how much to share right now.

Joanna nodded but didn't say anything. The pub was just up ahead. Fixed high up on the wall above the front door was a swinging sign with a huge sailing ship painted on it. Written on the hull in ornate letters was the name of the ship, and Alex presumed the name of the pub.

"The Hope and Anchor?" said Joanna, raising an eyebrow at Alex. "The coast is about seventy miles away. I doubt many pirates used to drink here."

Alex burst out laughing. "Well, maybe all the pirates grew old and retired to Milton Keynes, and they wanted a pub to remind them of the good old days."

Joanna stepped forward and standing on tiptoes, peered through the diamond leaded glass windows. "Well, the few that are in there appear half asleep. Shall we give it a go?"

"Why not?" replied Alex. He pushed open the door and held it open so Joanna could enter first.

* * * *

June 1961

Alex dabbed a tiny amount of glue onto the propeller mount and slid it into place. Finally, he had finished assembling the model plane. He picked up the Spitfire and admired it from different angles. Joanna had given it to him as a joke present. He had laughed after opening it yet was secretly thrilled as he had never assembled a model plane before. Every evening since, after hours of studying for his rapidly approaching final exams, he rewarded himself with some time to spend building and gluing the plane together. With the assembly now complete, all Alex had to do next was paint it. It was getting late. He glanced at the two small pots of ocean grey and dark green paint. They would have to wait for another night. Alex rubbed his eyes. They were dry and grainy. He was overdoing it. The air at college hung heavy with the expectation from tutors for the students to apply themselves in their last few months of the final term. There was no laughter in the corridors anymore. Instead, students scurried heads down from classroom to lecture hall, clutching folders and sheaves of paper. Even the Friday night visit down to the pub had stopped, which was a shame, as Alex's friends had welcomed a tentative Joanna into their circle as if she was one of their own. After setting the model plane down carefully onto its display stand, Alex sat back and admired it fondly. Although it had been given in jest, the plane symbolised so much more. He couldn't remember the last time that he'd been given a present, so the act itself had come as a complete surprise.

The week after they went for their first drink together at the Hope and Anchor back at the end of January, Alex had eagerly arranged to meet Joanna again at the local pub so he could introduce her to Roger, Alan and their girlfriends. Since then, he tried to see her at least twice a week, including once in the company of his friends. Roger had asked Alex how he was going to spend his Easter holidays, and when he replied that he would go home to Hastings, he had noticed Joanna's downturned mouth out of the corner of his eye.

Later that same evening, as he escorted her to the bus stop, he had commented upon how quiet she was. She'd said she was tired. Alex didn't press any further. Going home to Hastings at the end of each term was just what Alex did. He never questioned it or gave it any thought. This time, though, was different, and it was a strange feeling to consider changing one's schedule for someone else.

Once he had made his decision, out of courtesy, he had called his aunt from a phone box to explain that he wanted to spend the Easter holidays in Milton Keynes, closer to the college so he could prepare for his final exams. Her vague abstract indifference was to be expected, but Joanna's reaction had been one of pure joy. Alex moved across to the open bedroom window, intending to close it. It was now early June, and a balmy breeze rippled the thin curtains. He stood there for a moment, slowly breathing in the summer air in much the same way as he'd relished Joanna's scent when they'd kissed for the first time on the doorstep of her house.

* * * *

March 1961

"Mum wants to meet you," Joanna said out of the blue as they walked out of the cinema, her arm linked through his. She glanced at him. "Don't look so terrified."

Alex stopped in his tracks. "What, why?"

"Well," she began, "I've told her about you, and Mum thought it would be a shame for you to be alone over Easter, so you're invited to the house for lunch on Easter weekend." Joanna looked at him again, this time with hope in her eyes. "Please say you'll come?"

Alex wasn't sure how to answer. "It's very nice of her, but…"

"But what? It's just a bit of food."

Alex didn't reply. She removed her arm from around his. He looked at her. A deep frown creased Joanna's forehead. She was regarding him with an expression that he couldn't read.

"You don't want to meet my family?" she said softly.

Alex shook his head vehemently. "No, it's not that at all."

"Then what is it?" Joanna walked up closer to him, her head back and chin out as she stared him down. Alex shrank back against the wall of the cinema, and looked away from her challenging eyes.

Alex sighed, and let his shoulders deflate. There was no point making up an excuse. She'd get the truth out of him somehow. "Look, I'm sure your family are lovely, but I'm not very good in certain social situations. It took me a whole year just to pluck up the courage to talk to Roger and Alan."

Joanna's face softened and she reached out to stroke Alex on the arm.

"You must think me very silly," he continued. "I've led quite a sheltered life. Even when I was at school, I never went around to any of my classmates' houses. So to go around to my girlfriend's house to meet her parents is incredibly daunting to me."

Joanna's face lit up. "Did you just say girlfriend?" she whispered.

"What? No, I…" Alex backtracked and raised a hand in front of him, as if to ward off a blow. "I'm sorry, I didn't mean to assume…"

Joanna reached out and gripped both of Alex's hands. "Does this mean we're now officially going out together? As girlfriend and boyfriend?"

Alex gazed down into her beautiful hazel eyes. His face was reflected there. "I didn't know how to ask you out," he admitted.

"I think you just did," Joanna said, her voice muffled as she leaned her head against his chest.

Reaching around, he hugged her tightly, his hands pressed against the small of her back.

* * * *

April 1961

Alex looked up at the street sign, then back down at the curled piece of paper in his hand. This was the street. He checked his watch. It was just approaching two p.m. *Perfect.* Joanna's instructions had been easy enough to follow. The rows of terraced houses lining each side of the road were anonymous and nondescript. Each house had a tiny front garden. Some were a riot of colour, as flowers vied for attention, standing proudly in pots. Other gardens were overgrown, whilst some contained nothing but rusting dustbins. Alex found the correct house number. The front gate squeaked as he opened it, the black metalwork pocked with rust. The small front garden was well tended. Yellow daffodils swayed lazily in a flowerbed, and besides the front door, climbing a trellis, a rose displayed a multitude of fat dusky pink flowers. Alex rapped the polished brass door knocker and waited. He swallowed hard, determined not to let his nerves get the better of him. The door opened almost immediately, revealing a beaming Joanna, radiant and colourful in a bright flowery dress featuring blue irises and cornflowers. Her hair was slightly damp. She clapped her hands to her chest.

"You brought flowers," Joanna said, sounding both pleased and surprised.

Alex looked down at the wrapped bundle in his arms. "Actually, I bought two types." He handed over the smaller of the tightly bound stems.

"Tulips," she exclaimed.

"Those are for you, and these are for your mum. I bought some red wine, too," Alex said, lifting his arm from which a plastic carrier bag dangled.

Joanna held the door open. "Come on inside."

Alex stepped into a narrow, carpeted hallway. The smell of cooking filled the air, and the sound of clattering pots echoed from the kitchen.

"Come and meet Mum." Joanna closed the door and led Alex down the hall. They passed the front room. Alex glanced inside. It was small yet inviting and cosy. They passed another door, this one closed, before they entered the kitchen.

"Mum, Alex is here."

Alex wiped his sweaty right hand on his trousers and stepped forward. Joanna's mother closed the oven door and turned to him, wearing an open smile. She smoothed the folds of her apron and held her hand out.

"It's nice to finally meet you, Alex. My name's Carolyn, but everyone calls me Carol."

Her features were very similar to Joanna's although she had a larger frame and longer hair that was pulled back into a ponytail. Alex shook her hand gently and handed over the remaining bunch of flowers. "These are for you."

Carol looked from Alex to Joanna with obvious delight. She gently took the proffered flowers and raised them to her nose. "Lilies, how lovely. They remind me of my wedding day." Her smile faltered for a second and her eyes strayed towards the ceiling before returning to Alex. "Thank you."

"I bought a bottle of wine, too," Alex said, unearthing it from the carrier bag. "I hope it tastes nice."

"Alex, you're spoiling us," Carol said, as Joanna showed her the tulips. "Let's see if we can find some vases. Joanna, where are your manners? Sit Alex down."

Joanna's cheeks flushed. She took Alex by the wrist and moved towards the kitchen table where she pulled out a chair and gestured for him to sit. Alex perched himself stiffly on the edge of the chair and clasped his hands between his knees. He tried to appear at ease as he casually took in his surroundings. The contents of the room looked tired and well used. There were some nice feminine touches though sprinkled throughout. Red-and-white checked curtains framed the back window above the sink. A couple of plants in matching lemon-yellow pots sat on the tiled windowsill. Against the wall opposite the sink was a small kitchen dresser. Its upper shelves were festooned with ornamental plates. On top of the dresser, sitting on a cooling rack, was a large sponge cake covered in icing that was the colour of Cornish clotted cream.

"Here we are," Carol said, as she removed two vases from the cupboard she'd been rummaging in and set them down on the table. After unwrapping the lilies, she started to arrange them in a vase. Joanna followed suit. After a minute, Carol took a step back from the arrangement. "There. How beautiful. Joanna, can you put them on the dining room table please? And tell your sister that lunch is nearly ready." Joanna left the room clutching the vase, and Carol placed the tulips in the centre of the kitchen table. The petals were a pleasing mix of different shades of orange. "I hear that you go to Cranfield College?" she asked.

"Yes, I'm in my final year," replied Alex. Hopefully Joanna wouldn't leave him alone for too long.

Carol nodded but didn't say anything. She turned towards the stove and lowered the gas under the saucepans, before moving across to the fridge. "Let me get you a drink." From inside she removed a bottle of Guinness. "Here you go. It's my husband David's favourite. Have you tried it before?"

Alex shook his head. "Will your husband be joining us?"

"I don't know if Joanna told you, but he's been quite ill recently. It's best he stays in bed and rests. I'll take some food up for him later."

"I hope he gets better soon," said Alex. Carol poured the Guinness into a glass which she set down on the table in front of him. "Thank you."

"It's not really the sort of illness that you can recover from," said Carol quietly. "The best we can do is keep him comfortable." She placed a wire strainer in the sink and poured in the contents of one of the bubbling saucepans. Steam erupted upwards in a cloud.

Alex had no reply. Some things were best left unanswered. He picked up the glass and eyed the black liquid inside, then took a cautious sip. It tasted slightly bitter. Carol asked him a few polite questions about where he was from and other inconsequential things that he dutifully answered without giving too much away. He glanced at the kitchen door. Joanna was taking her time.

"Do you start your final term after Easter?" Carol asked in a conversational tone as she removed a joint of pork from the oven.

"Yes, and then depending on whether I get my degree, I'll need to go out and look for a job."

"Would that mean leaving Milton Keynes?"

It was a trap. Alex could tell exactly where this conversation was heading. Joanna's mum was being clever, not just by the way she spoke, but also because of the sort of questions she was asking. "I'll have to explore all the options if I get any job offers, but yes, I might have to possibly move somewhere else," he said. It was a considered yet honest answer.

Carol transferred potatoes from the roasting tin into a large china serving bowl. "My Joanna seems quite smitten with you. I know she seems a strong person, but inside she's still my little girl. Please don't hurt her by promising her things you can't give." Carol turned and regarded Alex for a moment. She wore a sad smile.

Alex didn't react, even though Carol's words had struck an immediate chord. He willed himself to relax his tightening grip around the glass of Guinness. Her words were unfair. She knew nothing about him. He'd never hurt a soul. Something hissed on top of the stove. Carol whirled around and quickly lifted a saucepan off the heat.

The moment was broken and Alex shifted his weight on the uncomfortable wooden chair. How could he promise anything to anybody? The future weighed heavily on his mind, mainly because it hadn't happened yet, and he couldn't predict where it would take him. All his life, everything had been mapped out for him. Now for once, he was the one who had the power to shape what happened next. Was Joanna going to play a part in that? Maybe, but he certainly had no intention of ever hurting her with hollow promises. Alex banished the questions that clamoured for answers. He could muse upon them when he was alone.

The sound of feet on the stairs heralded the arrival of Joanna, who was shepherding her sister into the kitchen ahead of her. "Alex, this is my sister Lizzie."

Alex stood up and stepped forward, holding out a hand. "Hello Lizzie. It's nice to meet you."

Lizzie took his hand and shook it once. Her gaze met his briefly before looking away. She looked to be a couple of years younger than Joanna, but Alex found her just as pretty, although she was wearing quite a bit of makeup. Joanna must have poked her from behind, because Lizzie jumped.

"Hello," she murmured, her voice barely audible.

"Right girls. Can you start carrying through plates and dishes to the dining room please?" Carol handed Alex a corkscrew. "Would you mind opening the wine? Goodness, I think the last time we had any was when my brother brought back a bottle from Italy last year."

Alex did as he was asked, and followed Carol as she carried the joint of meat through to the dining room where they all sat down and helped themselves to food. After the conversation in the kitchen, Alex realised he'd lost his appetite. He pushed the food around his plate knowing full well that to leave it uneaten would be regarded as an insult. Alex speared a potato on the end of his fork and dutifully put it into his mouth. He chewed and swallowed, then repeated the process without really tasting anything until his plate was cleared.

Chapter Seven

October 1987

Alex eyed the empty wine and beer bottles that were cluttering the kitchen countertop with distaste. He hoped that Luis hadn't felt too hung-over when he'd left earlier to prepare for his exhibition. Even if he had, Alex wasn't too guilt ridden. After all, it was Luis who'd persuaded him to open the second bottle of wine. Alex helped himself to a glass of water, his third already that morning. He'd woken late, and before showering and dressing, he'd checked outside to find Luis' car was no longer parked outside in the street. At least the painkillers were kicking in and his headache was receding. It had been a late night. Somehow they'd managed to eat both pizzas then moved down into the lounge where Alex had continued his story in between Luis refilling their wine glasses. At some point Alex had reminded Luis that he had an early start in the morning, and Alex was glad that he'd done so. The alcohol loosened his tongue and blurred the lines between how much he should tell and what should remain unspoken. Alex silently berated himself. He needed to be more careful. A lot of these memories had been buried deeply away for good reason, and if he was going to continue opening up to Luis, he needed to be cautious about which ones he was going to unearth. Now was not the time to go digging. He had this mess to clean up before he headed on out.

Alex checked the pad of paper he always kept by the kitchen phone. On it was scrawled the name of a gallery in Pasadena near to where Luis used to live. Alex had coaxed the name out of Luis in passing last night and had written it down whilst retrieving the second bottle of wine. Although he'd not been expressly forbidden from attending the exhibition, Alex had no intention of surprising Luis either. Instead, he would just drive down this afternoon, have a quick cursory look at the proceedings then leave. After clearing up the bottles and the grease-stained pizza boxes, Alex decided he had time to change the bedding in the guest cottage. He stepped out into the back garden and winced, raising a hand to shield his eyes from the sun. The sprinklers had left a late morning dew across the lawn which sparkled in the bright light. Alex followed the damp flagstone path down to the door of the cottage.

Inside, everything was neat and tidy. The bed had been made, although the pillow still bore the dent from Luis' head. Alex pulled back the duvet and picked up the pillow. He pressed it against his face and inhaled deeply. Besides the smell of fabric softener, there was another scent. Familiar and yet not. Alex filled his lungs a second time, relishing the subtle traces that Luis had left behind. He dropped the pillow onto the bed and stepped into the adjoining bathroom. The walls of the large room were clad in large travertine stone tiles that were the colour of honey. Besides the sink and toilet, the only other feature was an oversized shower head that protruded from the ceiling in a corner of the open-plan wet room.

On a rail fixed to a nearby wall hung a towel. The floor around the recessed drain under the shower was still wet. Alex reached out and pulled the towel off the rail and carried it back into the bedroom. He stood by the side of the bed and stared at the damp towel clutched in his left hand, acutely aware that Luis had used it to dry himself after showering. Alex ran his thumb over the rough cotton before closing his eyes. He slowly lowered his right hand and pressed it against the growing bulge in his crotch. A soft moan escaped him. Alex raised the towel and gently rubbed it over his face, whilst clawing at his belt buckle until it opened with a soft clink. He frantically pulled at the zip on his trousers and let them slide down his legs until they gathered in a heap around his ankles. Alex yanked his underwear down to mid-thigh, causing his engorged penis to spring free. It was hot to the touch. He gripped the stiff length with his hand. Craving release, Alex pressed the towel harder into his face and started masturbating. It didn't take long. After a couple of hard strokes, he let out a muffled groan as an orgasm overtook him, his body shuddering as he ejaculated. When he was done, he lowered the towel to discover streaks of semen splattered over the bed and pillow.

* * * *

Alex backed his car out of the short drive and onto the street. He checked his reflection in the rear-view mirror. His eyes still looked red and puffy after last night. He leaned over and removed a pair of sunglasses from the glove box. Alex slipped them on and inspected himself again. Much better. He ran the fingers of one hand through his short blond hair and tutted. Like an old piece of clothing, it had faded over the years, as if from countless washes. The vibrant yellow from his youth had bleached away and was now threaded with iron grey. In a few more years he suspected there'd be no trace of its original colour. Alex put the car into gear and pressed his foot gently down on the accelerator. The engine growled and the car moved smoothly forward. It made a welcome change to be doing something different. Otherwise he'd have just been slouching around the house or working in his home office. He wasn't ashamed about what had happened earlier in the guest cottage. Instead, he was more surprised by the impulsiveness of his actions and how sexually charged he'd been in that moment. Alex had sensed before in himself some form of attraction to Luis whenever he was in his company, but it had never manifested itself in this way before. Since arriving in the States, his libido had been practically non-existent. On occasion he would awake with an erection and masturbate desultorily, but that very rarely occurred. Immediately afterwards, he'd pulled his trousers up and stripped the bed sheets. After bundling everything in the washing machine, Alex had remade the bed and taken another shower. No one had seen anything. Any evidence was now washed away. There was no need to dwell on it.

Time to move on. The story he'd told Luis last night was still fresh in his mind, and although the part about the meal being marred by the preceding conversation with Carol, it suddenly struck Alex that afterwards, he and Joanna had said goodbye to each other whilst standing on the front doorstep. Looking back, that was probably the sweetest moment they had ever shared and was a sad reminder of what they could've had together if things hadn't turned out so differently. For the first time in years, Alex wondered what Joanna was doing right now. He glanced at the time displayed on the car radio. It was early afternoon here, so it would be approaching late evening over in England. She was probably getting ready for bed. Was there now another man lying beside her at night? Alex hoped so. He wanted her to be happy and loved. She of all people deserved it.

* * * *

April 1961

Joanna put the door on the latch and pulled it closed behind her. Alex breathed in the early evening air and stepped out into the front garden. The warmth of the day was nearly gone, yet the cool breeze was redolent with the scent of the different flowers growing in the gardens nearby.

"That went well, don't you think? I can tell that Mum likes you."

Alex smiled at her, but kept his thoughts to himself. "Your family are lovely and have been very generous. I wasn't expecting a fancy roast like that."

"Well, I told my mum that you were special to me, and so she thought you deserved a nice meal."

"I'm special to you? How?" asked Alex, moving closer to Joanna. She remained standing on the doorstep, rendering her the same height as him. The mischievous smile he'd grown to recognise in recent months flitted across her face.

"Are you fishing for compliments, Mr Spencer?"

"Maybe," he retorted.

"Let's see," Joanna said, raising a hand and tapping her forefinger on her chin. "Hmm, you're well groomed." She reached out a hand and ran it through his blond hair, then pretended to brush dandruff off his shoulders.

"Hey!" said Alex reaching up to grab her hand. He started laughing.

"Then of course there's the slightly above average intelligence and the passable features," she continued.

Alex covered his mouth to hide his laughter, then adopted a wounded expression.

"Aw, you look like a puppy that's just been punished." Joanna cocked her head to one side and scrutinised his face.

Alex dropped his hand away and let Joanna see him up close. Normally he wouldn't allow anyone to invade his personal space, but something about this was different. He leaned closer until their faces were only inches apart. Alex locked eyes with Joanna, and something unsaid passed between them. Their heads bent together, and her lips grazed against his. He put a hand around her small waist and pulled Joanna towards him. They kissed again, only this time more firmly. The heat from her soft moist lips seemed to pass through his whole body. Alex closed his eyes. Up this close, the perfume from her freshly washed hair and the natural scent of her skin filled his nostrils. It was spring and summer combined. Something fluttered in the pit of his stomach and inside his underwear his penis thickened. They parted. Joanna's chest was rising and falling rapidly, as if she was out of breath.

"I never knew you could kiss like that," she said, stealing a glance up and down the street.

Alex looked over at the front window which was only a few feet away. He didn't want to end a nice day with Carol catching him kissing her daughter on the doorstep for the entire world to see. "Look, I'm going to have to go. The next bus will be along soon."

Joanna pouted and gripped him by his forearms. "I know. I wish you didn't have to. Will I see you next week?"

"Of course. Why don't I meet you outside your store when you finish on Tuesday? That gives me a few days to catch up on studying."

"That sounds good. I can spend the rest of the Easter weekend helping Mum with Dad."

Alex looked down at his arms. "You're going to have to let me go, you know."

Joanna sighed. "Do I have to?" She started to giggle, then let go.

Alex turned and took two steps towards the gate, before spinning on his heels and striding back to Joanna. He pressed his lips against hers for one last kiss. A tiny whimper escaped her mouth as he stepped away and walked back to the gate, which screeched as if in pain when he opened it.

"See you next week. Please thank your mum again for me." Alex waved at Joanna, who remained on the doorstep with her hand raised in farewell, watching him go. Alex retraced his steps and soon found himself waiting by a bus stop that would take him back across Milton Keynes to Mrs Ellis' house.

He raised a finger to his lips and ran it over the surface. Joanna was the second person he had kissed with passion, and although it had been sensual, it had also been tender and sweet. A far cry away from the fervent, animalistic, sucking on each other's tongues that he had experienced with the boy under the pier. Although both kisses were very different, there had been no fear or shame whilst sharing that moment with Joanna.

Further down the street, a bus emerged from a turning and trundled towards him. Alex looked at his watch. He should be home in well under an hour. Then he would work on his latest paper that was due for submission at the college in a couple of weeks. The bus hissed to a stop in front of him. Alex climbed aboard the double decker and paid the conductor before taking the stairs to the deserted top deck. He sat at the front which offered an elevated view of the street ahead. The bus set off, and Alex settled back into his seat to enjoy the leisurely drive along the main roads and through neighbourhoods towards home. Eventually the bus began to pass through familiar areas. Streetlights started to flicker on as the sky darkened.

Off to the right was the entrance to the park which he had crossed late at night a few months back. The bus followed the road around the park's perimeter until Alex found himself on the other side where, from his elevated position, he could see the children's playground, dim in the gloom, silent, and still. The bus slowed as up ahead blue flashing lights lit up the street. Two police panda cars pulled up, blocking the road.

Four policemen emerged, two from each car, and raced up the same path that Alex had scurried down after his encounter in the public convenience. The policemen stopped outside the illuminated toilet block and conferred for a moment before disappearing inside. Even from inside the bus, the muffled shouts were audible. A man fled the entrance to the toilet closely followed by two policemen and headed for the road. The fear on his face was thrown into stark relief by the artificial glow of the streetlights as he tried to refasten his trousers whilst running. The man was slimmer and younger than the two portly officers who were trying to catch him, and he had a good head start as he ran up the street and disappeared down a side road. The policemen gave up chasing him and hurried back to their car, which then sped off in pursuit. Further back, another man with his head hanging low was being marched out of the toilet block by the two other policemen and towards the remaining police car. The bus started to inch forward, as the driver tried to squeeze the double decker past them.

Alex froze as the man being bundled into the vehicle suddenly looked up and locked eyes with him before the policeman bent his head down and pushed him into the back of the car. Although they hadn't passed on the stairwell for a number of weeks, Alex clearly recognised the lodger who rented the room above him at Mrs Ellis's. The bus made it through and started to pick up speed. Alex craned his neck to try and keep the man in sight, but the bus rounded a corner, blocking the view. Numb with shock, lunch and the afternoon forgotten, Alex sat back in his seat. It was obvious what the men had been caught doing, but what would the punishment be? Bloody idiots. Didn't they have anywhere else to go? It was a horrible smelly place, and there was nothing pleasurable about it, so why meet there?

Up ahead was Alex's stop. He rang the bell and waited for the bus to slow down. Alex descended the stairs and thanked the driver. He thrust his hands deep into his coat pockets and quickly walked the rest of the route home. Once outside Mrs Ellis's house, Alex stopped and looked up at the second-floor window. It was dark and the curtains hung open. He turned the key in the front door lock and let himself in. The hall light was on. The sound of the television came from the front room. Alex climbed the stairs and paused on the landing outside his bedroom door, listening hard. The rest of the house was silent. There was no one upstairs. Tonight, the lodger's bed would probably be inside a cell at the police station. Once inside his room, he closed the door. Witnessing the lodger being shepherded into the back of the police car had unsettled him. Alex moved towards the fireplace and began assembling a small fire — not because he was cold, but because he always associated the flames dancing in the grate with memories of being a young boy, warm and safe in the company of his mother. Once lit, he could begin to relax again.

* * * *

One evening, several weeks later, Alex jumped with a start as someone knocked on his bedroom door. He'd been daydreaming whilst hunched over his research papers. It couldn't be Mrs Ellis, as she had wished him a good evening in the kitchen earlier as he ate his meal, just before she left for her weekly bingo night down at the social club. He pushed back his chair and stood up.

"Yes? Who is it?" Alex had a sneaking suspicion it could only be one other person.

"It's Arthur from upstairs. I wondered if you had a minute."

Intrigued, Alex opened his door to reveal the lodger standing there, sheepishly clutching a couple of open bottles of wine and two of Mrs Ellis's glass tumblers, which he thrust forward at Alex.

"A peace offering."

Alex frowned, not understanding.

"I wanted to explain about what you saw the other week, you know, outside the park," Arthur continued.

Alex opened the door wider. "Come in."

Arthur looked relieved and stepped into the room. He put the wine and glasses on top of the desk and stood there, shifting his weight from foot to foot. This was the first time Alex was able to study the man more clearly. Normally they just shared an occasional glance and polite greeting when they passed on the dim stairwell or in the kitchen. Arthur was handsome, with dark coiffured hair that looked lightly oiled. He had piercing green eyes and an Irish accent. They were both about the same height and build, although Arthur had a thinner face, with pronounced sharp cheekbones. He dressed well, too. The grey woollen trousers were complimented by a white shirt and red tie that was flecked with gold. A pea-green waistcoat completed his attire.

"It's nice to finally talk to you. I'm Alex," he said, shutting the door. "I didn't know you were home this evening. Mrs Ellis says that you're rarely here."

"Ah that'll be me work. I'm a salesman of sorts. I travel around a lot." Arthur gestured at the bottles of wine. "I had these left over from some cases of wine I was selling, and they need drinking up."

Arthur still seemed agitated, so Alex took the lead and poured the wine into the two glasses. He handed one to the lodger and gestured for him to sit on the chair by the desk.

"Thanks," Arthur muttered, sitting down.

Alex retreated to the bed and perched on the edge. "No, thank you for bringing the wine. I had some a couple of weeks ago and think I'm developing a taste for it. Cheers." He raised his glass up in the air. Arthur followed suit, yet in an absent, dismissive fashion. Alex took a sip and waited. Although he had a pretty good idea of what had been going on in the public toilet, he wanted to appear ignorant in front of Arthur until he at least learned more.

Arthur drank half the contents of his glass and set it down on the desk. He leaned forward in the chair and looked directly at Alex. "Before I explain, I have to ask, did you tell anyone else about what you saw outside the park?"

Alex shook his head. "It's none of my business."

Arthur uttered a short bark of laughter. "If only the coppers thought the same." He fixed Alex with a shrewd look. "I like men, okay? You don't strike me as the judging type. I know it's illegal 'n all. Anyway, I do appreciate your discretion by not telling anyone about what you saw." Arthur reached up and smoothed back a lock of his hair that had fallen forward. "I just felt I owed you an explanation, even if you don't agree with what I do and who I am."

Alex shrugged, hoping it made him look as if he couldn't care less. He took another large sip of his wine.

"There are a lot of us out there you know," Arthur continued. "Problem is that we've nowhere to go. I can't bring a fella back here now, can I? Mrs Ellis would toss me out if she knew I had a man in my room. I only came down to see you 'cause she's at the bingo right now."

"It's up to you what you do," Alex said, looking Arthur calmly in the eye. "As long as you're not hurting anyone."

Arthur sat there regarding him for a moment. A small smile played around his lips.

"So, what happened in the park?" asked Alex.

Arthur's smile faded, and he looked a bit uncomfortable as he reached for his glass. He downed the contents and filled it up again, then leaned over and topped up Alex's. "I was passing by. I know that sometimes other men go there for, how shall I say..." Arthur thought for a moment. "A little bit of fun," he concluded. "Anyway, inside there was just one fella waiting at the pisser. He wasn't using it. So, I stood beside him. Used it myself and then we both waited. I was just about to reach over and grab his you-know-what when the police came in. They hadn't actually caught us doin' anything. Our trousers were open, but that's all. Still the fuckers had to make a big show of it and drag me outside and arrest me. The other guy bolted, and I think he got away, as I never saw him again. As for me, I spent a night in the cells and was let out in the morning with a caution. I got off lucky, I tell you."

"So why did you do it?"

Arthur smirked. "Why do we do anything? You'd have thought I would've learnt my lesson by now. Me mam threw us out of home after I was caught with another lad from down the road."

"What? How old were you?"

"I'd just turned seventeen. That was a while ago. I'm thirty-one now. I've not been back." He downed another deep swig of wine.

Alex couldn't believe that Arthur was telling him all this in such a nonchalant manner. "I'm sorry to hear that. It sounds like you've been on your own for a while now."

Arthur grinned at him and swatted the air dismissively with one hand. "I'm me own best company. Used to it. I get by." He gestured at Alex's glass. "You need topping up again. It's good stuff, right? A couple of glasses before bed and you'll sleep like a baby." Arthur stood up and grabbed the bottle. He stepped over in front of Alex and poured more wine, filling his tumbler to the brim.

Alex started to relax. Arthur seemed nice enough, and it was generous of him to share his wine. It was delicious but tasted stronger than other wines he'd tried before. He took another big swallow.

"I hope you don't mind me saying, but you look mighty young to be lodging here." Arthur observed. He sat back down, setting the empty bottle back on the desk.

"I'm a student. Final year," Alex said, by way of explanation.

"What are you studying?"

The words didn't come readily to mind. "Aero-nautical engineering," Alex said, after a beat.

"Something to do with planes then?" Arthur offered, reaching for the second bottle.

"Well, yes. It's a bit more complicated than that." Alex replied. He raised a hand to his mouth to stifle a giggle.

"Tell me."

Alex was aware that he was speaking, and that Arthur was nodding in all the right places. To accentuate a point he'd just made, Alex gestured with his glass, and wine slopped over himself and the bed sheets. He ignored it. Arthur was quick to stand and top up his glass again.

"Intelligent and good looking," exclaimed Arthur. "You'll go far, unless you get some girl up the duff, that is." He chuckled to himself. "Don't mind me. I say what I think."

Alex raised a hand to his cheek. It was hot. He was at a loss to say anything in reply. Arthur let out another chuckle and sat down on the bed next to Alex and patted him twice on the knee.

"The problem with the girlies is that they act all prim and proper and never put out for young lads like you. Where's the fun in that?" Arthur asked, turning to Alex. "I remember when I was your age, I was out looking for a bit of fun every day. And if you know where to look, you can usually find it."

Arthur winked and patted Alex on the knee again, but this time the hand stayed resting there. Alex looked down, his vision swimming. The room was starting to sway a little.

"So, if you ever come home after a hard day at college, and you fancy a little bit of light relief," continued Arthur, "you can always pay me a visit in my room when Mrs Ellis is out, like tonight. Maybe we can come to some regular arrangement?"

Arthur's hand moved slowly up Alex's thigh and stopped at his groin where it prodded and probed. Alex tried to lift his arms, but they'd become leaden. He didn't resist as Arthur removed the glass of wine from his hand and pushed him back so that he was lying on the bed with his feet still resting on the floor. There was a chink of metal as hands fumbled with his belt. Then his shoes were removed.

"Lift yourself up a bit," urged Arthur.

Alex obeyed, and lifted his bottom, allowing Arthur to pull down his trousers and underwear in one go. Without warning, his penis was suddenly engulfed by a hot wetness. Alex groaned as sparks of desire danced around his groin. A distant voice in his head told him that they shouldn't be doing this, but with Arthur's mouth and tongue working their magic, he didn't want the pleasure to stop. Alex lay immobile as Arthur's hands explored his body, pushing up his shirt and vest so his nipples could be pinched and sucked. He drifted on a sea of sensations, old and new, pliant and receptive.

When Arthur rolled him over, Alex couldn't lift his head. He was buried face down on the bed, the smell of Mrs Ellis's laundry detergent tickling his nose. From behind came the sound of a belt buckle being undone. Alex tried to speak, but he couldn't find the words. Instead, he closed his eyes and allowed himself to fall. Deeper and deeper, sinking and descending, endlessly towards the darkness that rushed up to meet him.

* * * *

Alex awoke. His mouth was dry and puffy as if full of cotton wool. A pounding rhythmic throbbing pulsed angrily in his head. He cracked an eye open and turned over onto his back, familiarising himself with his surroundings. He was sprawled across the dishevelled sheets of his bed. Alex sat up and the pain in his head doubled. An unpleasant burning sensation lined his bowels. Before he could reach around to check himself, Alex was gripped by a sudden rush of nausea. He swung his legs out of bed as his stomach contracted. Alex bolted for the door, not caring that he was only wearing a white vest and a pair of socks. The landing was empty. He ran into the bathroom and threw himself down on the floor in front of the toilet. Alex slammed the lid into the upright position with a loud bang. He leant over the rim as his gorge rose and vented the contents of his stomach. Remnants of his supper splattered the bowl, along with a hot torrent of red wine. The acrid stench assaulted his nostrils as he slumped down onto the floor with a groan. Another contraction gripped him. Alex pulled himself up into a crouching position, and let his body purge the remaining contents of his stomach into the toilet. More wine dribbled down the inside of the pan. He reached for the toilet handle and pulled. The water swirled his excesses away.

Alex staggered upright and lurched towards the sink. He turned on the cold tap and cupped his hands under the flow. After rinsing out his mouth, he gulped down the sweet-tasting water, relishing each swallow until his stomach revolted and he was sick again. When he caught his reflection in the mirror, his red puffy eyes gazed balefully back, daring him to justify his current state. In the background, the bathroom door was open.

He hoped no one had heard anything, or worse, was coming to investigate. Alex cupped his genitals and scurried back to the safety of his bedroom. He was furious that Arthur had got him drunk then taken advantage of him in his own room.

Alex paced the floor and marvelled at his own naivety. "I'm so stupid! Of course he offered wine to lower my defences," he muttered, banging his fists against his naked thighs. "Then find out who I'd told about what I'd seen by the park, and then ensure my silence by allowing him to..." Alex's voice faltered. "...do things to me," he finished.

Alex glanced down at the wine stains that marked his discarded clothes, puddled on the floor. He cursed. Even the ruffled bed sheets were marked. Alex looked closer and was alarmed to see what looked like spots of blood amongst the wine splatters. They were a darker, more crimson colour, drying to brown. A hazy recollection of last night came to mind. Arthur's weight bearing down on top of him, the sharp pain of being penetrated and the grunts and thrusts that followed. Instinctively, Alex reached around behind himself to check for the source of the blood but stopped short. He didn't want to know.

"What is it with all these men?" Alex couldn't ignore the anguish in his voice. "Why is everything they do so goddam furtive and dirty?" He wiped away a tear that threatened to spill down his cheek and moved over towards the bed where he carefully lay down, pulling the wine and blood-stained sheets up and over himself. Alex screwed his eyes tightly shut, wanting to close out the world.

"Happy thoughts," he whispered into the pillow. Memories of his mother slowly came to mind, and Alex grew calmer. Then an image of him kissing Joanna goodbye on the doorstep, drifted into view. Alex banished it. He didn't deserve to have her in his head right now. The guilt and shame over what had happened last night was immediate. "Sleep," he intoned. "Please sleep." He pulled the sheet up over his head, and imagined it was a shroud.

Chapter Eight

October 1987

Alex turned off the car engine. Silence descended in the cool gloom of the underground car park. He hadn't allowed Arthur to intrude into his thoughts for decades. Recalling what had happened to him was almost as shocking as the incident itself. Alex took off his sunglasses and threw them onto the passenger seat. He wiped his sweaty palms on his trousers. *Who am I kidding?* he asked himself. Calling it an incident did not disguise the fact that he'd been raped. There was no escaping that. Alex had never told a soul, nor had he any intention of doing so, but the fact that it had ever happened now filled him with an indignant anger that surprised him with its intensity.

"Not that there's a damn thing I can do about it," he said aloud, reaching down to release his seatbelt.

Alex climbed out of the car and slammed the driver's door shut behind him with more force than necessary. Keeping the painful memory alive was almost like saying that Arthur had won, even though there had been no competition. There was no way that Alex would allow that to happen. Hopefully, Arthur's predilections had caught up with him and he was in prison, or, even better, currently residing in hell. Although Alex wasn't a religious man, the image of Arthur screaming in agony as flames engulfed him for all of eternity brought a grim smile to his face.

After climbing two flights of stairs, Alex emerged out of the car park and onto the busy Pasadena Street. Blinking rapidly in the bright sunlight, he took a moment to get his bearings. It had been a while since he'd visited Luis' apartment when he lived here. Alex recognised a familiar restaurant across the road where they'd eaten a couple of times. If he was correct, the gallery should only be a block or two away from here.

It didn't take long to find, but once outside, Alex was reluctant to go in. He'd never visited a gallery before and wasn't sure if there was some kind of etiquette he should follow. Hanging back, Alex pretended to inspect the artwork hanging in the large plate-glass window. At first glance, the large square canvas was not much to look at. Its surface had been liberally coated with blue oil paint. There were no other features to command one's attention, yet for some reason, something about it drew Alex to lean closer. The swirl of the brush strokes indicated movement which was enhanced by the subtle drifting change in the shading. The bottom of the painting was an inky midnight blue, which rose and changed into a more pleasing aquamarine towards the top. The initials LB were printed neatly in one corner.

"It's the ocean," Alex murmured, stepping back to appreciate the piece as a whole.

"Can I help you?" interrupted a man standing in the gallery doorway holding a clipboard. "Do you have an invitation?"

"Sorry, I'm afraid not," replied Alex. "I am interested in this painting, though. Is it for sale?"

The man rather rudely made a point of openly looking Alex up and down. "We're hosting a private event at the moment." He glanced back into the gallery. "Wait here. I'll see if there is someone who can help you."

The man went back inside, leaving the door ajar. Inside was a reception area. Behind it was a large rectangular room that stretched back out of Alex's line of sight. Small groups of people slowly milled around, flutes of champagne in hand, pausing now and again to admire the various pieces of artwork adorning the walls.

A tall elegant woman dressed in a severe black dress strode into view walking towards him, her hand outstretched. "Jennifer Golding. I'm the gallery owner." Her warm smile was matched by the flaming mass of orange curls that graced her head. "I gather you're interested in one of our paintings?"

Alex shook her hand then pointed at the blue oil painting. "This one." He smiled apologetically. "I don't have an invite though."

Jennifer laughed. "A sale is a sale in my book. You have a good eye. That's one of Luis Batista's more recent pieces." She stepped aside and gestured for Alex to come in. "Let's go into my office. I can spare five minutes."

She ushered him into the reception area, then down a short corridor that led away from the main gallery. Her office was small and surprisingly non-descript. Alex had expected art to be hung on every wall, but they were as bare as the ones in his house.

"Please take a seat," Jennifer offered. She manoeuvred herself behind her desk and rifled through a small stack of papers. "Here we go." She ran a manicured finger down a page. "Piece eighteen is titled 'Hidden Depths'."

Alex's heart missed a beat as she read out the price tag. He'd never purchased a piece of artwork before, but wasn't expecting it to cost that much. "Will you take a cheque?" he asked, hoping his voice sounded nonchalant.

"Of course," Jennifer replied smoothly.

Alex reached for his chequebook and began filling in the cheque. Once his signature was added, he tore it free and slid it across the desk.

"I'll get my people to pack up the canvas securely," assured Jennifer as she began writing out a receipt. "All I need now is an address and we'll deliver it on Monday."

Alex leant forward and handed her a business card. "It's probably best to deliver it here."

Jennifer nodded and stood up. "Thank you for your custom" — she glanced down at the card — "Mr Spencer."

As they passed back through the reception area towards the gallery entrance, Jennifer touched Alex lightly on the arm, drawing him to a halt. "I know that it's invitation only today, but seeing that you've purchased one of his paintings, would you like the opportunity to meet the artist?" She pointed towards a group of people gathered in the main gallery.

Alex recognised Luis standing in the centre of the crowd, talking animatedly to them, and a sudden surge of pride and affection washed over him. He turned to Jennifer. "Thank you, but that might spoil the magic. I don't want him to explain his process. I prefer the mystery of viewing the finished piece without knowing how he created the artwork."

Jennifer nodded. "I understand completely. I'm sure Luis would, too."

"I'd like to think so," replied Alex. "I'll look forward to hanging the picture in my home soon." He shook her hand a final time and hurried from the gallery before he was seen.

* * * *

The phone kept ringing. Eight, nine, ten times. Alex was just about to hang up when a breathless voice answered.

"Hello?"

"Luis? It's Alex."

"Oh hey. Sorry, I've only just got in."

Alex glanced at his watch. It was approaching eight p.m. "That's a long day. Did the exhibition go well?"

"Actually, yes it did. There was a good turn out and I sold some pieces, too. Traffic was a bitch on the way back. That's why I'm home so late."

Alex toyed with the stem of his wine glass. "You should have stayed at mine again. You know you're always welcome."

"Yeah, maybe I should have. It would have been a nice way to end the day. I'm tired, so I'll probably just have an early night. What about you though? How was your day?"

"That sounds like a good idea." Alex took a small sip of wine before continuing. "My day was pretty quiet. I caught up on a few chores. I have to admit that I found myself pretty much at a loose end. Normally we both do something together on Saturdays, so it felt strange having the day free."

"I thought the same!" exclaimed Luis. "I tell you what. Why don't you come down after work next Friday and stay? Spend the weekend here. It seems silly to drive eighty miles down here most Saturdays, just to cook a meal and then spend another two hours driving back again in the evening. You can stay in the guest room."

Alex considered Luis' proposal. He had no plans and Luis did have a point. The drive there and back was pretty tedious. "Sounds good," he agreed. "Something to look forward to. Oh, I nearly forgot. When I was out and about today, on impulse, I purchased my first piece of artwork for the house."

"Oh, really? Who's it by?"

"I forget who," replied Alex dismissively. "I just liked it."

"I'm intrigued. I've always been interested in what it is that attracts a person to a piece of art. You know, that initial connection. It's a very personal thing."

"Mmm," Alex agreed. "I'm a complete novice, but I don't want to be told which pieces I should like and why. I like discovering the hidden depths of a painting by myself."

"Well, I look forward to the grand unveiling."

"I'll add your name to the guest list, although I'm making no promises," said Alex, with a smile.

"Ha, that sounds about right," replied Luis. He chuckled briefly. "Look, I'd better go. I need to fix myself something to eat before it gets too late."

"Okay. Have a good rest of the weekend and we'll catch up next Friday. I'll try and get away early and be down before six p.m."

"Sounds good. See you then and thanks again for letting me stay last night."

"My pleasure," said Alex. "Bye, Luis."

"Bye, Alex."

Alex reluctantly hung up. Part of him had wanted to say more. Without Luis actually being there, it would have been easier to reveal the conflicting tide of emotions that he always experienced in Luis' presence, but as usual, his reticence to discuss feelings had prevented that from happening. Alex still wasn't sure how to define his relationship with Luis. They were friends, that was for sure, but sometimes it seemed like there was more to it than that. Just silly things really, such as a glance that lingered a moment too long, or walking alongside each other, but maybe a bit closer than necessary. What frustrated Alex most of all wasn't the possibility that his feelings for Luis were unrequited but that it was inconceivable that he would ever pluck up the courage to divulge them.

* * * *

The week had passed uneventfully, which had suited Alex just fine. He was looking forward to spending the weekend with Luis. Hopefully it would be an unhurried, relaxing couple of days. The car left the on-ramp as Alex eased it into the heavy flow of traffic clogging the freeway. Although he'd finished work early with the aim of beating the rush hour traffic, it seemed that he was not alone in having that thought. At least each lane was moving and they weren't gridlocked. Alex was determined to keep his spirits high. He patted his overnight bag that rested on the passenger seat. Usually any nights spent away from home were because of work, so this made a nice change. The last thing he'd done before leaving the house was to hurry back down to the lounge to take a final look at Luis' painting, which had been delivered on Monday, and after much deliberation, now hung centre stage above the fireplace. It amused Alex that every evening that week, after finishing his evening meal, he had sat in the lounge and stared entranced at his new purchase. Buying art seemed such a terribly grown-up thing to do and Alex was proud of himself for being so impulsive. It made a welcome change. Luis was never far from his thoughts as he regarded the artist's painting, and towards the end of the week, Alex decided that since he'd started recounting stories from his past, he now needed to come clean and tell Luis about the incident that had brought about his divorce and subsequent life here in Los Angeles. He wasn't sure why, only that it was important to him and seemed the right thing to do. A long, oversized truck growled slowly past in a neighbouring lane. The container it was hauling was tall enough to block out the sun, casting Alex's car into shadow. All this talk about his youth was releasing a torrent of old memories, and even now, as the truck passed and the momentary shadows were replaced by golden sunlight, Alex remembered a long hot August when he returned to Hastings after finishing his degree.

* * * *

August 1961

The beaches of Hastings were already packed with people. It was mid-morning, early August, and Alex was standing at the top of the Tamarisk Steps. There was a viewing point here that looked down over the tall black fisherman's huts. He leant forward and looked to the right where the beaches and pier were. Throngs of visitors packed the pavements and promenade. Alex shaded his eyes from the merciless sun, incandescent, overhead. He had hoped to go for a walk on the beach, but that was out of the question. The idea of having to skirt around picnicking families, and screaming children, whilst dodging Frisbees and beach balls filled him with horror. All he wanted to do was escape the confines of his aunt's house and be left alone with his thoughts. It wasn't too much to ask.

Alex turned around to retrace his steps. He was resigned to spend the rest of the day inside. It wasn't being back in Hastings or staying back in Aunt Edith's house that was the problem. It was far simpler. Alex was completely and utterly bored, and although he wouldn't admit it to himself, he suspected he was depressed, too. Since his final exams, everything had been an anti-climax. June had been stressful. He'd submitted his final papers and sat various exams and now his three years of studying were over. The college had held an open day for various employers to visit and groom potential employees, and Alex had been offered numerous jobs contingent on him securing a good-enough degree. Now it was all about playing the waiting game.

Guilt plagued him daily because he had left Joanna behind. She called him most days after work from a phone box outside the department store. Mrs Ellis had already lined up another student to take his room, and after his encounter with Arthur, he couldn't move out quickly enough. It made sense to return to Hastings where his room was rent-free. He'd explained all of this to Joanna, except the part about Arthur, and imagined that her mother Carol would think harshly of him, as he had done exactly as she had predicted.

The first week back in Hastings, Alex had caught up on sleep as his mind and body were exhausted. The problem now was how to keep his mind active. He had spent the last three years studying hard, and now there was nothing to do. It was driving him crazy. His aunt wasn't much company as she spent most of her time in the back garden, weeding and planting. Whenever he looked out of any of the back windows, he would invariably spot her kneeling amongst the flowers and shrubs, wearing the wide-brimmed floppy sun hat that she favoured. It was out of the question to invite Joanna down to stay, even just for a weekend, as Aunt Edith had rather strict views about unmarried women staying in the same house as young men, so he had never bothered asking. Alex let himself into the house. The ticking grandfather clock in the hall chimed the hour. He sloped towards the kitchen and stopped in the doorway. His aunt was sitting at the small table.

"Ah Alex, I was hoping you wouldn't be too long. I've been waiting for you."

Alex frowned at her. "Is anything wrong, Auntie? I just went for a quick walk. I was going to stroll along the beach, but it's full of people."

"Yes, yes, never mind all that, come in, boy," urged Aunt Edith impatiently. She beckoned him closer and pointed at a letter that was propped up on the table, leaning against the salt and pepper shakers. "This arrived a short while after you left."

Alex sat down opposite his aunt, his eyes fixed on the envelope. His name was printed above the address. "Is that what I think it is?"

"There's only one way to find out."

Alex didn't move. His aunt leaned forward and picked up the letter and slid it across the table until it lay in front of him. He picked it up slowly and turned the letter over.

"Go on," Aunt Edith said.

Alex inserted a finger under the gummed flap and tore the seal. Inside was a folded piece of paper. He removed it and spread it out flat on the table.

"Let's see. Dear Alex Spencer…" He scanned further down the page reading aloud parts of the letter under his breath. "…the examining board…completed modules and coursework…submitted papers…awarded a first-class honours degree with distinction." Alex snatched up the letter and read it again. He looked up at his aunt who had clasped a hand to her mouth. Her eyes shone with tears. "I did it," he whispered. He dropped the letter on the table with a heavy sigh.

Aunt Edith stood up and moved around the table. "Yes, you did it," she said, her voice wavering with emotion. "I'm so proud of you. Your mother and father are proud of you, too. They'll be looking down on you right now." She stepped closer and held her arms out. Alex just stood there dazed and let her lean in and hug him. After a moment, Aunt Edith released him from her embrace. She dabbed at her eyes with a balled-up tissue that had appeared from about her person.

"You'd better call one of those companies that want to hire you. Strike while the iron's hot, as they say," she said.

"You're right," he answered. "I will do, but first I want to visit Mum and tell her the good news."

"Before you go, Alex, I have something for you. Hold on." Aunt Edith hurried into her parlour and emerged a moment later clutching a small rectangular piece of paper. "This is for you," she said, handing it over.

Alex read the first line of the cheque that was made out to him. "One thousand eight hundred pounds?" he said incredulously and looked at his aunt for an explanation.

"It's your inheritance from your parents," she said. "I held the money in trust and invested it for you. It's not as much as I'd planned on, seeing some of it was used to help pay for your lodgings and give you a bit of spending money whilst you were studying. Still, there is enough there to buy yourself a flat or possibly a house if you were to get a small mortgage. I would advise against renting. Put the money into bricks and mortar."

Alex was overcome with gratitude. "You've always looked after me. Thank you, Auntie."

A small smile appeared on Aunt Edith's face. "Someone had to, and I'm glad that that person was me. Now go and put that cheque somewhere safe and pay it into your bank account tomorrow. I'm going to go out shopping and get us something nice for a celebratory meal tonight. Do you think the occasion warrants a bottle of wine?"

"Most definitely," said Alex, and grinned.

* * * *

Alex leant against the balustrades as he sat on the bottom step of the stairs and waited for the phone to ring. The grandfather clock had just chimed six p.m., so Joanna should be leaving work around now. He was not looking forward to this call. Although the news today had been positive, the decisions he'd made came with repercussions. Alex stopped biting his nails and looked at them critically. Several had been bitten down to the quick and were starting to throb. The shrill sound of the phone ringing made him jump. He snatched up the handset.

"Hello?"

"Alex, it's me, Joanna. How are you?"

"Good thanks. It's nice to hear your voice. How was your day at work?"

"It wasn't great. Mr Purvis the floor manager was in a bad mood and made Cynthia cry. I spent most of the afternoon consoling her. How about you? I bet you're loving the hot weather."

"I tried to go for a walk on the beach today, but there were too many people." Alex paused. "Listen, I've got something I need to tell you. I got my university degree results today." There was a sharp intake of breath down the phone.

"Are you pleased? Did you get a good score? Alex, tell me."

"I got a first-class honours degree with distinction."

There was silence at the other end of the phone. "Is that good?" she asked cautiously. "I don't mean to be silly, but I'm not really sure how they mark these things."

"Yes, it's good. Actually, it's the highest mark you can get."

Joanna squealed. Alex held the phone away from his ear for a moment.

"Oh, Alex, I'm so proud of you. I can't wait to tell Mum. So, what will you do now?"

Alex winced and started pulling at his ear lobe. "Erm, well things have started to move along rather quickly. I've been reading all the information I was given by some of the companies that said they would offer me a job if I got my degree. One in particular looked good, so I rang them this afternoon." Alex paused, not wanting to elaborate.

"And?" Joanna prompted.

Alex closed his eyes and swallowed hard. "They want me to start in three weeks' time at the beginning of September."

"Okay, and where would you be working?"

"Dartford."

"Dartford? Where's that?"

Alex was beginning to detect an edge to Joanna's voice. "Outside London."

"How far outside London?"

"Well, the brochure they gave me says they're based eighteen miles southeast of London."

"Alex! That's too far! When will I ever get to see you?"

"I could come and visit you at weekends, or maybe you can come down and visit me." He tried to sound upbeat. "We'll work it out."

"And who's going to pay for that?" Joanna snapped.

"It shouldn't cost too much. I've worked out that Dartford is about eighty miles away from Milton Keynes. Some people travel that far to work every day."

"Eighty miles? Alex, I do not want a long-distance relationship. They never work." Joanna started crying.

"Joanna, please don't get upset. We'll come up with the answer soon, I promise."

"Alex, I'm not one of your bloody maths formulas! Couldn't we have talked about this first? It sounds like your career is far more important than I am." Joanna sniffed hard. "I've got to go. Mum's in a bit of a state. Dad's been moved to hospital so they can keep an eye on him around the clock. I said I'd cook dinner tonight as she's visiting him at the moment." She let out a deep sigh. "Goodbye, Alex."

"Wait, no, don't hang up. Hello? Joanna? Are you there?" There was no reply. The line had gone dead. He slowly put the handset back in the cradle. The grandfather clock ticked on.

* * * *

September 1961

Alex was aghast at how much he'd had to spend to secure a small furnished flat that he could rent. Firstly, there was the exorbitant deposit, then there was the monthly rental charge which, although he was outside of London, was still surprisingly high. Once he had accepted the job offer in Dartford, his aunt had practically pushed him out the door to go down there and get settled before he started work. A few days later, armed with two suitcases full of clothes, Alex had booked himself into a small bed and breakfast in Dartford. Whilst he familiarised himself with the area, he made enquiries about finding somewhere suitable to rent. A week later, the landlord handed him the keys.

Although the decor was not to his taste, the flat was at least clean. There was a double bedroom, a tiny bathroom and a living room with a small kitchenette in one corner. It would only be for a few months until he bought somewhere. Alex was sad that he had no one to share his excitement with. Joanna hadn't been in contact with him since he had told her about the job offer, and he had no way of getting in touch with her. There was no phone at her house, and he didn't want to get her in trouble at work by calling there. He doubted they accepted personal calls. Joanna's protracted silence was unsettling him. Was it over between them? He could always get on a train back up to Milton Keynes, but what sort of reception would be waiting for him? Probably not a pleasant one. Alex was at a loss about how to proceed and was acutely aware that the longer he left it, the worse things would be between them.

* * * *

Alex jumped in his seat as the office door opened and a man stepped out into the corridor. "Mr Spencer? Please come in."

Alex stood up quickly and followed him inside.

"It's Alex, isn't it?" The man closed the door and crossed the room towards a desk. He gestured at the chair placed in front of it. "Please sit."

"Yes, sir." Alex sat down and smoothed out the creases in the trousers of his newly purchased suit.

The man smiled benignly. "There's no need to call me sir. Mr Connolly will do. Now, let's see." He picked up a thin folder from off the desk and rifled through its contents.

Alex waited patiently, but not without some trepidation. This was his new boss, so it was important that he made the right impression. The man was probably in his late forties, and of average build. An unruly shaggy mop of brown hair crowned his head, the sides heavily streaked with grey. A thick-rimmed pair of black spectacles dominated his face, making his eyes look bigger than they were. Mr Connolly was wearing the obligatory shirt and tie that was standard office attire, but their colours were faded.

"Well, I can't fault your credentials, Alex, and your degree from Cranfield is exemplary. I think you are going to be a real asset to us here at Napier-Bell Engineering." Mr Connolly sat down behind his desk. "Just to give you a bit of background, in recent years we've become primarily subcontracted by the British Aircraft Corporation, specialising in research and development of a variety of aviation systems and technologies. You'll be mainly based in this building, although we do have a manufacturing facility just outside of Dartford where most of our prototypes are made. I'll schedule you in for a visit there during the coming weeks. For now, though, I think we'll just take a quick tour and introduce you to some of your colleagues."

Alex was quietly impressed as Mr Connolly showed him around. It was a three-storey oblong building filled with a multitude of offices and laboratories that branched off the central corridor than ran along each floor. Big glass windows allowed him to view lab technicians in white coats tinkering with scale models of prototype engines, whilst in another room, a small group of men huddled around a turbine which was hanging from a chain fixed to the ceiling. The smile on

Alex's face grew wider. This was his playground, and he was going to be paid to work here, doing what he loved most of all. Mr Connolly led Alex down another flight of stairs and stopped outside an office where he pointed through a large window at two men who were both bent over a large desk studying vast sheets of technical drawings.

"Right, this is you," said Mr Connolly. "You'll be working in different departments, but I thought we'd start in here. Smith and Matheson will show you the ropes, and I'll take you up to accounts later today so we can get your details put on the payroll. Any questions?"

Alex shook his head. Mr Connolly opened the door and gestured for him to go in. Alex's stomach was full of butterflies, yet he wasn't sure if it was due to fear or excitement. He took a deep breath and stepped into the room.

* * * *

As Alex settled into a routine at work, September slid into October, and the early evenings started to grow darker as he walked home every day. It was getting colder, too. Before long it would be Christmas. On impulse, one evening, Alex stopped at a phone box. There was no phone at the flat, and he hadn't spoken to his aunt in a while. He didn't fancy spending Christmas alone in Dartford. Alex dialled the number from memory, and after several rings, a familiar voice answered.

"Hello, Auntie, it's Alex. How are you?"

"Oh, Alex, I'm so glad you called." The relief in her voice was evident. "Your lady friend from Milton Keynes phoned me a couple of days ago asking if I had a number that she could call you on. She sounded very upset, and when I asked her what was wrong, she told me that her father had passed away in hospital the night before. I explained that you didn't have a telephone yet, and she asked me to pass on what had happened next time I spoke to you."

Alex froze. Poor Joanna and her mother and sister. This changed everything.

"Hello? Alex? Are you there?"

"Sorry, Auntie, I was just thinking. I'll catch a train up there on Saturday and go and see her. See if I can do anything to help."

"Good boy. When will I be seeing you next?"

"I was hoping to come home for Christmas if that's okay?"

"Alex, you should know better than to have to ask. I trust you're still enjoying the job? I look forward to hearing about it in detail when I see you."

"Yes, they're a good company to work for. It's hard work, but interesting, too. I'd better go. I don't have any more change for the phone."

"All right then, dear, we'll speak soon. I hope that poor girl will be all right."

"Bye, Auntie." Alex hung up. He suspected his aunt had consumed a couple of gin and tonics. She never called him dear. He left the phone box and walked slowly back to the flat, unable to dismiss the image of Joanna and her family sitting together at home taking solace in each other.

* * * *

As Alex stepped off the train, he stopped to briefly survey the familiar surroundings. Nothing had changed. Milton Keynes was exactly as he had left it. He'd timed it perfectly. It was late afternoon. Now it was all about supposition. Alex was banking on Joanna having returned to work. He didn't want to risk the possible hostility he would receive from an already traumatised Carol if he turned up on their doorstep unannounced. It was a grim featureless day. The sky was the colour of lead. The street was wet when he emerged from the station. Passers-by hurried along the pavements with their heads down. Alex joined them and set off walking briskly in the direction of the department store where Joanna worked. As he approached the store's front entrance, he looked at his watch. They would be closing the doors in ten minutes, and if Joanna was working, she should leave shortly after. The streets were still busy with traffic and shoppers, and to avoid being conspicuous, he passed the time by looking in nearby shop windows, all the while keeping an eye on the store entrance. When the store closed, the amount of people around him thinned out, and when some of the staff started to filter through the front doors, Alex had no problem spotting Joanna. She looked pale and drawn, but still as pretty as the first time he had set eyes on her. He called her name, and she stopped in her tracks, looking abruptly at him. Alex was mortified as her eyes widened and she promptly burst into tears. Shoppers regarded her with concern, but she paid them no mind. He rushed over and put his arms around her, hoping she wouldn't resist. She crumpled into his arms, sobbing uncontrollably.

"Joanna, I'm so sorry." He wanted to say more, but right now, just holding her seemed more important. Her hot tears dampened the front of his shirt. He waited until the crying began to lessen.

"No, I'm sorry. You must think me dreadfully silly." Joanna took a step back, her breath hitching as she spoke. "It was just a shock to see you standing there."

He gently led her over to a closed shop doorway to afford some privacy. "I feel awful," Alex admitted. "I haven't been there for you when you needed me. I only found out about your dad a couple of days ago when I phoned my aunt. I came up as soon as I could."

Joanna took a tissue from her purse and blotted her eyes then wiped her cheeks. "Oh, Alex, it's been awful. Mum's gone to pieces, and Lizzie won't come out of her room."

Alex put an arm around her and pointed across the street. "Look, there's a café over there. Why don't we go and have a nice cup of tea? You'll feel better, I promise."

Joanna nodded. They crossed the road and Alex held open the door of the café for her. A bell tinkled above the door as they walked in. There were plenty of empty tables, so they sat at the nearest. It was a cheap-looking place without any frills. No pictures decorated the walls. The air smelt of grease and cooking. The tabletop was clean, although there were cigarette burns on the chipped Formica. Joanna took her coat off and sat down. A formidable-looking waitress approached, holding a pencil and a dog-eared order pad. She looked at Alex, her lined face devoid of expression. "We're closing in thirty minutes, so there's no hot food."

"Actually, we just wanted a couple of teas if that's okay?" asked Alex politely.

The waitress licked the tip of her pencil and scrawled something on her pad. She turned her back on them and trudged towards the rear of the café where she disappeared behind a partition.

Alex leaned forward and placed his hands over Joanna's which were resting on the table-top. "Tell me what happened."

Joanna sighed. "There's not much to say, really. Mum had spent most of the day with him as she has done every day since he'd been admitted to hospital. Then later that evening, our neighbour came banging on our front door. It turns out that because we don't have a phone, Mum had given the hospital our neighbour's phone number in case of an emergency. Apparently, Dad had taken a turn for the worse. She drove back to the hospital, but it was too late." Joanna's eyes filled and fresh tears slid down her cheeks. "Now she can't forgive herself for not being there when he died."

Alex reached up and wiped her tears away. "Your poor parents. I'm so sorry. I wish I'd met your dad."

"He'd have liked you, for sure."

The waitress returned carrying a tray which she set down on the table then walked away without a word. Alex poured milk into both their cups before adding the tea.

"I wasn't sure if you'd be at work today. Did you not want to take some time off?"

Joanna stirred her tea listlessly. "Why? So, I could sit at home and listen to Mum crying upstairs?"

Alex had no reply to that. He picked up his cup of tea and blew on it before taking a cautious sip.

"I wish you hadn't left me," Joanna said, her voice barely a whisper.

Alex slowly set his cup down on the table. He needed to choose his words very carefully. "I never left you. I'm here now. I simply moved away, as I had to pursue something that was, and still is, very important to me."

"Boys and their toys," Joanna muttered sulkily, staring down at her cup and saucer. "You and your planes."

"No, not at all," Alex said gently. "It's not the job itself. I could be a farmer or doctor. It doesn't matter. What does, though, is how I live my life. I feel I owe it to my parents, and especially my aunt to make something of myself and not waste it."

"And where do I fit into all of this?"

Alex looked away and gritted his teeth. The pain and anguish she was enduring needed a salve. Joanna deserved an answer. Something that would thaw her defiant stare. "Why not move down to Dartford with me?" he offered impulsively. "I'm buying a house. My aunt gave me my inheritance. It's a two-bed semi-detached place in a nice area. You could see if the department store you work at has any branches nearby and ask to be transferred."

"But what about my family? Mum would never allow it." Joanna frowned and shook her head.

"Your mum wouldn't be alone. Lizzie still lives there. You're an adult. You can do whatever you like." Alex pressed the point home. "You need to think about where you want your life to lead." Joanna still wore a frown, but she now looked uncertain. Was he being cruel by asking her to re-evaluate her life so soon after the death of her father?

"My mum needs me at the minute. We're going to the undertakers on Monday to sort out the funeral arrangements."

"Of course she needs you. I wasn't thinking about now. Maybe next year? It would be a big step. You need time to think about it." Alex smiled. The redness in her eyes had faded and been replaced with a small glimmer of excitement.

"I don't know, Alex. I don't think it's the done thing for unmarried couples to live together." Joanna bit her bottom lip. "Imagine it, though—you and me living in our own house."

"Anything's possible if you want it enough," said Alex. "Look, right now I think it's really important that you look after your mum and help her with the funeral. Focus on that. Would you like me to come?"

Joanna looked apologetic. "Actually, Mum just wants it to be close family. Is that all right?"

"Sure, I understand. Listen, let me know if there is anything I can do. I'm sorry I don't have a phone, but you can always write to me. I'll give you my address." Alex looked up at the waitress who was staring haughtily at them both from behind the till. "I think they want us to go so they can close." Alex swigged down the rest of his tepid tea. "I'll go and pay."

When Alex returned to the table, Joanna gave him a reassuring smile as she started to put on her coat. "I feel much better now. Seeing you has really helped."

"That's good. Here, let me help you." Alex held open her coat so she could slide her arms into the sleeves.

Outside on the pavement, Alex could tell that things weren't how they used to be between them. The formality that existed on their first couple of dates had returned. It was as if they were getting to know one another all over again.

"I haven't even asked you how the new job is going," said Joanna.

"Well, that's understandable, but if you've got time, why don't we go and get a proper drink and I'll tell you all about it? I've missed our visits to the Hope and Anchor. I can catch a later train."

Joanna slipped an arm around Alex. "I'd really like that."

As they walked slowly along the road, Alex mulled over the conversation in the café. He'd asked her to move down to Dartford. Had he really thought this through? Although protective of Joanna, he had doubts about where this relationship was heading. For some reason, the face of Arthur the lodger appeared in his mind. Angrily, he cast the image away. Although Alex occasionally saw men in the street who, he admitted to himself, were attractive enough to look back at as they passed him, there was no way he could ever consider living the kind of life that Arthur enjoyed. He didn't want to. He wasn't a homosexual. With Joanna there were other possibilities. Stability. Companionship. They could start a family. *Baby steps*, he told himself. *One thing at a time.* Right now, though, all he wanted was to see her wear her beautiful smile once more. Alex pulled her closer against his side as they walked off into the evening.

* * * *

October 1987

Alex was glad when he turned off the freeway and started driving down Laguna Canyon Road. It meant there wasn't far to go. In the distance, the ocean sparkled enticingly as the late afternoon sunlight covered it with a blanket of glittering gold. Very soon he'd be in the company of Luis and they could talk about other things. He didn't want to dwell on that period after Joanna's father had died, but looking back, it was now easy to realise how much the tragedy had changed her. In the years that followed, the sweet girl he'd escorted to the bus stop on the first night they'd met had vanished and been replaced by someone deeply hurt and resentful at the cruel twists of fate that life gleefully threw their way.

Chapter Nine

October 1987

Alex turned over and let out a sigh of exasperation. He couldn't sleep and that always annoyed him on the rare occasion it ever happened. The bed in Luis' guest room was comfortable, so it wasn't that. His stomach was full after the fabulous meal that Luis had made for them both, and they had shared a fine bottle of Italian red wine. Even the brief after-dinner walk along the beach where they'd enjoyed the evening air hadn't induced a soporific state. Alex stared into the gloom of the room. A muffled cough broke the silence, reminding him that Luis was only a few metres away in his bedroom next door. *Maybe he's awake too?*

An image of Luis lying in bed staring at the same section of wall that was behind Alex's head came to mind, as did the question of whether he was also similarly naked. Alex resisted the urge to reach down under the covers and idly play with himself. There was no point getting aroused. The memory of what he'd done in the guest cottage with Luis' damp towel wouldn't stay buried and that disconcerted him, as did the urgency with which he'd sought sexual release. Desire hadn't reared its head that many times throughout Alex's life so far, for which he was thankful. The few times it had, in his eyes at least, had taken him along a path that led to events which over time had their own disastrous consequences. Even something as tender and innocent as the night he'd lost his virginity.

* * * *

December 1961

Christmas came and went. As much as Alex loved being by the sea, he left Hastings early to return to his flat. He liked the idea of seeing in the New Year by himself. Joanna had called him at home in Hastings on Christmas day from the phone box at the end of her road, and they'd talked about this and that. Alex found it strange that Joanna didn't once mention his suggestion that she move to Dartford. Maybe she thought it was the wrong time to discuss it with her mother. Losing a daughter from the family home might be too much for Carol to bear.

Alex moved over to the lounge window. Even though it was New Year's Eve, the street outside was deserted, except for a taxi that was slowly cruising along the road. Alex closed the curtains. He eyed the solitary radiator in the room with disdain. How he wished the flat was furnished with a fireplace. Outside, a car door slammed, followed moments later by the chime of his doorbell. Alex tutted with irritation. Who the hell was at his door? He left the lounge and walked up the short hallway. A shadowy figure was visible through the frosted glass of the front door. Alex reached for the latch, determined to give them short shrift for bothering him.

"Joanna," he said in amazement, as he pulled the door open. "What on earth are you doing here?"

"Surprise! Look at your face." Joanna started to laugh.

Alex grinned and ushered her inside. It was freezing outside. She was wearing a thick full-length coat and a pale blue scarf. A bright yellow bobble hat graced the top of her head. Two round circles of red stood out on her cheeks as if she had applied rouge without the aid of a mirror. They hugged briefly in the hallway, then he led her through to the lounge where she placed a small holdall she'd been carrying on the floor.

Alex had so many questions. He wasn't sure where to start. "I can't believe you travelled down here without telling me." He shook his head in mock disapproval, but couldn't stop smiling at her. "Well, first of all, welcome to my flat. What do you think? It'll do for now, at least until the house purchase is completed."

Joanna walked around the room, inspecting the furniture. "It's perfect, really. I can see why you chose it." She pulled back the curtain. The streetlights outside bathed the side of her face with a yellow-white glow.

"I thought you were spending Christmas and New Year with your mum?" asked Alex.

Joanna turned to him wearing a guilty expression. "I may have told a little white lie. Mum decided that she wanted to travel up north with Lizzie to stay at her sister's in Derby for a few days. She wanted me to go too, but I said I had to work and didn't mind staying at home by myself." Joanna bit her lip. "Actually the store is closed over New Year, so I thought I would catch the train down here and surprise you."

This was the first time Joanna had deceived her mother, at least to Alex's knowledge. "You'll be in big trouble if she finds out."

Joanna looked at him reproachfully. "Well, she's not going to find out, is she?"

Alex held his hand up in surrender. "My lips are sealed." He moved over to her. "Let me take your coat off, and then we can have a drink."

Joanna undid her coat and Alex held the back of it so she could pull her arms free of the sleeves. When he stood this close, the air was suffused with the scent of her hair and perfume. He draped her coat over a nearby chair, then put his arms around Joanna and pulled her to him. She inclined her face towards his, and their lips brushed together. A little sigh escaped her mouth as they kissed more passionately. Alex broke contact first so he could catch his breath.

Joanna reached up and laid her palms flat against his chest. "I've wanted to do that for a while now." She blushed furiously.

Alex laughed and gently lifted her hands away. "I think we need to celebrate your surprise visit." He moved over to the kitchenette where he retrieved two wine glasses and a bottle of red from a cupboard, then took them across to the coffee table and gestured for her to join him on the sofa. "Tell me about your journey here."

Joanna kicked off her shoes and sat down. "There isn't much to tell you, except it was long and boring."

She sank back into the sofa with a sigh. "Finally, I can relax. The seats on the train were so uncomfortable."

Alex uncorked the bottle and filled two glasses, before passing one to Joanna.

"Thank you." Joanna frowned at Alex. "I really don't understand why people enjoy travelling."

"You're here now. That's all that matters," said Alex soothingly. "Here's to us." He touched his glass against hers.

"To us," Joanna echoed.

Alex took a long sip of wine. He glanced across the room at her holdall. It was big enough to contain a few changes of clothes and some toiletries. His stomach turned over. Did she intend to stay and sleep in the same bed with him? The idea was exciting and terrifying in equal measure. He would be a gentleman and offer to sleep on the sofa. She would probably expect that of him anyway.

He sat back and turned to Joanna. "What prompted your mum to go and visit family?"

Joanna ran a finger around the rim of her glass, her eyes focused on the plum-coloured wine. "I'm not sure really."

When she didn't elaborate any further, Alex just waited patiently. After a short comfortable silence, she continued.

"Mum never said why. It wasn't planned. We were meant to be spending the holidays together, just the three of us. I think she found the idea of us all alone in the house over New Year too suffocating a prospect, especially after Christmas, which was bad enough. What was there to celebrate? Dad's presence followed us from room to room. God knows how Mum sleeps in their bed alone at night." Joanna stopped playing with the rim of the glass and dropped her hand down into her lap. "Visiting her sister is Mum's way of keeping busy."

She raised the wine glass to her lips and drank half the contents down in one swallow. Joanna grimaced and shifted her gaze to Alex. "I think we all needed to get away for a bit. Y'know, get out of the house. It's the silly things you notice that you always ignored before. His favourite mug is still sat on the shelf in the kitchen cupboard. There's a bottle of Guinness in the fridge that'll never be drunk." She offered him a pained smile. "I found his shaving cream in the bathroom cabinet. I don't know why, but I took the lid off and held it under my nose. It was the same cream that he always used, and smelling it reminded me of being a little girl again and Dad picking me up and holding me. I used to bury my face in his neck where he'd smell of aftershave and soap."

Alex put down his glass, then reached out and retrieved Joanna's hand from her lap. He held it loosely in his, and ran his thumb slowly back and forth over her fingers. "I know what it's like," he said. "How much it hurts. The panic you feel knowing that the one person who made you feel safe is no longer there to protect you." Alex squeezed her hand.

Joanna closed her eyes and let out a wavering sigh. "Oh, Alex, it's so unfair. I miss him so much. I want my dad back." Her shoulders began to hitch up and down as she started to cry.

With his free hand, Alex reached over and took her glass away before she spilt wine on herself. He set it down on the coffee table and turned back to Joanna, pulling her closer. She flung her arms around him and he held her tightly. As she wept, Alex rubbed her back, his hands describing slow repeating circles that he hoped would soothe. Eventually, Joanna's sobs started to subside. She relaxed her hold on Alex and drew back so they were facing each other. Joanna looked away. "I'm sorry. I've been doing that a lot recently. Crying suddenly for no reason."

Alex reached up and gently turned her head back towards him until her eyes met his. With his other hand, he wiped away the tears that streaked her wet cheeks. "Don't apologise. You have every reason in the world to cry. You're grieving."

Joanna nodded. "I know. It doesn't make it any easier though." She let go of his hands and reached for her wine glass.

"Here, let me top you up," said Alex. He grabbed the bottle and filled both their glasses.

Joanna took a sip and relaxed back against the cushions. "It's my mum that I feel sorry for. She's all alone now."

"She's got you and Lizzie though."

"I know. For now. But that's all. What else has she got? When Mum married Dad, she gave up her job as a teacher."

"Why?" asked Alex.

Joanna shrugged. "They both wanted children. Dad had a good job. Someone needed to look after the home and cook dinner."

Alex nodded. "Maybe she can start teaching again?"

"Mum's older than she looks. I don't think she could cope with teaching kids nowadays." Joanna tutted. "It makes me angry that she did that. Gave up everything that she'd achieved. What a waste."

Alex didn't reply. Joanna had a point, but Carol must have had her reasons. Maybe the promise of creating a family had been too much of a temptation?

"That's why I needed to get away," continued Joanna. "I was angry at my dad for dying and angry at my mum for being left with no real life of her own. I wanted to be with the only person who would understand what I'm going through." She bit her bottom lip and took a hasty sip from her glass.

"Come here," said Alex, patting the gap on the sofa between them. "I'm so happy that you decided to surprise me. You've been through so much recently and I've missed you. I know that I can't turn everything back to the way it was, but I hope that at least here tonight I can make you feel special and loved."

Joanna leaned forward slowly and kissed him. She tucked her legs up on the sofa and curled up against Alex like a cat. He wrapped an arm around her, privately surprised by the naked candour of his words and ran his tongue over his lips, tasting her kiss.

* * * *

Alex lay still, listening to Joanna's measured breathing. It had been inevitable, really. The two of them together, alone. The first bottle of wine hadn't taken long to finish, and their inhibitions had diminished after they'd finished the second. Sometime after that, Alex had found himself being led by a giggling, flush-faced Joanna towards his bedroom. In the dim glow of the bedside lamp, they'd kissed and caressed in-between undressing each other. Joanna had whispered for him to be gentle as it was her first time.

Alex had nodded dumbly, not wanting to admit that he was a virgin too, as she revealed her milky-white breasts for the first time. He'd pulled Joanna close, and her dusky-pink nipples had tickled his chest. They'd explored each other's bodies, and he'd groaned when she'd reached down and her hand encircled him. Sensibly, he had some protection—something he'd bought in a moment of madness whilst picking up a prescription for his aunt at the chemist in Hastings, never expecting he would ever have cause to use them. The act itself was short lived, and although at the end Alex had experienced an intense burst of pleasure, something was not right. He wasn't sure what it was and put it down to first-time nerves.

Alex hoped that Joanna had enjoyed her first time. She had lain beneath him, breathless, occasionally whimpering, whilst her nails dug into the skin on his back. Afterwards, lying there, side by side, lost in their own private reveries, Joanna drifted off to sleep. Alex's eyes were growing heavy. He looked at his bedside clock. It was nearly midnight. In the distance was the muffled sound of fireworks. Next time he awoke, it would be at the start of a new year and whatever that was going to bring him.

* * * *

October 1987

Alex jolted awake. Everything was dark. He sat up and peeled off the sheets that were tangled around his naked body. His breathing was laboured, so he exhaled slowly and concentrated on calming himself. It was just a bad dream. Something had been chasing him. He rubbed his eyes and blindly reached over to the bedside table where he always kept a glass of water. The table was empty. Realisation dawned. Alex groaned and reluctantly climbed out of the guest bed. His mouth was dry. The bathroom was just down the hall. Taking care to be quiet, Alex opened the bedroom door and tiptoed out and along the silent corridor.

"Alex? Are you all right?"

Alex froze, suddenly no longer thirsty. Just ahead of him was Luis' bedroom door. It was open a crack. "I'm fine. I had a bad dream," he said. "I'm sorry if I woke you. Go back to sleep." He waited a moment but there was no reply, so he took a step back towards his room.

"Alex?"

Alex paused but didn't answer.

"If there's something wrong, I'm here for you. I hope you know that."

Alex leant back against the wall of the corridor and clenched his fists in frustration. He was so tired. Tired and lonely. Tired of living a lie. Alex willed his hands to relax and turned around. He stepped in front of Luis' door and gently pushed it open. Inside the room, silvery moonlight spilled through the half-closed curtains. Night air wafted through the partially open window and tickled Alex's bare chest. On the bed, a shadowy outline shifted as Luis turned to face him.

"There's been something wrong with me for a long time now," Alex admitted, ignoring the waver in his voice.

Luis pulled back the sheet covering the empty side of the bed. For a brief second, Alex caught a flash of his naked frame. He hesitantly approached under Luis' gaze, then slipped under the covers.

"Do you mind if we just lie here? It's been a while since…" Alex sighed, not wanting to finish the sentence. He closed his eyes.

"Hey, calm down. Relax." Luis reached over and rested his hand on Alex's bare chest. "You're trembling. Just breathe… Slowly… That's it."

Luis' hand rose and fell as Alex concentrated on slowing his breathing. Minutes passed by in silence.

"When did you know?" Alex asked.

"That you like men?" Luis lifted his hand and stroked Alex's chest with his fingertips. "I suppose I guessed pretty much straightaway."

"What!" Alex opened his eyes and tried to sit up.

Luis chuckled and gently pushed him back down. "Don't look so panic stricken. There's no neon sign flashing above your head advertising the fact."

Alex relaxed. "How could you tell?"

Luis shrugged. "Call it intuition or a hunch. I don't know."

Alex stayed silent and chewed on his bottom lip.

"I know you're not happy about it," Luis added. "That's fine. You don't have to be. These things take time. If you want to talk about it, then great, but if you don't, then that's okay, too. Take all the time you need."

"Why didn't you ever let me know that you might have been interested in me?" Alex asked.

"What? Like now? Inviting you into my bed?"

Alex nodded.

"Because you weren't ready," replied Luis. "I just waited till you were."

Alex had no answer to that. He stared up at the ceiling. Beside him, Luis settled back on his pillow, his hand never leaving Alex's chest. The ghost of a breeze stirred the bottom folds of the cream cotton curtains.

Alex closed his eyes and let himself be lulled by the slow rhythm of Luis' breathing. It was probably his imagination, but in the distance, carried on the wind, the faint sound of waves could be heard crashing upon the shore.

* * * *

Alex awoke to find himself alone in Luis' bed. He sat up and stretched. The faint sound of music drifted up from downstairs. Alex considered taking a shower but decided it could wait. It was more important that he talked to Luis. In his head he replayed the conversation they'd had in this bed last night. Alex rubbed his eyes and threw back the sheet. *Luis has known all along.* He allowed himself a rueful smile as he climbed out of bed and padded over to the bedroom door. Alex peered out into the empty hallway, then trotted naked back up the corridor to the guest room where he quickly pulled on a pair of shorts and a T-shirt before making his way downstairs. Unsure about what to say, Alex paused, unnoticed, in the kitchen doorway. Luis was standing at the sink washing up. He was wearing an old paint-splattered T-shirt and frayed denim shorts. The calf muscles on the back of his bronze legs flexed as Luis tapped his foot in time with the music. A woman's sultry voice accompanied the soft jazz that was playing on the radio. Even though they had only slept naked in the same bed together, things had now changed and Alex wondered if there would be any embarrassment between them.

He coughed discreetly. "Morning."

Luis looked over his shoulder, his whole face lighting up. "Morning, handsome. You're finally awake."

Alex's cheeks flushed at the compliment. "What do you mean finally?"

Luis turned back to the sink. "I've been up for over an hour. I've made us a fruit salad and there are fresh croissants on the table. Let me finish this and I'll make us some tea to go with it. Did you sleep okay?"

Alex shifted his weight from foot to foot. He didn't know how to reply to that. "I guess so," he said. "I've never spent a night sleeping with another man before."

Luis turned and flashed him an impish grin. "And was it as terrifying as you imagined it to be?"

Alex shook his head. "It was nice," he admitted. "It would have been nicer if you'd been there when I woke up." He looked away as the heat in his cheeks flared up again.

"Sorry, I'm an early riser. Always have been." Luis removed a plate from the sink and stacked it on the drainer. "What would you like to do after breakfast? It's going to be a beautiful day."

"I was kind of hoping we could go for a walk on the beach. I need to finish telling you the rest of the story about what happened between Joanna and me. You know, the divorce and all that."

Luis pulled out the plug and the dirty water gurgled down the drain. He turned around and leant back against the sink. "Alex, I'm not a priest. I hope you're not expecting me to absolve you of your sins." He reached for a tea towel and dried his hands. "I don't understand this sudden need to confess things from your past."

Alex sighed and pulled out a kitchen chair from under the table. He dropped down into it. "You wanted to know about my time in England. Growing up in Hastings, marrying Joanna, having a son. It wasn't a fairy tale where everyone lived happily ever after…" His voice trailed off.

"Whose story ever is?" said Luis as he pushed himself off the sink and joined Alex at the table. Once he'd sat down, Luis leant forward and lifted one of Alex's hands out of his lap and rested it on the table. He covered it with one of his own.

"But there's still more I have to tell you," Alex insisted.

"Why?"

"Because of this! Us!" Alex pulled his hand out from under Luis'. There was no hiding the anguish in his voice. "Whatever it is that we have together!"

The kitchen fell silent apart from the steady ticking of the cuckoo clock. Luis sat stock still, his expression one of shocked surprise.

"I'm sorry. I just don't want there to be anymore secrets," Alex added softly. He rested his hand back on top of Luis' and gently squeezed it.

Luis stared at their hands on the table for a long moment before nodding slowly. "I guess you're right. Neither do I." He slid his hand out from under Alex's, then stood up and moved across to the kitchen counter where he selected two mugs and a box of teabags from the overhead cupboards.

"I didn't mean to raise my voice to you," said Alex.

"I know," replied Luis as he held the kettle under the kitchen tap. "It's okay." Once it was full, he set the kettle on the countertop and turned it on. "I guess things have been a bit one sided recently. I think it's about time that I told you a story about a little boy born in Mexico City."

"Luis, you —"

"Ssh," interrupted Luis, turning around to frown at Alex. "Let me speak." He stepped over to the refrigerator and removed a carton of milk. "I'll keep this brief and give you the short version or we'll be here all day."

Alex said nothing and let him finish preparing their tea, noting that Luis had remembered to add half a teaspoon of sugar to Alex's mug without asking. Sometimes it was the little things that made a big difference.

Once the kettle had boiled, Luis filled their mugs, then carried them over to the table and sat back down. "When I was a small boy, I rarely saw my father. He followed the work wherever it took him and he would be gone for weeks at a time, leaving me alone with Mom. I thought that was normal. He worked hard, despite the low pay and the long hours, but when he came back, the money never lasted long. There was always overdue rent to be paid and I remember my mother complaining that I grew out of my clothes so fast." Luis reached across the table and slid the plate of croissants closer to Alex. "Help yourself. I've had one already. They're delicious."

Alex took one of the crescent-shaped pastries and tore off a segment. He popped it in his mouth and let the buttery flakes melt on his tongue.

"We moved around a lot, too," Luis continued. "That is, until my mom insisted that we settle down somewhere and buy a place. She didn't want me to keep changing schools. Said it wasn't good for my education. They had some savings by that point. Not much, but enough to put down a deposit on a one-bed, three-room apartment in some shitty rundown neighbourhood. I slept in a corner of the living room until I was twelve. We used to make our meals in that room too, as there was no proper kitchen. My clothes and bedding used to always smell of my mom's cooking. I never went hungry, though." Luis picked up his mug and blew on the tea before taking a sip. "Then things changed. For the better really, I suppose, depending on how you look at it. Dad went and got himself a new job. A proper one with a salary and everything. I forget now, doing what. It doesn't matter. Anyway, it meant we could afford a bigger place to live. In a nicer area, too. I had my own bedroom for the first time in my life." He placed the mug back down on the table. "It was around this time that my mom started to get invited to events in the local community. There were a lot of nice well-meaning people where we lived and it felt good to be included. What my father and I didn't know was that most of the socialising revolved around the local church."

Alex smiled, remembering Aunt Edith's withering disdain of all things religious.

"Now, don't get me wrong," said Luis. "I was brought up Catholic just like my parents. There was no cussing inside the house, and my mother used to regularly make the sign of the cross, but we were never regular church-goers. That is until my mom was introduced to Father Nestor and became one of his converts."

Alex opened his mouth to speak, but Luis raised his hand to silence him. "I know what you're going to ask. Was he one of those old-school priests who terrorised his flock with preaching sermons full of hellfire and brimstone?"

Alex let out a small chuckle and nodded.

"Actually, when we were first introduced, I found him to be very friendly and engaging. He was handsome, charismatic, and all the women doted on him."

"So?" Alex prompted.

"It turned out that he was also very persuasive, and that any community fundraising went straight into the church coffers. I remember my parents arguing once when my father found out that my mom was handing over a portion of his monthly income to Father Nestor's new church roof appeal. My dad was a meek man, though, and my mom always won those battles." Luis exhaled loudly, then picked up his mug. He gazed at Alex over the rim as he took another sip before continuing. "Anyway, I didn't pay much attention to what was going on back then as I'd discovered new interests. Or to put it another way — boys." Luis let out a short bitter laugh. He reached over and picked up a few loose crumbs of pastry from the plate and licked his fingers. "I was so scared of someone finding out, even though I didn't get up to much. I never got caught, but somehow my mom must have guessed that something was going on because she went straight to Father Nestor."

Alex winced. "Oh no. How do you know that's what she did?"

Luis smirked. "It was just another normal evening. I'd gone to bed and was trying to sleep. It was late but I could hear my parents in another room. They were arguing in loud whispers. I crept out of my bedroom to listen. I'm glad I did, as it turned out that Father Nestor had arranged for me to be sent away somewhere with my mother's blessing."

"Where?" asked Alex, leaning forward, his croissant forgotten.

Luis shrugged. "I never found out. Instead of going to school the next day, I caught a bus north and never went back."

"What?" Alex exclaimed. "Please tell me you're joking. You ran away?" Luis nodded. He seemed amused by Alex's reaction. "How old were you?"

"I was fifteen, nearly sixteen. I went to stay with my dad's sister. She hated my mom."

Alex didn't reply. He was dumbstruck by Luis' revelation.

Luis drained the rest of his tea and stood up. "Of course there's more to that story," he added, "but that's for another time." He walked over to the sink and started rinsing his mug.

"Did you ever hear from your parents again?"

"Sure. The first time was in my first year of Art College, here in California. One evening I was in my dorm and another student said I had a phone call. It was my mom. God knows how she tracked me down."

"What did she want?"

"She said it was time for me to come home and that if I repented my sins in a house of God, I would be welcomed back with open arms." Luis mimicked what he was saying and turned to Alex, spreading his arms wide.

"How did you answer?"

"I just told her that I thought we were taught that Catholics must forgive the sins of others in order for God to forgive our own sins. She said that was correct, so I replied with just three words."

"Which were?"

"So, forgive me."

"What did she say to that?" asked Alex.

"She didn't. She hung up instead." Luis dropped his arms to his sides. "I spoke to my father a few times after, and he visited me once after lying to my mom and saying that he was going to see his sister. It was a long time ago. Both my parents have since died."

Alex stood up and walked over to join Luis at the sink. He placed a hand on his shoulder. "Luis, I'm so sorry." Luis slowly turned around and regarded Alex with a sad smile, before leaning forward and embracing him. Alex stiffened for a moment, then folded his arms around Luis and patted his back awkwardly a few times. Luis must have sensed the tension in Alex's body as he took a step back after they'd briefly hugged. "Why did you tell me that story?" Alex asked, cautiously.

Luis was silent for a moment. His limpid brown eyes regarded Alex. "I just wanted you to know that I understand how hard it can be to achieve what you want in life and along the way, sometimes people get hurt. Maybe I shouldn't have poked into your past. Don't think that you are in anyway duty bound to explain or justify yourself to me. You're not an evil man, Alex. Do you really think I'd invite you into my bed if I thought you were?"

Alex nodded. "I get that," he said. "I truly do. But, if we're going to have any future together, I want to be completely transparent and finish the last part of my story. I'm not proud of what I did and you might think less of me because of my selfish actions. I lost everything and hurt my family because I was tempted by the offer of experiencing just a brief taste of another life. To be honest, I think it's been eating me up inside for years now, and talking to you has made me realise that."

Alex moved back to the kitchen table and sat back down. "I bury myself in my work. The only people I know on a first-name basis apart from you are my employees at work and a couple of waiters at my favourite restaurants. I don't want to confide in them. I want someone who's just willing to listen and not pass judgement, and so far that person has been you."

Luis bit his lip. "I'm sorry. I didn't realise how important it's been for you to talk about the past. I'll always listen if you have something to say. I hope you know that." Luis moved closer and reached his hand out to tousle Alex's hair. "Judging by your bed hair, you haven't showered yet. Why don't you go and get ready and then we can take that walk on the beach? Sound good?"

Alex laughed and batted Luis' hand away. "Sounds good," he said, standing up and moving away from the table. At the kitchen door, he paused and turned around. "Thank you for telling me your story."

Luis looked up from where he was clearing the table. "Maybe it's because I recognise a kindred spirit when I see one. You're the only person I've ever told it to."

"I'm glad you did," said Alex solemnly as he turned to leave the room.

Chapter Ten

October 1987

As they ambled along the couple of streets that separated Luis' house from the Laguna Beach boardwalk, Alex recounted the story about Joanna's unannounced visit to his flat on New Year's Eve all those years ago. He omitted the part about them sleeping together for the first time. Although it wasn't a secret, it was a private memory and he decided that it should remain so.

"I proposed soon after. I still don't know why. She just seemed so fragile and vulnerable at the time. We were both young and I was impulsive. The wedding was a quiet affair at the Milton Keynes registry office later that summer." Alex laughed out loud. "I just remembered the moment when Aunt Edith arrived in a taxi. She nearly eclipsed the bride by wearing a white turban."

Luis raised his eyebrows. "There are not many people who could pull off a look like that."

Alex nodded. "Rest assured, Aunt Edith certainly could."

"So, after that you settled down to a life of wedded bliss?" asked Luis. He glanced at Alex and gave him a wry smile.

Alex let out a snort. "Hardly." He slowed to a halt. On their left was a small grassy park divided by short paths. Alex gestured with a hand for Luis to go first. "Lead the way." Alex followed Luis along one of the paths that led onto the wooden slats of the curved boardwalk. "I wouldn't call it bliss," he continued, "but I've got some fond memories of back then. It was all new and exciting. Both at work and at home. We soon fell into a routine. To be honest, I really liked the monotony of life. The weeks and months flew by and turned into years. It's all rather hazy now, but I do remember coming home one wet November evening to find Joanna sitting on the bottom step of the stairs waiting for me. She'd not been feeling well and had seen a doctor. They'd carried out a urine test and the results showed that she was pregnant. We were going to have a baby."

They strolled along the winding boardwalk until Luis stopped by a vacant bench that was facing the ocean. "Let's sit here for a moment. I always like watching the surfers fall off their boards."

Alex sat down next to Luis and shaded his eyes with one hand as he gazed out at the roaring surf. A couple of bronzed surfers rode a couple waves for a few brief seconds before they tumbled from their boards and disappeared momentarily beneath the roiling waves.

"That must have been a scary time for you both," said Luis, still looking out to sea.

"That's putting it mildly," replied Alex. "We were both terrified." He leaned forward and rested his elbows on his knees. "Luckily Joanna's mother Carol was a big help."

Alex didn't elaborate any further. He didn't want to admit that even after Daniel was born, he was ashamed of the trepidation that having a son instilled in him. As Daniel had grown, it intensified. Early on, looking down at the helpless bundle, so tiny and fragile, asleep in the cot, Alex had been certain that whilst raising Daniel, he and Joanna could inadvertently shape and mould their son's character and personality. Of course, right and wrong were basic tenets, but other much more subtle nuances could be picked up and absorbed on a daily basis. Did he want to dictate who his son became? Without the memory of his father's voice to guide him, Alex had approached his son's upbringing the only way he knew how, as he did with one of the many projects he oversaw at work—a challenge to be overcome. Joanna had a natural aptitude for motherhood which at the time surprised him, and a new equilibrium settled as he and Joanna had adapted to their new addition.

During the week, Alex worked as normal, but weekends were set aside for them to spend together as a family. It was during this time that Alex grew envious of the bond between Daniel and his mother. As Daniel grew, this connection became more apparent. When the family strolled through the local park, Alex used to hoist Daniel up to sit on his shoulders and run around in lazy circles, making the boy squeal with delight. This was always short lived, as after a minute of this, Daniel would demand to be set back down on the ground, preferring the reassuring grip of his mother's hand. Even when Daniel took the occasional careless tumble and ended up with skinned knees, he would ignore his father's outstretched arms as, crying, he made a beeline for Joanna. The ritual of reading a bedtime story though was something that Alex had liked to regard as his exclusive domain. On the rare occasions when Alex came home from work early enough, he would read stories to his son that he too had also listened to as a child. Daniel would listen, wide eyed and entranced, which had made Alex pine for the innocence of childhood before things had started to go awry. For Alex though, his favourite closest moments with his son had been in the months after Daniel had been born. Interrupted sleep was to be expected, Carol had lectured to them, and Alex had soon become accustomed to being woken by his son's cries during the night. Lifting him from the cot, Alex would place Daniel over his shoulder and take him downstairs, so that Joanna could sleep. There in the twilight hours where time lost its meaning, Alex would stand looking out of the lounge window, stroking his son's back and listening to his breathing. Even after Daniel had fallen back asleep, Alex would remain there, imagining how many times his father had done the same as the grey fingers of dawn crept over the dark horizon of night.

Luis sat back on the bench and turned slightly towards Alex. "I guess that being a parent is something that I'll never experience. I don't know if that's a good or a bad thing."

Alex shrugged. "I don't think it's for everybody," he said. "Like anything, it has its pros and cons. Looking back though, I wouldn't change a thing. Joanna and I may have gotten a lot of things wrong, but having Daniel was the best thing we ever did."

Luis reached down and took off his plimsolls. He stretched out his feet and wiggled his toes. "You must miss him."

"Every day," replied Alex automatically.

Luis nodded and stood up, clasping his shoes in one hand. He pointed at Alex's deck shoes. "Why don't you take them off? Let's walk along the shore. I'd like to feel the waves wash over my feet while you talk. I'm guessing this is where the story takes a turn?"

"Something like that," muttered Alex as he kicked off his shoes. He followed Luis over to a short set of wide wooden steps which led down onto the pale-yellow sand. There were a few people dotted along the beach, but not many, as the tourist season had long passed. They walked the short distance to the shoreline and the accompanying steady roar of the crashing waves. Alex gritted his teeth as a shallow wave broke over his ankles. He was expecting the water to be freezing but it was cool instead. A gentle breeze rippled the front of his T-shirt. With the sun on his face, Alex realised that at that moment there were far worse places he could be. "I can see why you wanted to move here. It's beautiful," he said, turning in a slow circle to admire the beach and its surroundings.

Luis retreated back a few steps as a wave splashed up his legs dampening the hem of his denim shorts. He padded over to stand next to Alex. "I took a walk on this beach straight after the realtor showed me around the house. That's when I knew I had to have it."

"I'm glad you did," replied Alex. "It suits you, living here."

"As does it you, although I still don't know how you ended up here."

"Let's walk a little," said Alex, turning to face along the beach, his feet sinking slightly into the damp sand, "and I'll tell you about the time an American called Brad visited a small aeronautical company based in Dartford near London."

* * * *

May 1981

"Internationalisation is key to our expansion and future, ensuring that Napier-Bell Engineering remains an innovative aeronautical company that is always one step ahead of the game."

Alex was only half listening to the irritatingly upbeat Jeff Harris who had recently been appointed and put in charge of overseas development. As Jeff continued with his introduction to the assembled staff in the conference suite, Alex shifted his focus to the tanned good-looking man who had entered the room alongside Jeff, and who now stood quietly to one side next to an overhead projector. Alex hazarded a guess that he was a similar age to him, putting them both in their early forties, although the chiselled features made the man look younger. His eyes shone Egyptian blue, and the blond hair on his head was cropped short, complementing his handsome face. Alex looked around at the colleagues closest to him. They were all pasty, pale and grey in comparison to their exotic-looking guest.

"So it gives me great pleasure to introduce Mr Brad Anderson from Miller Aviation Corp," Jeff concluded, turning to the man by the projector. He started clapping, and after a slight hesitation, the rest of the room joined him. The man called Brad raised a hand in acknowledgement. He reached down and pulled out a sheet of paper from a leather satchel at his feet and laid it down flat on top of the projector. Up on the screen hanging from the front wall appeared three magnified words — *Research, Development and Production*.

Brad took off his suit jacket and hung it carefully over the back of a chair. He grinned at his captured audience and started rolling up his shirt sleeves. Alex was startled by how impossibly white Brad's teeth were. His gaze flicked to the muscled brown forearms now on display. From where he was sitting, the hairs on Brad's arms looked golden under the florescent ceiling lights.

"Good morning. Thanks for the introduction, Jeff. My name's Brad, and I'm here today to tell you a little bit about the work we're doing over in Los Angeles."

The thick nasal American accent sounded strange in the room. People were exchanging excited glances. Alex smirked. They were acting as if they hadn't seen an American before. True, this was the first time one had visited Napier-Bell Engineering, but Alex had spoken to many on the phone over the years about different overseas projects, and when he visited London, there were always plenty of American tourists around. Alex shook his head slowly. Surely his colleagues, especially in this line of work, realised that the advances they made in aeronautics were making travel easier and bringing people from other continents closer?

Brad sauntered up to the screen, and Alex couldn't help but stare at Brad's well-muscled buttocks that flexed inside the tight trousers he wore.

"You heard Jeff mention internationalisation." Brad pointed at the words on the screen. "In a nutshell, this is all about developing existing cooperative manu-facturing programs, where firms from different nations share research, development and production costs." He extended a hand out towards the audience. "You help us, and we'll help you."

Alex had to admire Brad's patter. His easy smile and good looks had already won over most of the audience. All eyes were focused on the American. What he was talking about was nothing new. Alex had read many articles about different countries pooling their aeronautical knowledge and resources to further global technological advances. As Brad carried on talking, Alex let the words wash over him. Instead, he concentrated on the man standing before him. He couldn't remember if he had ever seen a man as attractive and alluring as Brad Anderson before. Physically he was perfect. Alex could see the front of Brad's shirt clinging to the contours of his pectoral muscles. His gaze trailed down to the impressive bulge at the crotch and lingered there for a long moment, before following the powerful legs down to the feet. The leather shoes looked expensive and foreign. Possibly Italian, although what did he know? Alex had also spotted cufflinks on Brad's shirt before he had rolled his sleeves up. Impressed that someone could look so effortlessly classy, Alex looked down and frowned at his years' old suit. The knees on the trousers were shiny and worn thin. The cut and style were from the seventies. Some of his colleagues dressed similarly, but most dressed down nowadays. Over the years rules had been relaxed. Maybe it was time to update his wardrobe a bit? He could certainly afford it. Alex folded his arms and dismissed the thought. "This is a workplace, not a catwalk," he murmured. Half the time they wore lab coats anyway. The people sitting either side gave him a quick uncertain glance. Alex was no fool, and recognised envy when it reared its ugly head, but another long dormant sin was also now awake. Lust.

* * * *

Joanna lifted the lid of the casserole dish, and both Alex and Daniel leaned forward to smell the steam rising off the bubbling contents.

"Ah, *coq au vin*," said Alex, smiling up at his wife. "This has to be one of my favourites."

"Yes, Dad, we know," said Daniel, helping himself to potatoes. "You say that every time we eat this."

"Well, imagine if I'd said that this was my least favourite meal that your mother makes. Do you think that would go down well?" Alex countered, enjoying the smile that Joanna wore as she listened to their banter whilst spooning the chicken onto their plates.

"So, what is your least favourite meal that Mum makes?" asked Daniel innocently.

Alex could read his son's mischievous intentions a mile off and burst out laughing.

"I think your father would like to eat his meal and leave the table in one piece, rather than answer that question, don't you think, Daniel?" said Joanna, sitting down and casting Alex an amused glance. "How was work?"

"We had an American come in to give a talk to all the staff today. His name is Brad Anderson," said Alex, trying to pronounce the name in an American accent.

Daniel started laughing with his mouth full of food. "Dad, that accent was rubbish," he spluttered, and began coughing.

Joanna leant over and patted him on the back. "Was he nice?" she asked Alex, her eyes focused on her son.

"He seemed an affable sort of chap. I was introduced to him afterwards. Apparently, he's staying here for a month to get an idea of the sort of work we do. Best practices and so forth. See what he can take back with him."

Joanna nodded. "You realise he is probably on the phone right now, speaking to his wife or girlfriend, and telling them how he met a frightfully English-sounding gentleman called Alex Spencer." She mimicked Alex and pronounced his name in an exaggerated upper-class English accent.

Daniel chuckled and echoed Alex's name in the same manner.

"I do not speak like that," Alex said in mock indignation.

Daniel and Joanna looked at each other with eyebrows raised, then collapsed into giggles.

Alex tried not to laugh but failed. He looked fondly at his wife and son in turn. It was good to see them happy. This was what it was all about. Spending time together. He ignored the voice in his head that piped up and reminded him that it was Friday, and this was the first time this week that he had been able to finish work and join his family for dinner. *It's a busy time*, he reminded himself. Things were gearing up at Napier-Bell, and now with the arrival of the American, Alex could sense that changes were afoot. He opened his mouth to say something but thought better of it and picked up his glass of wine instead. Alex took a sip.

Telling his family that they should do this more often would not go down well. Especially as Joanna and Daniel did this every day.

* * * *

Over the next few weeks, Alex rarely had any contact with the enigmatic Brad Anderson. That was not to mean that he wasn't around. In fact, Brad popped up pretty much everywhere Alex went. In the cafeteria at lunchtime, Brad was always surrounded by staff who wanted to bask in the exoticism of him being American. Whenever Alex passed by, carrying his lunch on a tray, Brad would always give him a nod of acknowledgement. There were times in the lab, whilst running tests with some of his junior staff, when Alex would turn and catch Brad quietly observing them through a window. Even when they passed each other in a corridor, Brad was always with someone. Alex never had a moment alone with him and was beginning to suspect that Brad was doing this intentionally. Had he guessed that Alex found him attractive, and this was his way to gently rebuff him?

Always pragmatic, Alex knew that in no time at all Brad would be on a plane back to his life in Los Angeles, and things here would return to normal. Until then, Alex would allow himself this fanciful infatuation, because that was all it was and ever would be.

When it was announced a week later that Napier-Bell Engineering would be hosting a farewell dinner for Brad in one of the top hotels in Dartford, Alex was surprised that he received an invitation. Joanna was rather miffed that she was not invited to accompany him upon his arm. Alex had patiently explained that it was not going to be that sort of social get-together. It was a meal for just the upper members of management and department bosses. More of a display of affluence and affiliation to their American friend and the company he represented. He was quietly relieved, as the rather desperate sight of all of his colleague's wives trying to outdo each other, flaunting their jewellery and dresses in a preening peacock display always made those kinds of events uncomfortable. As usual, Joanna had the last word, and asked him to try and remember when he had last taken her out for dinner. Rather guiltily, he'd still been wracking his brains long after she'd left the room.

* * * *

Alex hurried through the grand foyer of the Metropole Hotel, cursing under his breath the taxi that had turned up late. His brand-new black shoes echoed on the marble tiles as he approached the reception desk.

"Could you tell me where the Napier-Bell dinner is being held?" he asked, brandishing his embossed invitation at the receptionist who was wearing a polished, yet well-worn smile.

She gestured towards the corridor off to the right. "Follow the signs to the private dining rooms. Your party is in the Churchill suite. Enjoy your evening."

Alex flashed her a grateful smile, and followed her directions until he was standing before a set of double doors upon which a copper-plated sign announced he'd found the right place. A babble of voices could be heard from inside. Alex resisted the urge to knock, then opened the door, irritated by an irrational rush of nerves. The square room was designed to impress. The back wall was taken up entirely with a well-stocked bar, all glass and chrome. In front of him were a collection of his colleagues spread out upon an array of leather sofas and armchairs that were artfully scattered around the room, their drinks resting on low small circular wooden tables. A few people raised a hand in greeting before returning to their conversations.

Alex stepped forward onto the highly polished wooden floor that glowed a soft honeyed brown. The walls were covered with green velvet wallpaper upon which the ghost of a paisley pattern flowed sinuously, its design inviting him to caress it. He fiddled with his uncomfortably starched collar and straightened his bow tie. The suit wasn't a perfect fit, but it was all they'd had left at the hire shop. Looking around, it seemed that everyone else had beaten him to it, judging by the black and white attired throng. Alex's trepidation vanished as he took a deep breath and crossed the room towards the group of men standing in front of the gleaming bar. A waitress approached him bearing a tray of brimming champagne flutes. She offered a dimpled smile which Alex returned as he plucked a glass from the tray.

Over the years, he'd attended the obligatory staff party usually held at Christmas, as well as other gatherings when the company had reason to celebrate, but none of them had been as lavish as this. Alex allowed himself a rueful smile. It was clever. Speculate to accumulate. Impress the American and the company he represented, and further down the line, the payoff could be immense if Miller Aviation Corp and Napier-Bell Engineering developed a strong working relationship.

He took a long sip of his drink. The bubbles fizzed on his tongue as he swallowed. Off to his left was an archway, through which was another room. Inside was a long table covered with a white tablecloth, place settings spaced out evenly across the surface. Alex's stomach rumbled. He'd skipped lunch in anticipation of tonight's meal. As he neared the men, a distinctive voice could be heard. There was no mistaking that American twang. In the centre of the group, Brad was holding court. He was telling an anecdote. Alex hung around at the periphery and joined in with the rumble of appreciative laughter when Brad had finished.

"Drink up, Alex," urged a voice at his elbow. He turned to see Graham, the head of accounts, who was beckoning one of the circulating waitresses over. "If the company's paying, it's only proper that we dutifully enjoy ourselves. Right?" Graham, whose face was already flushed and blotchy, chortled as he helped himself to two glasses from the tray. Alex quickly downed his first drink before accepting his second from Graham.

"Cheers," they saluted, chinking their glasses together.

A hand fell heavily on Alex's shoulder. Startled, he whirled around to find Brad standing in front of him.

"Woah, go easy there!" Brad hastily stepped back as champagne slopped over the side of Alex's glass.

"I'm sorry," blurted Alex. "I do apologise."

Brad rocked back on his heels. "Ha, you Brits. Only you can say sorry and apologise in the same sentence."

Alex laughed without humour and cursed his Englishness. The small group had dispersed, although a few men loitered around Brad, orbiting like moons.

"This is quite the shindig you guys have put on tonight," observed Brad, looking around the room. He placed his hand casually back on Alex's shoulder and guided him towards the bar. "C'mon, let's go get ourselves a proper drink."

Alex was bemused. Apart from being introduced to each other after Brad's presentation on his first day, and the occasional exchange of pleasantries whilst passing by in corridors, they had never had a proper conversation, yet here was Brad acting like they were old friends.

"Two bourbons straight up," Brad instructed the barman, then turned around and leant back against the bar, his arms extended either side, resting on the copper countertop. "I must be costing your company a goddamned fortune." His eyes flicked upward towards the ceiling. "Did you know that I've been staying here for the past month? All expenses paid."

Alex dutifully raised his eyebrows. "Your charm offensive must have worked," he said, maintaining a neutral expression.

Brad paused and regarded Alex quizzically before letting loose a booming laugh. He reached around behind him, and grabbed the two tumblers that were waiting on paper coasters. Brad handed one to Alex and shook his head. "I'll never get used to your sense of humour over here." He downed the drink in one and looked at Alex expectantly. Alex followed suit, and suppressed a grimace as the fiery liquid burnt his throat.

"Attaboy," said Brad, slapping him on the back. "You know I can see big things further down the road for our two companies." He leaned closer and lowered his voice. "Who knows Alex? We both might be working a lot more closely together, going forward."

Brad was dangling a line, but Alex was damned if he was going to bite. He just nodded. Being this close to Brad was both thrilling and nerve-wracking. He smelt good, too. A bizarre mix of freshly cut wood and lemons. Up close though, Brad's tan looked unnaturally orange, and there was something artificial about his uniformly perfect rows of bright white teeth. His breath smelt of mints and alcohol. The man exuded something else, though. Alex couldn't decide what it was, but he wanted more of it.

The bright sound of a shrill bell ringing cut through the chatter in the room. Outside the dining room stood a man holding a tiny bell aloft.

"Gentleman, please make your way to the dining room and find your designated seat."

"Shall we?" asked Brad, gesturing expansively for Alex to go before him.

Alex nodded and joined the steady flow of men as they filed slowly into the dining room. The decor was the same as the bar area. Dotted along the walls were sconces holding fat candles, the small flame on each casting a pleasing glow that reached up to the low ceiling. Candelabras were spaced out along the middle of the table, illuminating the name cards placed at each setting. Alex walked slowly around the table, which looked like it could seat thirty people. He checked behind him, but there was no sign of Brad. Alex concentrated on greeting colleagues and exchanging a few words, whilst skirting chairs that people pulled out as they found their seats. Halfway down the other side, Alex finally spotted his name and sat down. Alex looked up as Jeff Harris and Brad walked through the archway into the dining room. Jeff was laughing and patting Brad on the back. They exchanged a few more words, then separated. Brad strode over to the middle of the table and pulled out the empty chair directly opposite Alex. He sat down and greeted the men either side of him by their first names, whilst flicking out his folded napkin with a flourish.

* * * *

Alex set down his knife and fork. The food so far had been exquisite. He'd chosen the pork terrine and toast to start, followed by grilled Dover sole paired with a lovely, chilled Chablis. Across the table, which was just that bit too wide to comfortably talk across, Brad was ignoring him completely, focusing only on the men either side of him. Throughout the meal, the three of them either bent their heads close together whilst talking intently, or broke apart, leaning backwards in their chairs to laugh uproariously at a shared joke. They were starting to get on Alex's nerves.

The main course plates were cleared, and the dessert was served. On the plate set down before him was a showcase of sugar and cream, a meringue swan floating regally upon a thin lake of raspberry coulis. Alex hesitated. It seemed a shame to ruin the illusion that had been painstakingly created. He sighed, then used the edge of his spoon to break the swan's graceful, curved neck. The taste was at once sublime and overpowering. Alex closed his eyes in appreciation. Something brushed against Alex's ankle under the table. His eyes snapped open as he jumped in his seat, banging his knee painfully on the table. Alex glanced around the table, but no one gave any indication of having touched him inadvertently.

After dessert, it was announced that coffee and brandy would be served in the bar area, followed by a few words from the chairman of the board. A few barely stifled groans sounded around the table, followed by laughter. Alex sat back and swirled the remnants of his wine around the bottom of the glass. There was no rush. Chairs screeched as they were pushed back, and bit by bit, the table emptied as the men made their way leisurely into the other room.

It had been easy to leave the private dining room on the pretext of using the gents. Alex just followed the lead of other guests, but once in the corridor, he had turned in the opposite direction and hurried along to reception where he could grab some fresh air outside. He abhorred speeches, and the collective back-slapping that inevitably went with them, but Alex also knew how to play the game. Part of him wanted to slip away unnoticed and go home. The chances of that happening were good, but he couldn't risk the slightest possibility of being seen leaving early. That was bad form, and not to be expected from a team player. Alex sighed and looked at his watch. He'd give it ten minutes, then go back inside, make sure he was seen, and hopefully soon after, the evening would draw to a close.

After the appropriate amount of time had passed, Alex went back inside and passed back through reception, hoping that he wouldn't encounter anyone. Luck prevailed and a moment later, he cracked open the double doors of the Churchill suite and rejoined his colleagues. A wraith of silvery-blue cigarette smoke hung above the bar. Below, slouched against the counter-top, were a few die-hard drinkers, determined to polish off just one more free drink at the company's expense. Alex was pleased that the evening was over. He'd worked the whole room efficiently, only ever pausing for a brief chat before moving on. Now it was time to go. Alex joined the stragglers heading for the door. It was quarter past ten. Not too late, but it was a weekday. He would order a taxi at reception. Alex walked down the corridor and out into the reception area. The woman behind the desk was dealing with a guest, so Alex took his time crossing over towards them.

"Here's your replacement key card, sir. Enjoy the rest of your evening." The receptionist slid a slim plastic card across the desk's polished surface.

"Thanks. You too, ma'am." The guest pocketed it, half turned then sauntered off towards the lift.

Alex froze. He hadn't recognised Brad from behind. The receptionist looked questioningly at him. Alex held up a hand to stall her, and flicked his eyes back to Brad, who was pressing the lift call button. It was a moment of pure indecision. Should he call out? The lift doors opened, and Brad stepped inside. Before Alex could make up his mind, Brad had turned to face outwards, and the doors of the lift started to close. A hand shot out between them. The doors stopped, then smoothly retracted. Even from the reception desk, the whiteness of Brad's grin was visible. Brad beckoned Alex over with quick hand gestures. He shot the receptionist an apologetic glance, and hurried over towards the lift which Brad was holding open.

"Hey, Alex, good night, huh? Guess what? I made it upstairs only to find I'd lost my key card." Brad fished in a pocket with exaggerated movements before triumphantly brandishing the replacement card out in front of him. "What are you up to?"

Alex pointed over his shoulder towards the receptionist. "I was just about to order a taxi. It's getting late."

Brad nodded, then cocked his head to one side. "Care to join me for a quick nightcap? Just the one. Like you said, it's getting late." Alex paused a moment too long. Brad leant out and pulled Alex into the lift. "You missed my speech. Don't think I didn't notice. C'mon, the least you can do is join me."

The inside walls of the lift were mirrored. Brad pressed a button on the panel and after a moment the lift juddered upwards. "I couldn't help but see you staring at me during my presentation on my first day here."

Alex was startled by Brad's observation, spoken so nonchalantly and out of the blue. The contents of his stomach shifted uncomfortably as he tried to come up with a reply, but no words came to mind. Brad's lips curled in amusement as the cheeks of Alex's reflection burned in the mirrored door.

"Was I really that obvious?" asked Alex cautiously.

"Well, you certainly weren't being coy about it. I wasn't sure if I should've been scared or flattered." Brad looked up at the digital display above the doors. "Something I've noticed about you is that you're quite the dark horse."

Alex frowned. "What do you mean?" he asked Brad's reflection.

"I've been asking around."

Alex waited. Was Brad playing games with him? "And?" he prompted, when Brad didn't elaborate further.

"It seems that you are held in a somewhat high regard by everyone you work with. At first I thought you were just another of the worker ants, but slowly I found out that over the years, you've quietly climbed the corporate ladder here at Napier-Bell."

"I didn't end up sitting opposite you at the table by accident, did I?" asked Alex. "If you were seated in the middle as guest of honour, then surely people far senior to me would've been seated there as well?"

"It's probably the fault of one of the waiting staff who mixed up some of the name cards whilst laying the table," replied Brad, not missing a beat. He frowned at his reflection and smoothed the front of his dinner jacket with one hand.

Alex didn't buy it but wasn't going to press the matter. "Was that your foot under the table?"

"Maybe. You'd fallen into a trance and were staring at your plate for most of the meal." The lift slowed to a stop. A ping sounded and the doors opened. Brad stepped out and immediately turned left, leaving Alex in his wake as he strode up the carpeted hallway. Alex followed, and caught up with Brad outside one of the many wooden panelled doors lining the corridor. Brad inserted the key card into a slot located beneath the door handle, and a small light turned green. He opened the door wide and motioned for Alex to go in. Brad followed, and once inside, reached out and pressed a light switch.

Alex hadn't stayed in many hotels over the years, but just by glancing around, he could tell that Napier-Bell Engineering were hefting out a tidy sum to accommodate Brad and keep him happy. The short hallway opened out into a large spacious room. A large cream-coloured rug covered most of the dark hardwood floor. Brass wall mounted lights cast a soft glow. A giant king-size bed dominated the left side of the room. The white sheets looked crisp and inviting. Alex moved over towards the window which took up half of the back wall. Outside it was dark, but from this elevated position, the twinkling lights of Dartford could be seen. As could Brad's reflection, watching him. The right side of the room was furnished with a brown leather sofa and a couple of armchairs.

"I didn't know such hotel rooms existed in Dartford," Alex said drily, turning to look at Brad.

"Hey, I'm worth it," joked Brad. He crossed the room to some recessed cupboards and removed a bottle and two glasses from inside.

Alex inspected the two oriental wall hangings, the only art in the room. On each, a dragon had been rendered in blue ink, the body elongated and winding. Their faces leered at Alex, whilst their long tongues danced, tasting the air. He turned away and leant back against the wall.

Brad poured them both a drink. "Is whiskey okay?"

"Sure. Thank you."

Brad brought the drinks over. "Oriental art not your thing?" he asked, gesturing with his glass at the wall hangings.

Alex accepted his drink and took a small sip, suddenly aware that Brad wore no rings on his fingers. "It's beautiful to look at, but to be honest, I've never really had much interest in art before," he admitted.

Brad grunted and walked over to stand at the foot of the bed. He pointed at the padded headboard, which carried on the oriental theme. Another dragon had been woven into the fabric, this one portrayed in emerald green. "Tell me, is that a Chinese or Japanese dragon?"

Alex looked helplessly at him. "Chinese?" he guessed at random.

Brad grinned and shook his head. "Look at their toes. Chinese dragons have five, and Japanese have three."

Alex counted the toes and nodded. "I'm impressed."

"Not just a pretty face, huh?"

Alex smiled thinly and looked away, embarrassed.

"I'm a mine of useless information," said Brad, moving back over towards Alex. "Maybe I should start concentrating on remembering the important stuff."

"Such as?" asked Alex. He lifted his glass to his lips and drained the contents, hoping the whiskey would calm the fluttering in his stomach.

Brad shrugged. "I don't know. Maybe I should remember to always ask the right kind of questions?"

Alex frowned, not understanding.

Brad stepped closer until he was facing Alex. He paused and bit his lip, his eyes never leaving Alex's. "Why is it," he began, "that every time I see you, I get the very strong feeling that you are undressing me in your head?"

Brad took the empty glass from Alex and placed it on top of a nearby desk. He stepped closer and grabbed both of Alex's hands, lifting them up and over his head, pinning him to the wall. Brad took yet another step. Their faces were now only an inch apart. They were both breathing hard. Alex closed his eyes and leaned forward, pressing his lips hard against Brad's. Alarm bells rang in his head, imploring him to stop, but he paid them no heed. Brad responded, opening his mouth. Alex pushed his tongue inside, relishing the heat and wetness. Having his arms restrained excited him, and Alex thrust his groin forward, rubbing it against Brad's, encouraging the growing hardness there.

Brad released Alex's arms and leaned his head back, breaking their kiss. "Woah there. I didn't know you were this fired up."

Alex didn't reply, and instead put an arm around Brad's thick neck and tried to pull him closer. Brad flexed his muscles as he resisted Alex's attempts. He chuckled and reached out to slide Alex's dinner jacket back and off his shoulders, allowing it to fall to the floor. He fumbled with the buttons on Alex's shirt, and in his haste, a button pinged off the front and glanced off the nearby desk. "Shall we move over to the bed where we'll be more comfortable?"

Alex nodded, as he followed suit and started removing Brad's clothes. Together they staggered across the room, trading fervent kisses, and leaving a trail of discarded garments in their wake. Now fully naked, Alex pressed his body against Brad's, his hands in constant motion as they roamed down Brad's back and squeezed his well-rounded tanned buttocks. They fell onto the bed, legs entangled. Alex rolled over on top of Brad, straddling him. He looked down and planted his hands on Brad's chest, marvelling at his muscled physique that for the past month had lain hidden under layers of clothing. It was as if he was riding a chiselled slab of brown marble. Something twitched beneath him. Alex reached down and his hand encircled Brad's stubby thick cock. Brad groaned and reached up, pulling Alex down and easily flipped him over onto the bed.

"It's my turn now," Brad instructed, reaching for him.

Alex nodded and lay back as Brad gripped his legs and dragged him closer. "Yes," he whispered as Brad bent over his pale body. "Yes, yes," he urged, his voice growing louder. Alex threw back his head and let himself be devoured.

* * * *

Alex awoke with a start. Soft snoring sounded from the prone figure next to him. Light from a lamp atop the desk, opposite the bed, suffused the room with a dim glow. "Shit," he whispered angrily as he glanced at the bedside table. The green glowing hands on the alarm clock were both pointing upward. It was a few minutes past midnight. Not good, but it could be worse. He berated himself for his stupidity. How could he have dozed off? Alex gathered up his creased clothes which were scattered around the room and dressed quickly and silently. Satisfied that he hadn't forgotten anything, Alex headed for the door, but paused by the bottom of the bed. Brad was still asleep, sprawled naked, lying on his front with the bed sheets twisted around his body like a toga. The dim light threw shadows across him, highlighting the contours of his muscular frame. Alex swallowed hard. It was time to go.

In the lift, the mirrored walls would not allow Alex to look anywhere but at himself. Multiple reflections gazed back silently, waiting. Waiting for what? Did he have to justify to them what had happened in that hotel room tonight? The things he'd done to Brad? The things he'd whispered and pleaded for Brad to do to him? Alex reached out and stabbed the lift button. As the lift started to descend, he turned around in a slow circle and looked every reflected Alex defiantly in the eye. So, he had derived pleasure from another man? And willingly too. He waited, but not one of them dared to raise a finger and point at him and accuse him of doing wrong. The absence of shame was surprising. As was the way he had greedily demanded Brad to obey him in fuelling their desires, and more so in that Brad had willingly complied. Afterwards, the two of them had lain back on the bed panting and grinning at each other. There had been nothing furtive or fumbled in their actions. Nothing done against anyone's will. It was just two men enjoying sex together, and for once, Alex *had* enjoyed the sensation of being both satisfied and complete in a way he couldn't describe.

He raised a hand to the threads of grey that were gathering at his temples. They were a constant reminder of how quickly time passed. Was he already beyond his prime? It seemed like only yesterday when his son was born, but in a couple of months Daniel was about to turn fourteen, and he had been married for how many years now? Eighteen? The lift doors opened with an accompanying ping. The warm post-sex afterglow dissipated instantly as Alex stepped back out into the reception area. Dwelling upon his family was the equivalent of a cold bucket of water thrown over two rutting dogs. Although there was no remorse, there was guilt. Of course there was guilt. He'd been unfaithful. There was no escaping that. Even though sex had gone out of the marriage years ago. Alex hurried over to the woman at the reception desk. He needed to get home. Now was not the time to wrestle with his demons.

Back at the house, Alex closed the front door and winced at the dry click of the latch sliding into place.

He slipped off his shoes and crept upstairs to the bathroom, where he stripped silently and filled the basin with hot water. He inspected himself in the mirror. His lips looked puffy, and his neck was red. Otherwise there were no other marks or bruises that would need an explanation. Alex used his flannel to quickly scrub himself all over. He wanted to remove any trace of the odour of sex which he was sure not only still clung to him but had invaded his pores. Alex picked up his clothes and folded them into a tight bundle. Out on the landing, he blindly found the bedroom door and turned the handle slowly. Inside, the only sound was of Joanna sleeping. Alex dumped his clothes carefully in a corner of the room and found his side of the bed. He slid in under the covers and lay still, hoping that his movements hadn't disturbed her. Alex closed his eyes. The desire to sleep was overwhelming. He let his mind drift away and didn't dwell on the sound of Joanna's breathing, which wasn't as slow and measured as his.

* * * *

October 1987

Alex fell silent. He'd been painfully transparent in the retelling of his transgression, not wanting to hide any of the details from Luis. They walked on, accompanied only by the unceasing thunder of the waves crashing on the shore. Alex stole a glance at Luis, but looked quickly away, alarmed by his furrowed brow and eyes fixed on the sand in front of him.

"I'll understand if this changes things between us," said Alex.

Luis stopped abruptly mid-step and turned to him. He shook his head slowly as if in wonder and a small smile of amusement creased the corners of his mouth. "Do you know how exasperating you can be at times?" He held his left hand up in front of him. "No, don't answer that. It was a rhetorical question." Luis resumed walking and Alex kept pace alongside him. "Why should events that occurred years ago on another continent affect us here in the present at this very moment? I completely understand what you are trying to do. I totally get it and appreciate your honesty, but you have nothing to apologise for or prove to me."

Alex stayed silent. He would let Luis say his piece. The last thing he wanted was an argument.

"So you did something you shouldn't have done in the heat of the moment," Luis continued. "Welcome to the real world, Alex. We're human. We make mistakes. It's also worth noting that it takes two to tango, you know. This Brad guy doesn't sound completely innocent in all of this."

"I know," said Alex. "I just never intended for anyone to get hurt."

"Of course you didn't. Why would you?" Luis reached over to touch Alex on his arm. "Tell me though, was it something to do with that encounter with Brad that led to you living in America?"

Alex considered the question for a moment. "Maybe, maybe not. It's difficult to say. Everything happened so fast, starting with the following day."

Chapter Eleven

May 1981

There were a few pale faces in Napier-Bell Engineering the following day as Alex strode down the corridors to his office. Physically he was fine. A couple of glasses of water, first thing, had quenched his thirst, but nothing could alleviate the sickening guilt that he had been unfaithful. It would've been so much easier if he could've blamed it on the booze. Sure, he'd had some champagne and wine, plus a few whiskeys. Inhibitions had been lowered, but there was no way Alex could dress up or mask the truth. He'd been in control and had acted on his impulses in that hotel room. Alex had woken early, still tired after a troubled night's sleep, and left the house before Joanna or Daniel stirred. He needed time to process the maelstrom of conflicting emotions that were demanding his attention. Even in the cold light of day as Alex lowered himself into his office chair, there was still no remorse.

He didn't regret what had happened, but couldn't condone that he, a married man, had cheated on his wife. In front of him on the desk lay his work planner. He stared blankly at the week's schedule, unable to concentrate. The phone rang. Alex snatched up the receiver, irritated at being disturbed.

"Yes?" he snapped. Alex winced as he recognised the voice on the other end of the line. "No, Paul, I'm fine. Sorry, I was just in the middle of something. What? Yes, I'll be there in a couple of minutes. Okay, bye."

Alex gently placed the receiver back down. His anger had dissipated and been replaced with curiosity. It had been five years since Mr Connolly retired and Paul had replaced him, and in that time he'd only been summoned to Paul's office twice. Alex grabbed his suit jacket from the back of his chair and hurried from the room. Outside Paul's office, voices were audible from within. Alex checked he was presentable. He ran the fingers of one hand through his blond hair then knocked on the door twice.

"Come in."

Alex opened the door and stepped inside. "Morning, Paul, you wanted to…" His voice petered out as Brad, leaning nonchalantly against a filing cabinet next to Paul's desk, gave him a nod of acknowledgement.

"Ah Alex, there you are. Please, sit down. Now you know Brad, of course." Paul gestured to his left.

Alex nodded dumbly, then quickly sat in the chair opposite his boss. He arranged himself so he was not adopting a defensive posture, resisting the urge to cross his arms. The brief nod from Brad had not in any way passed on a secret message alluding to last night. Was that a good or bad sign? Even if Brad had winked at him, Alex would still be none the wiser about why he had been summoned here.

"Thanks for joining us, Alex," said Brad, his posture straightening. "Now as I'm sure you know, I've been here for the past month as a grateful guest of Napier-Bell Engineering. In that time, I've been trying to gain an understanding of the way you guys do things over here. In a few days I'll be flying back to LA where I'll present my findings to my boss, and suggest ways that, going forward, we can work together." Brad paused. "You with me so far?"

Alex nodded again, perplexed as to where this was going.

Brad moved over and perched on the edge of Paul's desk. "What I didn't reveal to most people here was that I was also visiting for another reason."

Brad paused. Alex smiled to himself. Brad's formulaic approach to speech had become painfully transparent. Yet again he was dangling a carrot to keep the listener enthralled. Alex had to begrudgingly admire how clever and effective it was. That didn't stop it being annoying, though.

"I've been looking to headhunt a European employee for a six-month placement in LA at Miller Aviation Corps. Someone who is excellent in their field, but also a team player. Both Paul and I think that person is you. Do you think you've got what it takes?"

Alex looked at them both in turn, unsure how to answer. They were waiting expectantly.

Paul pushed back his chair and stood up. "It's a lot to take in. I appreciate that. Have a think and get back to us." He moved around to the front of his desk and patted Alex on the shoulder. "Congratulations, this is a huge opportunity for you."

"We need an answer in the next twenty-four hours," said Brad. "Forty-eight at the most, as we'll need to go to the consulate in London with your passport and get your visa approved so you can enter the US."

"Go home," said Paul. "Take the rest of the day off and give it some thought. We appreciate that you'll need to discuss it with your family." Paul glanced at his watch. "I've got a meeting I'm late for. Stay here for a bit and Brad will answer any questions you have." He picked up a folder from his desk and after murmuring his thanks to Brad, left the office.

Brad clapped his hands together and stood up. "Okay," he said, then walked around the back of the desk. He sat heavily in Paul's chair and leaned forward, propping his elbows on the desk. "So, Alex, are you ready to come and play with the big boys?"

Alex was still trying to wrestle with the implications of what he'd just been offered, but the not-so-subtle innuendo in the way Brad phrased his question immediately silenced the clamouring voices in his head. He looked directly at Brad, aware of a twitching in his groin. "Oh yes, I'm ready."

Brad's mouth broke into a wide grin, displaying his unnaturally perfect white teeth.

* * * *

Alex hadn't made the connection before. Although the crow's feet that framed Joanna's eyes had become more pronounced in recent years, Alex was only ever aware of them when she screwed up her face in anger.

"Can you hear yourself? What you're asking of us? Daniel's at school! What on earth are you thinking? I hope you haven't said yes!" Joanna buried her hands in her new haircut. A couple of plastic shopping bags lay forgotten at her feet.

"I said I'd discuss it with you. I need to tell them tomorrow. Brad is flying back Friday morning."

"What, and you're meant to be going with him too?" Joanna's arms fell limply to her sides.

Alex shrugged helplessly. "I don't know all the details yet, but yes." He held his hands out to stall Joanna from replying. "Please, hear me out. I just thought it would be great if we all lived there together whilst I grab this once-in-a-lifetime opportunity. After all, it's only for six months. Once I've found us somewhere to live, you and Danny could fly out and join me. I'm sure we can find him a school that he can attend for a term or two. He'll love it." Alex paused and searched Joanna's face for the slightest trace that she understood how big a deal this was. "I know that it's all very sudden, and I'm sorry," he added.

Joanna's shoulders slumped in resignation. "You know, Alex, there comes a point when saying sorry just isn't good enough." She turned away to look out of the kitchen window. "I should have known right from the start that it was always about the bloody job. I don't think I even came second or third. I think your pride and stubbornness did. After all these years, you'd have thought I would have learnt that by now." Abruptly, Joanna turned around and stalked from the room, hurling words over her shoulder. "Do what you want. You always do anyway, but leave our son out of it."

Alex closed his eyes and willed himself to stay calm. Rather than make the mistake of going after her, he pulled out one of the dining table chairs and sank heavily onto it. This had not gone according to plan. On the walk home from work, Alex had weighed up his options. His inner conflict was not about whether or not to accept the six-month placement. That decision had already been made, and he'd be a fool not to go. Instead it had been about choosing the best approach to use when he told Joanna that he was going to LA. That was when he'd hit upon the genius idea of asking them to come along with him. It was only for six months, and of course he wanted them both to experience the trip of a lifetime with him. That way he could enjoy the best of both worlds. Joanna's reaction had been unexpected. It had caught him off guard and Alex had been shocked by her ferocity. He considered how he might assuage the situation and realised that he didn't have a single clue about what to do next.

* * * *

The train slowed, brakes squealing until it came to a complete stop. A loudspeaker heralded its arrival as Alex descended the couple of steps onto the station platform. He was home. It was instinctive to call Hastings that, even though he hadn't lived here for nearly twenty years. The idea of spending the rest of the afternoon and evening in the house back in Dartford hadn't appealed to him. Especially after the way Joanna had reacted so badly to his plan. He was hurt and bewildered that she couldn't understand how much it would mean to him if they all went to LA together.

At least there was always one person that he could rely on who would side with him. He hadn't told his aunt he was coming. It had been an impulse decision based purely on a need to see a friendly face. He had last visited Aunt Edith in early December, nearly six months ago. He always extended an invitation for her to join them in Dartford over the festive period, but every year she politely declined. As usual, Alex walked down to the seafront first. The beach was still busy as people took advantage of the warm late afternoon. Cotton-wool clouds rolled across the china-blue sky. A balmy breeze carried upon it the scent of salt and rotting seaweed. Wheeling overhead were the ever-present gulls, their abrasive screech strangely comforting. Alex walked slowly along the promenade towards the tall black fishermen's huts, then climbed the Tamarisk Steps and headed along the road towards home. He paused outside the front gate.

Aunt Edith was sitting on a wicker rocking chair in the shade on the front veranda. Her knitting basket was at her feet, and the clack of her needles reached his ears. Alex pushed the gate open and stepped though. The gate clanged shut behind him. Aunt Edith looked up, and her knitting needles fell silent as he walked up the path.

"Hi, Auntie. I was hoping to surprise you." Alex mounted the couple of steps up onto the veranda. "You look like you've been waiting for me," he joked.

"I have," she stated, with no glimmer of a welcome in her voice. Her face was a mask, devoid of expression.

Alex froze. "Let me guess," he said softly. "Joanna?"

Aunt Edith nodded. "I received a call a couple of hours ago. She sounded quite distraught."

"She told you my news then?"

"She did."

Although Aunt Edith was getting on in years and had to be approaching her seventies, if she wasn't already, Alex still found her forbidding. Even now, just by the virtue of her presence, she had the capacity to render him into a childlike state once more. Her body had shrunk, and she could no longer walk completely upright with the regal air that used to turn heads on the street, but her eyes and voice still commanded attention.

"I thought you'd be pleased?" Alex frowned. This was not going as expected. "It's an amazing opportunity for me," he added. He searched his aunt's heavily powdered face, the lines and fissures of old age carefully hidden from view. There was no sign of the pride or satisfaction that he was hoping for.

Aunt Edith, in turn, regarded him with her clear sharp eyes. She slowly shook her head. "Oh, Alex. How can someone so clever be so stupid."

There was no reply to that. Alex just stared at her. She had never called him stupid before. It hadn't even been spoken in the form of a question. What hurt was that it had been uttered as a statement laced with despair.

Aunt Edith muttered under her breath and tossed her knitting into her basket. She struggled up and out of her seat, batting aside Alex's attempts to help with a baleful glare. A bony hand reached out to snatch up a walking stick leaning close by. "I think it's time I told you some home truths. Then maybe you'll understand. Come with me."

Alex followed Aunt Edith as she made her way inside. Instead of moving down the hall towards her parlour, she crossed to the staircase and started to ascend, one step at a time, her knuckles white as she grasped the banister for support.

"Where are we going, Auntie?"

There was no reply. Either she hadn't heard or had chosen to ignore him. Alex stayed close behind her in case she slipped, but Aunt Edith was as sure footed as a mountain goat. They stopped when they reached the first landing. Mirroring downstairs, it consisted of a long hallway, all wooden panels and locked doors. At the far end was another set of stairs that led upward.

"It must have puzzled an inquisitive young boy when he first arrived in this house and found locked doors on every floor." Aunt Edith pointed at one such door with her walking stick and fixed him with a shrewd look.

"There was a lot to take in at the time," replied Alex lamely.

Aunt Edith nodded. "Ah, that there was." She smiled, the dry powder around her mouth cracking in hairline fractures. "Still, a curious young mind won't let a locked door stop him. Am I right?"

Alex just stared at her. How stupid he'd been after all these years to have assumed that she'd never discovered that he'd borrowed her keys to sneak into a few of the locked rooms.

She leaned forward and patted him on the arm. "Don't look so terrified, Alex. When I was a young girl, I used to creep into my mother's bedroom and play with her jewellery box which was always out of bounds. Children will always explore where they should not. It's a law of nature."

The wooden floorboards creaked as Aunt Edith walked off slowly down the hallway. They passed the bathroom, the door open. The hollow, slow drip of water from the cistern echoed off the bathroom tiles and out into the hallway. She stopped outside a door next to her bedroom. From within the folds of her dress,

Aunt Edith removed a key. She inserted it in the lock. It turned easily. "There was never any harm in looking inside any of the rooms, you know," she said, turning to face Alex. "None of them were hiding anything. There was just no reason to use them anymore." Aunt Edith chuckled briefly. "You look confused, Alex. Let's go inside and maybe you'll understand why." She turned the door handle and pushed the door open wide. Inside it was dark. Indistinct objects stood shadowy in the gloom. Alex followed her into the room. Aunt Edith bustled over towards the window where heavy velvet curtains hung from ceiling to floor, sealing out the world outside. With difficulty, she yanked them apart, the curtain hooks screeching with each jerky movement.

Light poured in, illuminating the large room. Three tall wooden chests of drawers lined one of the walls, which were all painted a dusky shade of pink. The centrepiece of the room was a giant white cot. Directly above it hung a circular mobile from which an assortment of wooden animals dangled. Alex walked over and rested his hands on the cot railings. It rocked slightly from side to side. Inside it was empty, although the bed was made. The sheet and woollen blanket were folded back beneath a small, plumped pillow. He looked up to find his aunt calmly observing him from her spot in front of the window, her hands clasped together against her midriff.

"It was never used in the end," said Aunt Edith, pointing at the cot. "We didn't get to bring her home. She only lived for a couple of days. I named her Rose. Because of her rosy cheeks, you see? The same colour as these walls." She walked over towards Alex until she was standing opposite him. Aunt Edith gripped the edge of the cot and leaned over, peering inside. She reached in and smoothed out a dimple on the pillow with one hand. "There were complications. The doctors were scratching their heads. They thought something had gone wrong whilst she was growing inside of me. Then like a flower, she faded and was gone."

Aunt Edith stepped away from the cot and walked slowly around the room. Alex kept silent. She pulled out a drawer in one of the chests and inspected the contents before shutting it. It was packed full of knitted clothing. She repeated the process a couple of times with different drawers. The contents were all the same. Dotted around the edges of the room were an assortment of full bags leaning against the walls. Some were plastic. Others were made of paper. Alex turned on his heels to survey the room. There were a lot of bags.

"I never knew. I'm so sorry," Alex said softly.

Aunt Edith picked up a silver photo frame that was standing alone on top of one of the chests of drawers. She handed it to him. "Of course you weren't to know. You hadn't been born yet. You came along a few years later."

The photograph mimicked the one resting on Alex's bedside table upstairs. The black and white picture featured a young couple in formal dress, both smiling at the camera. "Is this you?" he asked.

Aunt Edith nodded. "My husband and I."

Alex frowned. "Where is he? What happened to him?"

Aunt Edith scowled. "He left me a few weeks after Rose died. We hadn't even buried her body yet." She gently took the frame out of his hands and placed it back on top of the chest of drawers. "All my husband ever wanted was a family. When the doctors told us that I couldn't have any more children because it was too dangerous, well..." Aunt Edith shrugged. "One day he just didn't come home. He left everything behind. His clothes, possessions, money...me. I never saw him again."

"Auntie, I don't know what to say. How could he do that to you?"

"He had his reasons," she replied bitterly, and glared at Alex. "I'm telling you all this to try and open your eyes to what's around you. You're willing to risk your marriage and give up what I lost and then never had? I thought that you of all people would understand the importance of family, yet now you plan to just throw that all away? I brought you up to be better than that. This bizarre notion that they are something you can just uproot and take with you on a whim is preposterous, as is the alternative, which is you abandoning them. Your wife and son need you, and you will do well to remember that."

"But it's only for six months!" There was silence. Alex had never raised his voice to his aunt before. "I'm sorry. Joanna doesn't understand. This could change everything."

"For who, Alex?" she asked gently. "Ask yourself that. Your wife is scared that if you go, you won't come back."

"But that's ridiculous," he spluttered.

"As is putting your work before family," Aunt Edith finished. She headed for the door. "I'm visiting an old friend for dinner this evening. I need to get ready. Your room is as you left it if you decide to stay the night." She paused in the doorway and looked back at him. "If I were you, I'd put that brain of yours to good use and have a long hard think about what it is that you really want going forward."

Alex shook his head with bewilderment as she left the room. Why couldn't anyone see things from his point of view? Alex trudged towards the door. Maybe a lie down on his bed would help. His eyes were drawn to the piles of bags leaning up against the walls. His curiosity got the better of him, and he crouched down so he could rummage amongst them. He picked one at random and pulled out a tiny woollen cream cardigan. From another he unfolded a pair of lilac woollen trousers, so small they would only fit a baby. Alex went from bag to bag. They were all full of miniature items of knitted clothing. He put everything back and stood up. He didn't want to stay in this room anymore. There was nothing but sadness here. Out in the hall he made sure the door was closed properly behind him before climbing the stairs to his bedroom. Alex was in complete agreement with his aunt. Some rooms definitely deserved to stay locked.

* * * *

The bell above the door tinkled as Alex walked out of the chemist with his purchases. The carrier bag swinging from his hand banged against his leg. Besides the new toothbrush and toothpaste, it also contained his mother's hairbrush and the framed photo of his parents. He had decided to stay the night at Aunt Edith's. The idea of travelling back to Dartford and arriving late hadn't appealed to him. Nor the frosty reception he would have undoubtedly received. After scraping together the remnants of a meal from cold leftovers in the fridge, he had gone to bed and risen early to catch the first train out of Hastings. Before departing the house, he had left his aunt a hastily scribbled note on the kitchen counter detailing his intentions. He was already an hour late for work, and still wearing yesterday's clothes. Alex increased his pace. He should be in his office within the next fifteen minutes. A quick visit to the staff toilets to brush his teeth and wash his face should be sufficient before he tracked down Brad to accept his offer.

Alex couldn't believe how quickly everything fell into place once he'd officially said yes. Tomorrow morning, he was travelling with Brad to London to get his passport stamped at the American consulate. Then on Friday, their flight was due to depart at ten a.m., bound for Los Angeles. Alex had spent the rest of the day reassigning various projects he was working on. Word had spread about his posting abroad, and his colleagues presented him with a good luck card and a small basket full of English provisions to last him during his time in LA.

The house was empty when he arrived back. He'd dragged his heels and taken the long route, all in an attempt to delay another confrontation with Joanna. He needn't have bothered. The note attached to the fridge accused him of running away to hide behind the folds of his aunt's skirt, and consequently, Joanna was visiting her mother for the night whilst Daniel was having a sleepover with a school friend. Alex crushed the piece of paper into a small ball and hurled it into the kitchen bin. Time was running out. They needed to talk and work out what was to happen going forward. Alex still couldn't understand Joanna's reticence about moving abroad for six months. Earlier, his colleagues had worn their envy and admiration on their sleeves.

Most people would jump at this chance. But then Joanna wasn't 'most people.' Upstairs, Alex brought down a couple of suitcases from the attic so he could pack for the trip. It made sense to do that now, without Joanna here trying to stop him. Then he should consider having an early night. Tomorrow was bound to be a long day.

The late spring, early evening sky was starting to darken as Alex inserted the key into the front door. Déjà vu accompanied him inside. Just like the day before, the house was empty. He called out to Joanna and Daniel, but there was no reply. Alex checked his watch. It was nearly seven p.m. Daniel should have been home from school hours ago, and Joanna's note had said that she would only be away for the one night.

It had been a long stressful day. Alex headed upstairs. He needed a shower to wash off the residue of grime accumulated during the visit to London. Alex had been looking forward to spending time with Brad as they hadn't been alone together outside of work since the night in the hotel. Journeying across London had proved to be a nightmare. An unexpected tube strike and a lengthy slow-moving queue at the American consulate did nothing to brighten Brad's mood. He was clearly irritated to be spending his last day in the UK babysitting Alex. It was somewhat of a relief when they parted company back at Napier-Bell. Brad's parting words had been that he would pick Alex up the following morning at seven a.m. sharp. Alex turned on the shower and quickly stripped, leaving his clothes in a pile on the bathroom floor. He smiled. Joanna would have a fit if she saw them lying there crumpled like that. He stepped beneath the spray and reached for the soap.

Alex hoped that it wouldn't all be about work once he was in LA. Maybe Brad would show him the sights? Brad had certainly shown him a thing or two in the hotel room. Alex reached down. His penis was starting to grow hard as he conjured up future scenarios of the two of them together. He would give it a week or two then invite Brad over one weekend so they could spend some leisurely time getting to know each other better. He would then seduce and strip him. Order him into the shower. Soap him all over and kiss him. Their tongues would fill each other's mouths as their hands explored and pleasured each other. From downstairs came the muffled sound of the front door opening, jerking him from his fantasy. After hastily turning off the shower, he snatched a towel from the rail and quickly blotted himself dry.

Alex bent down to gather up his clothes, then crept along the landing on his way to the bedroom. The sound of kitchen cupboards being opened and the rustle of plastic drifted up the stairwell. Alex dressed hurriedly and made his way downstairs, past his two suitcases waiting in the hall, and into the lounge. Visible through the kitchen doorway was Joanna's coat and a small overnight bag which had been unceremoniously dumped on top of the small dining table.

"You're back then?" Alex stepped into the room and positioned himself by the dining table, his hands resting lightly on the back of a chair. Further down the kitchen, Joanna was unpacking a bag of groceries. She didn't answer or acknowledge his presence.

"Where's Daniel?"

"Staying at a friend's," Joanna replied, her voice clipped.

"What, again? I need to say goodbye to him. When does he get back?"

"When you've gone," said Joanna.

"Are you trying to prevent me from saying goodbye to Daniel?" Alex asked, calling her bluff. She wouldn't dare.

Joanna set a tin of tomatoes down on the counter and stared at Alex. "I'm protecting Daniel. He doesn't even know you're leaving. You only found out forty-eight hours ago, remember?"

Alex willed himself to relax. The wood beneath his gripped fingers ceased creaking. "I need to explain to my son why I must go. Make him understand."

Joanna chuckled and shook her head. "Oh, Alex. Really? He's not a child anymore. How do you think he'll react to you breezing off to America for six months at the drop of a hat? Sure, Dad," Joanna mimicked, parodying Daniel. "Don't worry about us, or that you'll miss my birthday. I'll look after Mum. You have a great time."

Alex suppressed a yell of frustration and instead threw his arms up and out towards her. "Then come with me!" he pleaded, raising his voice.

Joanna shook her head slowly. "I will not uproot our family for some vanity project. You expect me to fly halfway around the world just so I can cook your dinner every night? You may be clever, Alex, but I can assure you that I'm not stupid either."

She batted the open kitchen cupboard closed and walked towards him, pausing only to pick her coat up off the table before leaving the room.

"Where are you going?" Alex called out.

"Out."

"Why? It's getting late." He hurried after her. "Joanna, wait!"

In the hallway Joanna opened the front door then turned to him. "Why am I going out?" she asked.

Alex stopped in his tracks. With practiced ease, his wife threw him a scornful look.

"Has it ever occurred to you, Alex, that other members of this family have lives, too?" There was a pause. Joanna nodded as if satisfied. "I thought not." She stepped outside and pulled the door firmly closed behind her.

* * * *

An unfamiliar beeping sounded. Alex reached out and grabbed his newly purchased travel alarm, silencing its piercing shrill. Beneath his head, Daniel's pillow carried the same unmistakable scent of his son's hair, transporting him back to the time when he used to hold his new-born son over his shoulder during the dreamlike hours whilst the world slept. Alex sat up and gazed around his son's room, rubbing the sleep from his eyes. Everything lay ready for him. Fresh clothes. Wallet. Passport. He had twenty minutes before Brad was due to turn up. Hopefully Joanna was still asleep. He was pleased that he'd had the presence of mind to assume he'd not have been welcome in the marital bed last night, so had laid low in here instead. Alex swung himself out of bed and dressed quickly. He carefully opened the bedroom door and crept into the bathroom where he cleaned his teeth and emptied his bladder as quietly as he could. He left the room without flushing the toilet and went back to Daniel's room and gathered his things. Out on the landing, the house was silent. He hated leaving like this, but he couldn't bear another confrontation. At the top of the stairs, Alex looked down and stopped, his breath caught in his throat.

Joanna was waiting for him at the bottom of the stairs, fully dressed, blocking his path. "Don't do this, Alex," she said grimly. "You can still change your mind."

Alex shook his head and descended a couple of steps. Joanna didn't move. He cursed himself for telling her when Brad was flying back. "I get that this is all unexpected," Alex began. "I really do, but I need you to look past that. Think about it," he impassioned. "By making sacrifices like this, I can secure a better future for us in the long term." He braved another couple of steps.

"Sacrifices? Don't you dare pretend you're doing this for us. Instead, you're single-mindedly determined to wreck this family. We barely see you as it is, but this is the final straw. I'm warning you. If you do this, you're going to have to choose between your job or this marriage." Joanna stepped aside.

Alex winced, not only at her ultimatum, but also at her physically giving him free reign to choose his path. "Come on, you don't mean that," he reasoned, taking a step lower, then another. "We can still turn this around. There's time. How many families get the opportunity to move abroad for six months? Our home will still be here when we get back."

Alex reached the bottom of the stairs and stood there facing his wife. Outside a car horn hooted. He moved past her and opened the front door, then grabbed the two heavy suitcases from down the hall. "Look, I've got to go. Please at least reconsider what I've said. I'll call you once I get there." Alex leaned forward to kiss his wife. Joanna recoiled. He froze. For a moment, their eyes locked. Alex stepped back. There was nothing more to say. Without another word, he turned and dragged the cases towards the car. He heaved them into the back seat before climbing into the front and slamming the door.

Brad looked at him questioningly. "Is everything—"

"Just drive," snapped Alex, staring straight ahead.

Brad put the car in gear. He gunned the engine and the car jerked forward. Out of the corner of his eye, Alex caught him flipping a jaunty salute towards Joanna, who was standing motionless on the doorstep. He closed his eyes, wishing he was back in bed where life was so much simpler.

* * * *

As they passed through the airport, Alex followed Brad's lead with feigned nonchalance, not wanting him to guess that he had never been abroad before. Joanna had never expressed much of an interest in foreign travel. Alex had always suspected that she didn't want to stray too far away from her mother, even for a week or two. For Alex, the idea had always held some sort of allure, but that was all it ever was—an idea. As a family they had only ever holidayed in the UK. This trip was perfect. For the first time in his life, he could enjoy a working holiday abroad.

On the plane, Alex willed his fingers to unclench as he gripped the armrests during take-off, hoping Brad wouldn't notice. An hour into the flight, Brad ordered them both double whiskeys. It was now late morning, but morning, nonetheless. Alex gulped it down and requested another. Brad kept them coming.

Alex drifted awake. His head throbbed and his mouth was dry. The drone of the engines, a constant irritant. Brad snored, head back, next to him. The cabin was dark, but out through the window on the distant horizon, the sun splayed out vivid streaks of orange and red that stretched out across the unblemished blue sky. His eyelids were too heavy, or it was too bright. He couldn't decide, so he just let them close.

* * * *

Alex accepted his meal from the stewardess and placed it on the folding tray in front of him. He pulled back the foil covering the plastic dish. "What the hell? Where's my dinner?"

Brad pointed at the congealed steaming yellow mass with his fork. "That's scrambled eggs. You're on west coast time now. It's nine a.m. there. Eat up. We land in four hours."

* * * *

Alex stared out of the window. This trip was not playing out the way he had imagined it. He was bored and his back ached. Brad had slept most of the flight, his muscled left leg stretched out so it pressed up against Alex, encroaching into his confined leg room and keeping him in a state of semi-arousal. Alex shifted in his seat trying to get comfortable, but it was useless. He looked down at his hands pooled in his lap. Brad's leg was only a couple of inches away. Impulsively, Alex extended his right forefinger and ran it gently along Brad's thigh, following the seam of his trousers. The muscle tensed under his touch. Alex looked up and gasped as Brad gripped his hand and squeezed it painfully.

"What the fuck are you doing?" Brad whispered fiercely, his voice furred by sleep.

"Nothing. I'm sorry." Alex yanked his hand free and rubbed it. He turned away from Brad's bloodshot glare and focussed once more on the void outside.

Brad let out a deep sigh. He leaned over towards Alex, his voice low. "Please tell me you've heard of the phrase 'don't shit where you eat'?"

"I've heard something similar," Alex muttered to the window.

"Okay. Good. Now look at me."

Alex reluctantly turned to find Brad extending his left hand towards him, palm up, upon which lay a ring. It was plain and gold in colour.

"I'm going to spell it out for you anyway, just to make sure it's perfectly clear between us. Understand?"

Alex nodded. There was something in Brad's tone of voice that was unsettling.

"You and I, we had a little fun and let off some steam. It's something I like to do on the rare occasions I travel abroad." Brad pointed at Alex's wedding ring. "We're very similar, you and I. Happily married. Kids." He chuckled. "Hell, I'm an all-round family guy." Brad paused and leaned closer, his face now a couple of inches from Alex's. "And I intend to keep it that way. You get me?"

Alex swallowed, trying hard not to recoil from the smell of sour whiskey and egg. "Yes," he whispered, dumbstruck that he'd not seen the pale band of skin on Brad's tanned ring finger before.

Brad stared at him. Alex waited, stock still, as the seconds passed. Brad smiled his movie star grin and sat back. He patted Alex lightly on his thigh. "I'm pleased we now understand each other."

The plane juddered as they hit some turbulence. A soft chime sounded. Above Alex's head, the fasten seat belts sign glowed red.

* * * *

October 1987

"Jesus!" Luis exclaimed, stopping to stare wide eyed at Alex. "That guy is one serious asshole."

Alex nodded. "There are a number of other words that best describe Brad, but that one will do just fine." He bent down to retrieve a small shell that lay half buried in the sand. "God, I remember feeling such an idiot."

"What did you do next?"

Alex straightened up and brushed away the particles of sand that clung to the surface of the shell. "Well, I could hardly stay on the plane and wait for it to take me back to London. Don't forget that I was there representing my company. Expectations ran high, as did the prospect of future dividends earned from me being there. Any repercussions as a result of my performance would have been far more damaging."

Luis looked troubled. "Just please tell me that you didn't have any further encounters with that asshole."

Alex handed the shell to Luis, who turned it this way and that before holding it up to the light. "No, thankfully not. In fact, after he introduced me to my new boss, I only saw him fleetingly in passing at work. I've no idea where he is now." Luis offered the shell back to Alex, who shook his head. "You keep it. Add it to that bowl of seashells you keep in your bathroom."

Luis nodded and slipped the shell into the back pocket of his shorts. He turned and pointed back towards the distant boardwalk. "Shall we head back? It'll take us a while if we walk slowly. I have a sneaking suspicion that there is still a bit more to your story."

Alex grinned. "There's not much more, I promise. I'll make you a deal. Let me finish by telling you about Frank, my new boss, and what happened after, and then I will take you out to lunch. My treat."

"I can't argue with that," said Luis as they started walking back. In front of them, they were accompanied by two short shadows cast by the sun, still climbing overhead.

Chapter Twelve

May 1981

Alex was thankful that Brad took charge and navigated them through immigration and along to baggage claim where they retrieved their luggage from the carousel. From there, they passed into the crowded arrivals area. Struggling with his suitcases, Alex hurried along in Brad's wake towards the exit, trying not to lose sight of him amongst the teeming throngs of people. On his left, bright sunlight streamed in through a vast wall of glass that separated him from outside. Alex didn't want to admire the view. It was all too much to take in. He was still trying to process what had happened as they came into land. Brad's harsh rebuttal had been a verbal slap in the face, instantly shattering the fantasies that Alex had daydreamed about over the past few days.

At times Alex cursed his analytical approach to reasoning, as inescapable as it was. He couldn't ignore that part of the cause for being here was due to him succumbing to the deluded prospect of enjoying unbridled sexual abandon far from home and his real life. Alex didn't want to dwell on how much that might have swayed his decision to come here. Up ahead, Brad stopped and gestured for Alex to catch up with him.

"Hurry up, Alex. I've been waiting a whole month for this." He pointed towards the glass fronted exit that led out onto a wide expanse of pavement and the road beyond that ran in both directions. Further down, a long line of taxis were parked.

Alex's arms ached with the weight of his oversized bags, but he increased his pace as Brad strode off and passed through the automatic doors. Outside, Alex recoiled as he stepped into the sunlight and a wave of heat washed over him.

Brad, who had turned around to watch him, burst out laughing. He set down his luggage and leaned forward, resting his hands on his knees. "Ha, you Brits are all the same. Obsessed with the weather in a country where it's always grey and raining. Welcome to the real thing. Give it a month and you'll be as brown as a nut, I promise you. Nothing beats the California sunshine. God, I've missed this." He stood upright and inclined his head back, wearing a smile of contentment.

Alex didn't reply. He dropped his bags to the ground and stretched a hand out towards the azure sky to block out the blinding glare. Any trace of the undisguised menace that'd darkened Brad's voice earlier had vanished. He pictured the packed beaches of Hastings in the summer, irritated by Brad's attempt to pour scorn on the admittedly insipid English weather, so proudly defended by the British.

Even though the heat outside wasn't oppressive, it had been a surprise. It was good to breathe in fresh air after having been cooped up inside the plane for so long. Alex tried to place the mixture of scents carried on the warm breeze, but the odour of high-octane jet fuel was too prevalent. He turned to face the road. At least three lanes ran in both directions, separated by a grass verge upon which a long row of tall palm trees stood. Alex craned his head back, admiring the elegant slim trunks as they tapered upwards. At the top hung wide fans of dark green fronds that rustled in the sultry air. There was nothing here that would remind him of home, he concluded, and turned to Brad, eager to find somewhere quiet where he could collect his thoughts.

"So where next? Are we dropping off our bags? I don't even know where I'm staying."

Brad was still basking in the sunlight. He turned and squinted at Alex. "Relax. Mr Miller wants to see you first." Brad stretched out his arms and yawned, then picked up his bags. "You're right. Time to go. Let's grab a taxi."

Alex caught his reflection in the glass doors of the exit. His clothes were rumpled and his face bore an unhealthy pallor. This was not the best way to make a good first impression. He wasn't in any position to call the shots, so stayed silent and followed Brad over to the nearest taxi which resembled an oversized shoebox without a curve in sight. After getting in, Alex pulled the car door closed with a satisfying clunk, shutting out the muted roar of jet engines. Brad slid onto the seat next to him and rattled off an address to the driver. The car pulled out smoothly and picked up speed.

Alex closed his eyes and surrendered himself to the here and now, ignoring the alien world outside the window. All recognisable, yet different. There was time to appreciate that later. He'd only just landed, and everything had changed. He'd been duped, taken for a ride, whatever he wanted to call it. Used as a plaything, then cast aside. Beguiled by a charlatan. Maybe it served him right? Alex shifted in his seat, inching himself closer to the window. Anything to put a bit of distance between himself and the man who'd so recently occupied his fantasies. Brad and the driver fell into a loose, easy conversation about the traffic problem in LA. Alex ignored them and focused on what was now important. He was about to meet the head of a much larger American aeronautical firm. He'd been handpicked, Alex reminded himself. That was the reason he was here. Brad had merely been the icing on the cake. It was time to show them what he was made of. He didn't need to rely on fancy leather shoes and cufflinks to make an impression. A childhood memory of Aunt Edith sprang to mind and Alex smiled at the recollection. She had been patiently explaining to him why they always burnt coal instead of wood during the winter.

"A log fire smells nice, but needs constant attention. The wood is expensive and burns quickly. It pops and sparks, so you should always remember to use a fireguard," she instructed. *"Coal, on the other hand, burns much more slowly and provides a steady heat. It's cheaper, reliable and quietly glows. It gets the job done."*

Her voice in his head was comforting, although Alex was glad that he hadn't been there to witness her reaction to his note explaining that he was still intending to travel to America. Over the years he had stored away lots of snippets of their shared conversations. He reflected upon them when he needed to, and right now, like the coal fire, which he'd always preferred, he was here to get the job done.

* * * *

"Alex, wake up!"

Alex jerked, the seatbelt snapping against his chest. Brad was shaking him by the shoulder. They were still in the taxi, but it had slowed to a crawl. "Sorry, I dozed off. Where are we?"

Brad pointed at a low white building ahead, its perimeter surrounded by a tall chain link fence. "Miller Aviation Corps." He leaned forward towards the driver. "Stop just ahead. I need to show my I.D."

The driver nodded and the car inched forward towards a red-and-white striped barrier that blocked the entrance. Brad pressed a button and his rear side window slid down. A uniformed guard stepped out from a small booth next to the barrier. The tinny sound of a sports match echoed from a hidden radio.

"Hey, Jerry. Good to see you. Is that the Dodgers game?" asked Brad, fishing a laminated pass from inside his jacket and holding it out for inspection.

Jerry nodded. "Hey, Mr Anderson. Welcome back. Valenzuela's just about to pitch." He wrote something down on the clipboard clasped in one hand.

Brad grunted. "If they're playing against the Reds and the guys are running a sweepstake, put me down for twenty, would ya?"

Jerry nodded eagerly. "Sure thing, Mr Anderson." He stepped back inside the booth and pressed a button on the wall. The barrier started to rise and once it was clear, the taxi glided forward towards the parking area ahead.

Alex leaned forward in his seat, impressed by the wide gleaming building in front of him. It looked brand new. Brad paid the driver and they stepped back out into the harsh glare of the sun overhead. After collecting their luggage, they walked down the wide path that led to the front entrance, guided by low box hedging and shrubs which softened the ultra-modern minimalist feel. They passed through darkened glass doors into an air-conditioned lobby where Brad greeted the receptionist and flashed his laminated card at her. Alex was issued with a guest pass and after being assured that his luggage would be safe, he and Brad went through a set of doors that led deeper into the building. The corridors were well lit, and the beige walls reflected off the polished white floor tiles, making them appear taller than they actually were. The hollow echo of their footsteps accompanied them as they walked on, passing the occasional anonymous closed door. The only clue to what lay behind them was a numerical code stencilled in red above the top of each doorframe. It reminded Alex of a hospital where everything was antiseptically clean. It was a far cry away from the gloomy corridors of Napier-Bell Engineering, where underfoot, cracked faded linoleum marked the passage of time, since the building had originally been constructed and used as a munitions factory. Not that Alex had ever minded. History left stains, and rightfully so. There was no evidence of that here.

"Does anybody work here?" Alex asked in a low voice as they turned into yet another deserted featureless corridor.

Brad glanced at him and smiled thinly. "Sure. There's lots going on. Different levels of security. Here, we like to keep things behind closed doors. It's a state-of-the-art facility and is completely soundproofed. There's two more levels underground." Up ahead, the corridor ended in another set of doors. Brad pressed his plastic card against a black panel set into the wall and the doors buzzed. They stepped through into another smaller reception area. Sofas lined the room and a fan of magazines was spread across the top of a low coffee table. Soft pastel art hung on the walls. A smiling receptionist sat half hidden behind a pine desk, speaking into a phone.

"Yes, Mr Miller. Actually they've just arrived now. Would you like me to send them on through?" She nodded. "Of course, sir."

"Did you miss me, Martha?" asked Brad as he sauntered over to her desk and leant over it, invading her space.

Her cheeks coloured as she hastily put down the phone. "Ssh, he might hear you," she whispered fiercely, glaring at Brad. Martha smiled at Alex. "I trust you had a pleasant flight, Mr Spencer?"

"Yes, thank you," Alex replied politely.

Martha's gaze flicked back to Brad. "He's waiting for you."

Brad pushed himself off the desk and beckoned to Alex. "Time to meet the boss." He walked across the room towards a big wooden door that swung open as he approached. Brad gestured for Alex to go first.

Alex smoothed out the worst of the wrinkles creasing the front of his suit and walked into a large, well-lit, oval-shaped office. Opposite him sat a man behind a desk which appeared to be made from a single slab of honey-coloured marble. It was cantilevered at one end to give it the illusion of floating in mid-air. The surface was bare except for a telephone. The man was old. At least in his seventies, Alex guessed. He had a full head of pure white hair and pale blue eyes that appraised Alex from across the room. His weathered face was bronzed with an ingrained tan that could only have been achieved by spending many years exposed to the sun. A road map of wrinkles was chiselled into his handsome features. The man pushed back his chair and stood, wearing a warm smile that revealed bright, even, white teeth mirroring Brad's. He moved with surprising agility around the desk and stepped forward to grip Alex firmly by the hand.

"You must be Alex. I'm Frank Miller. It's a pleasure to finally meet you. I've been hearin' some great things about you guys over in the UK, ain't that right, Brad?"

"Yes, sir," said Brad, from where he was standing further back near the door.

"Please sit," said Frank, steering Alex by the elbow to the one empty chair in front of the desk. "How was your flight? All good?"

Alex nodded and lowered himself into the chair, whilst Frank perched on the edge of his desk. Alex was taken aback. He was expecting a formidable sharply dressed guy in a sombre suit. Instead, the tanned old man, with penetrating, kind eyes and a heavily lined face was wearing a blue pair of jeans with a blue denim shirt. Leather boots adorned his feet. His accent was from another part of the country. God knew where. All he needed was a cowboy hat, Alex decided. He quickly glanced around the sparse office. Above him, in the centre of the vaulted ceiling overhead, was a giant glass skylight. It was angled so that rays of sunlight poured in and illuminated the left wall of the room upon which three massive oil paintings hung, each one depicting a grand mountain range.

Frank followed Alex's gaze. "You'd never guess that I grew up in Wyoming," he said, gesturing towards the paintings. He let out a wheezy laugh.

"Are those the Rocky Mountains?" asked Alex cautiously.

Frank slapped his hands against his thighs with obvious delight. "Goddamn! What did I tell you, Brad? They sure do take their education seriously over there on the other side of the pond." He winked at Alex. "There's not many Americans who'd recognise the Rockies, let alone a Brit." Frank stood up and pointed to the wall opposite the paintings. "I've got somethin' else over there which I'm sure will interest a man like you, Alex. Come and take a look."

The other side of the room was in shadow, and there hanging low above the floor, suspended from the ceiling by two thick links of chain, was a large cylindrical piece of machinery over three meters long end to end. Alex walked slowly alongside its length, marvelling at the complicated array of pipes, tubes and vents. Parts of it were similar to jet engines he'd worked on, but this was something different altogether. "It's beautiful," he whispered.

Frank rested his hand on a metal fin. "What you're lookin' at, Alex, is a tiny segment of the propulsion system that powered the Saturn V rockets that took astronauts into space. This part came from the very one used for the Apollo 15 mission. Be my guest. Touch it."

Alex bent closer and traced his fingers lightly along a series of interconnecting slim pipes. "These are designed to carry liquid hydrogen, so this must be a part of the second or third stage of the rocket, am I correct?" He glanced up at Frank, who was watching him intently.

"Exactly right."

Alex could detect the satisfaction in Frank's reply and decided not to comment any further. He was ahead of the game and didn't want to risk making a mistake. Astronautics was a field he had only a rudimentary knowledge of.

"This is the future, Alex," said Frank, patting the metal fin. "Like Napier-Bell Engineering, we've prided ourselves here with our long history in aeronautical design and research, but you have to move with the times if you want to succeed. Agreed?"

"Of course," replied Alex, standing upright.

"Last year I set up a department to look into the viability of Miller Aviation Corps diversifyin' into astronautical research and development. It's provin' to be a very lucrative market and I want a slice of that pie." Frank leaned closer. "That's partly why you're here," he said in a stage whisper. "I wanted a fresh pair of eyes to see what we've achieved in a year, and you came highly recommended. Maybe suggest some improvements?"

"I, I...I know nothing about astronautics," spluttered Alex.

Frank smiled at Alex and nodded. "Indulge me."

Frank turned and headed back towards his desk. Alex followed. Instead of sitting, Frank stood next to the large window that took up most of the wall behind his desk. He beckoned for Alex to join him, and pointed outside. Through the glass, a large courtyard was visible, boxed in on all sides by the main building. In the centre was a barren-looking garden. Large rocks and small pruned bushes were sparsely arranged across a perfectly square bed of sand coloured gravel that had a pattern of even, undulating waves raked into it. A simple small backless bench waited in front of the middle of the far wall opposite.

"It's meant to be calming," Frank explained. "A place where the staff can take some time out. Apparently it's an exact replica of a famous garden in Kyoto." He frowned. "Brad, is that in China or Japan? I always forget."

"Japan," confirmed Brad from across the room, not missing a beat.

Frank nodded. "Personally I don't go in for any of that zen crap, but then what do I know? As long as my employees enjoy it, then that's good enough for me."

Alex was confused. First the paintings, then the engine and now the garden. Where was this leading?

Frank looked at his watch and frowned, "Where are my manners?" he muttered to himself. "Let's see, it must be nearly eleven p.m. in London." He glanced at Alex. "You must be tired. Sorry to drag you over here after your long flight and all, but I wanted to put a face to the name and see the new addition to Miller Aviation Corps. I know it's only approachin' three in the afternoon, but I think we need to get you settled. My secretary has booked you into a motel. I'm afraid it's not the Ritz, but I thought it best you stayed somewhere close by. Then next week we can look into findin' you somewhere more permanent for the months ahead. You've got the weekend to get over the jetlag and we'll meet up again Monday mornin'. Give you the tour, show you what's what." Frank held out his right hand.

Alex grasped it and shook firmly. "Thank you, Mr Miller. It's very exciting to be here, but yes, I'll admit I could do with getting some sleep."

Frank clapped his hands together. "Brad will drive you to your motel. Get you checked in. Okay with you, Brad?"

"Of course, sir," replied Brad. Alex swore he caught a flicker of irritation flash across Brad's face.

Frank nodded. "Well then, gentlemen, I'll bid you a good weekend and see you bright and sharp on Monday mornin'." He turned back around to face the window.

Alex realised he'd been dismissed and walked quickly back towards Brad. As the door swung open automatically, Frank called out his name. Alex spun around. Had he forgotten something? "Yes, Mr Miller?" he asked.

"It's just a small thing really," said Frank, still facing the window. "Seein' you've made the effort to come all this way to join our little family, I think it would be nice if we dispense with some of the formalities. From now on I want you to call me Frank. Sound good?"

"Erm…yes, certainly…Frank," Alex answered haltingly.

Frank nodded. Alex hurried after Brad who was already striding out of the waiting area, completely ignoring Martha. Alex threw her an apologetic glance.

"Your British accent seems to have done the trick. There's not many people Mr Miller allows to call him Frank." Brad scowled and cast Alex a dark glance.

They collected their luggage from reception, and exited the building. Brad led them to a corner of the parking lot and opened the boot of a car that looked twice as big as any British model. It was an ugly shade of green and had wooden panelling down the sides.

"It's my wife's car," Brad explained, his cheeks colouring.

Alex said nothing as he struggled with his bags. Ten minutes later, Brad eased out of the slow-moving traffic and swung the car around in a wide arc onto the forecourt of the Five Palms Motor Inn. Alex stared through the windscreen at the building's flat roof where a giant garish, red neon sign was advertising vacancies.

"It's only for the weekend," said Brad.

"I'm sure it will be fine," muttered Alex, as he opened the car door. It certainly was a step down from the hotel in Dartford where Brad had stayed, but Alex appreciated Frank wanting to keep him close to Miller Aviation. Trying to traverse an unfamiliar city on Monday morning would not be the best way to start his first week here.

The motel room looked tired, albeit clean. Alex couldn't conjure up another word to describe his surroundings. He commiserated, understanding how it felt, as he took stock from where he was sitting on the edge of the bed. The mattress was hard and unyielding beneath him.

"So where will you go now?" he asked Brad, who was standing in the open doorway.

"Back home to fuck my wife." Brad regarded him with what looked like pity and slowly shook his head. He jerked a thumb towards the television. "I'm sure you'll find a porn channel on cable, but you'll have to pay extra for that. You don't want Frank's secretary going through the room charges and telling Frank that he's been paying for you to jerk off all on your lonesome in here." Brad chuckled, and jiggled his car keys in one hand. "I'll leave you to make yourself at home. See you around."

Alex quelled a bubble of panic that threatened to rise up at the prospect of being left alone. Although he didn't want him to leave, and for an insane moment was going to suggest that they went for a drink, Alex remained silent as Brad stepped back outside into the parking lot. The loud drone of traffic from the nearby road was instantly muted as Brad closed the door behind him without a backward glance. A television clicked on in the room next door. Alex stared at his two oversized suitcases and considered unpacking, but couldn't muster the effort required. He lay back on the bed. *Just for one minute*, he promised himself, and awoke nine hours later, disoriented and bewildered in the early hours of the morning.

The weekend passed in a surreal blur for Alex. At times, he experienced a sense of disassociation with his surroundings which he put down to jet lag. It didn't seem real that he was actually here in another country.

That first morning as he waited patiently for daybreak, Alex had showered and dried himself using scratchy towels that were the colour of old bones. Dressed in fresh clothes, he'd ventured out and explored the streets in the surrounding area, his spirits buoyed by the warmth of the sun in a cloudless sky. He took his time, taking in the shop fronts and the people strolling past. Dotted around and lining some streets, the ever-present palm trees stood tall. He'd tried calling home several times that Saturday, using the phone in his room, but there had been no answer.

That evening, he'd eaten alone in the motel dining room, where he suspiciously prodded the meatloaf that the waitress had recommended, whilst rehearsing in his head what to say when Joanna eventually answered the phone. On Sunday morning he walked in a different direction and arrived back to his room early afternoon, his face and forearms already pink from the sun. Trepidation was starting to kick in at the prospect of tomorrow which was to be his first day at Miller Aviation Corps. Alex checked the time. It was one p.m. That meant it was nine p.m. back in England. Alex wanted to hear a reassuring voice. Danny would have school in the morning, so Joanna must be home. He sat on the bed and picked up the phone. After dialling, Alex waited patiently and was rewarded with a ringing tone. Eventually a voice answered.

"Hello?" said Joanna.

Alex closed his eyes and smiled. He could picture her sitting on the bottom steps of the stairs. "Hey," he said softly. "It's me." There was silence at the other end. "Joanna? Are you there?"

"You arrived then."

Alex paused before replying, surprised by the coolness of her tone. "Yes, I'm in a motel at the moment. It's sunny here. I just wanted to let you know that I'm all right. How's Danny? I miss you both." Again, more silence.

"As you might have guessed," began Joanna, ignoring his question, "it's been rather quiet around here the last few days, so I've had a lot of time to think. Something doesn't add up. You're a clever man, Alex. There's no way you'd rush off abroad without considering all the possibilities very carefully. And then when I tell you that Danny and I aren't coming, you don't bat an eyelid and just leave anyway."

At times Alex forgot just how intuitive Joanna was. Along with her smile, it was another of her qualities that had initially attracted her to him. The need for the sound of a familiar comforting voice dissipated and was replaced with a growing sense of unease.

"Was it really the job offer that lured you away?" she asked. "I still can't believe you went ahead and left us. Just because of work."

Alex stayed silent.

"Something happened," Joanna continued. "The few times I spoke to you last week, I could tell. You couldn't look at me for more than a couple of seconds before you had to turn away."

The line between them hissed, and occasional clicks filled the silence.

"I'm not stupid, Alex," Joanna added. "Who is she?"

Alex's shoulders sagged. He could tell a lie, but she would see straight through it. It was useless to pretend otherwise. He sighed and rubbed his eyes. "Yes, something happened," he admitted, speaking slowly. "Something that shouldn't have, and I regret it. Please believe me when I tell you that it was not planned in any way, and it'll never happen again." Joanna didn't answer. Alex carried on, eager to absolve himself and admit what he'd done in the hope that she would forgive him. "It was after that dinner last week. Remember? At the hotel? I was just leaving, and our American guest of honour, Brad, invited me up to his room for a quick drink before I came home."

"And?" prompted Joanna, after a long pause, punctuated only by the sound of her breathing, controlled and measured.

"I'd had a few drinks..." Alex began. His bottom lip trembled. He clenched his teeth before continuing. "We drank some more, and then, I don't know how...he was very charming and persuasive, but one thing led to another." The silence that followed was so protracted that Alex wasn't sure if Joanna had hung up until she spoke.

"My mother used to say that there was always something about you that she couldn't put her finger on," Joanna said, then laughed.

It used to be a sound that was music to Alex's ears, but now laced with bitterness and scorn, it was rendered discordant.

"What a stupid expression, but still, I guess she was right all along."

"I'm sorry…" began Alex.

"What have you done to us, Alex?" she yelled, interrupting him. "Your family? What do I tell your son? That his dad's a bloody poof?"

She spat the last word, and Alex jerked, recoiling away from the phone receiver. There was silence. Alex wanted to reply, but what was there to say? A maelstrom of images and accompanying sounds flashed inside his head, assaulting him with their intensity. He closed his eyes to banish them, but relentlessly they continued. The first time Joanna smiled at him across a crowded pub. Holding Daniel as a baby and rubbing his back till his cries subsided. He heard his mother's laugh and his aunt's clipped tones. They overlapped and blurred in a cacophony, only to be replaced by an image of Brad, naked and reclining on a bed amongst crumpled sheets. Brad winked at him. Alex raised a hand and brushed a couple of fingers against his lips. Shockingly, he could still recall the taste of Brad's cock in his mouth. Joanna whispered three more words, and the images flew apart like a flock of startled birds.

"Don't come back."

The line went dead. Alex froze. Eventually an automated voice echoed from the phone, asking him to replace the handset. He obeyed and set it down. Only then did he start to cry.

* * * *

October 1987

Alex hadn't realised just how painful it would be to speak about memories that were now maybe best forgotten. It had been six years since he'd last heard the sound of Joanna's voice, yet he recalled the final three words she'd spoken to him with perfect clarity. He finished the story just as they were approaching the boardwalk. Alex led the way and climbed the couple of steps up off the beach. The bench they had used earlier was still vacant. He sat down heavily with a sigh and dropped his deck shoes beside him. Luis followed suit and they began brushing off the sand that coated their feet and ankles. Most of the fine grains fell between the small gaps separating the wooden slats of the boardwalk.

"Alex," Luis began. "What you just told me...I don't know what to say. I'm so sorry."

Alex reached over and patted Luis on the arm. "You don't need to say anything. I just wanted you to know. That's all." Luis fell silent and busied himself by putting on his plimsolls. Alex finished lacing up his deck shoes and stood up. "Why don't we pop back to your place and change into something a bit smarter? Then we can go and find somewhere to have lunch."

"Sounds good," Luis replied.

They left the boardwalk for another day and walked the short distance back to the house in comfortable silence. Once they were inside and the front door was closed, Luis took Alex by the hand and without a word, led him upstairs and back into the bedroom they had both slept in last night.

He guided Alex to the centre of the room where they stood in a square of warm sunlight that spilled through the window. Facing each other, Luis reached for Alex's hands and interlaced their fingers together. "I know that the guilt over what happened to your marriage has been eating you up inside, but if you can salvage one thing, it's that we would've never met if you had carried on living a lie." He lifted their joined hands to his lips and gently kissed them. "We've both told each other things about ourselves that no one else knows because we have a mutual trust and bond that I think is very special. I'm so happy to have you in my life and I hope you'll let me become part of yours." Luis kissed their hands a second time then gently lowered them and let their fingers part.

Alex had no words with which to reply, and none were needed. Everything he wanted and had dreamt of all of his life was now standing in front of him. He couldn't imagine spending any time going forward without this beautiful man by his side. Alex brought his face closer to Luis', not wanting those brown eyes to ever look away. He moved nearer and placed his hands on either side of Luis' slim waist. Without waiting for permission, he leant forward and kissed Luis on the lips, savouring their warmth and softness. Luis responded, pressing his lips hard against Alex's. His arms encircled Alex's back and he pulled him into a tight embrace. Their mouths parted for a second before fusing back together, tongues entwined and their hands exploring the contours of each other's bodies. Alex lifted Luis' T-shirt up and slid his hand over the smooth skin underneath. His trembling fingers moved slowly upwards until they found a nipple. Alex gently squeezed it and Luis let out a soft moan.

They pawed at each other's clothing whilst kissing fervently until they were both naked. The warm sunlight caressed them with its heat as Alex pressed Luis' body against his, relishing the exquisite sensation of their hard erections rubbing against each other. Together they fell onto the bed, their limbs entangled. Alex reached down and grabbed Luis' long cock, which jutted out in a proud curve from his neatly trimmed groin. In turn, Luis caressed Alex's balls and gripped his achingly hard penis. As they pleasured each other, Alex ran his tongue over the soft cinnamon-coloured skin of Luis' neck. A residue of salt from the ocean spray clung to it and Alex eagerly licked it off. The urgency of their movements increased as they both sought release. Alex found Luis' mouth and filled it with his probing tongue just as their orgasms overtook them. Their bodies shuddered as they ejaculated, both of them crying out in unison. The sound of their harsh breathing filled the room. Luis' head fell back on the pillow.

Alex paused for a moment to enjoy the afterglow. Although the sex had been brief and hurried, for once it had not been tainted by shame or guilt. In his head, the boy under the pier, Arthur and Brad clamoured to be remembered but he banished them away. They would not ruin the sanctity of this moment. Alex lay back and turned on his side so he was facing Luis, who was wearing a serene smile with his eyes closed. Alex waited patiently for him to open them again. He was in no hurry. In fact there was nowhere else, right now, he'd rather be.

Chapter Thirteen

May 1993

"Why can't success be achieved anonymously?" muttered Alex to himself as he stepped out onto the wide balcony. The door swung shut behind him, cutting off the babble from the noisy crowd inside. He exhaled loudly and looked up. It was early evening and the sun had already set, but there were still streaks of red and orange smeared across the darkening sky. Tonight was the culmination of twelve years' hard work, and Alex had been told many times tonight by well-wishers just how happy he must be. Earlier, he'd walked onto the stage of this hotel's conference centre in downtown LA, and shaken hands with the director of the American Institute of Aeronautics and Astronautics, who'd presented him with an award. It was an ugly thing – all chrome and Perspex.

As he'd gazed out at the sea of faces, he had been hit by the truth that there was not one person in that vast room who was truly proud of his achievements. Sure, Juliette and his other employees would be pleased for him, but that fell well short of familial pride. Not that either of his parents were alive anymore. Even Luis couldn't be here tonight. He was hosting his own art exhibition down in Laguna Beach. That left only three other possible people. His ex-wife who he hadn't spoken to for twelve years, and his son Daniel, both of whom he doubted would be thrilled by his success at their expense. Only Aunt Edith, who was still sequestered away in the house he'd grown up in, still maintained a vested interest in him. After leaving the stage, he'd been swamped by the other guests who'd all wanted to congratulate him. It had taken a considerable amount of effort to wade through them all in search of a moment's respite. Alex leaned on the balustrade that ran around the edge of the balcony and gazed down into the hotel's manicured back garden. The sound of water from an ornate fountain, coupled with the breeze that was stirring the tops of nearby palm trees, calmed him. Behind him, the door opened. Alex smiled, not needing to turn around. It could be only one person.

"People are asking where you are," said Juliette, walking over to join him, her stilettos clacking against the tiles.

He turned to face her, and she handed him a flute of champagne. A demure black dress clung to her slim figure. Juliette looked every inch a movie star. She was also wearing a knowing smile that he'd seen many times before. They knew each other too well. The irony was not lost on him that, although he hadn't seen his son for twelve years, often he regarded Juliette as the daughter he'd never had.

"Sorry, I just needed some air. All those people. It was getting a bit suffocating."

"Well, tonight is meant to be all about you, which unfortunately means that you can't hide out here all night."

She was right. That didn't mean he had to enjoy it though. "It's like being at the Oscars in there. Why do the Americans insist on all that glitz and glamour? Aeronautical engineering is not very Hollywood now, is it?"

Juliette threw him an amused look. "Maybe not, but there are some important people in there who sign the really big cheques. It won't kill you to do a bit of schmoozing."

Alex groaned but allowed Juliette to guide him by the arm back across the balcony. She opened the smoked glass door, and the cacophony of voices buffeted them both causing Alex to take an involuntary step back. Juliette tightened her grip on his arm.

Alex leaned closer to whisper in her ear. "Don't worry, I'm fine. Let's do this. Just stay close. You're far better at this sort of thing than I am."

He walked through the doorway and immediately someone called out his name. Alex conjured up a winning smile. The door closed behind them as they stepped forward and into the fray.

* * * *

The midnight-blue Mercedes-Benz emerged from the hotel's underground car park and eased out into the evening traffic. Even after all these years, Alex still couldn't get used to the sheer number of cars on the roads in LA, not just during the day, but at night too.

New York wasn't the only city that never slept. He didn't mind. There was no rush. Tomorrow morning he would drive down to Laguna Beach to spend the weekend with Luis. Alex couldn't wait to show him the ugly award he'd been presented with. He glanced down at the monstrosity lolling heavily on the passenger seat. Since his aesthetics were drawn from nature, it was doubtful that Luis would allow it in the house.

The traffic thinned as he hit the freeway. Alex reached forward and pressed a button. Above his head, the roof of the car folded back, exposing him to the evening air. Depending on the wind, sometimes he could smell the ocean, but tonight the hot, dry, Santa Ana winds carried down a myriad of scents from the mountains mixed with the ever-present odour of asphalt and traffic fumes. Alex took the off ramp and followed signs leading him towards home in Calabasas. The residential streets were his favourite to drive along. There one would find a jarring mish-mash of architectural styles abutting each other. Beautiful gardens either showcased or shrouded the houses they grew around, often displaying a sea of different colours, including his favourite, the red and purple varieties of bougainvillea.

There was one flower that always reminded him of his early days in Los Angeles. In those first few months, he'd been amazed at how prevalent it was, and even now, as he drove down the street towards his house, he could detect the cloying, pervading smell of jasmine in the air. Alex turned into his driveway and parked. He sat there for a moment, relishing the sound of a light breeze blowing through the tops of the shade trees behind him lining the street. Soft clicks emanated from the car engine as it cooled. Inside, the house was dark and still. Alex placed the award next to the front door so he wouldn't forget it in the morning. It would make a good door stop. After scooping up the mail, he carried on through to the kitchen and set it down on the white marble countertop. Ruminating on his old life and the new was nothing unusual. Rattling around an empty house usually meant that Alex only ever had his own thoughts for company. And that was fine. He'd been in this house for six years now and whenever Alex cast his mind back to that first year here in LA, he would never have imagined living somewhere like this. Alex had Frank Miller to thank for that. Good old Frank. They'd only worked together for three years but Alex still missed him every day. Like the tired old cliché, Alex now considered Frank as the father he'd never really had.

* * * *

March 1981

On his first day at Miller Aviation, Frank proudly gave him a tour of the facilities and introduced Alex to a number of the different teams that he was going to be working with. After that, Frank faded from view, leaving Alex to fend for himself.

Unfazed, Alex worked long hours and studied late into the night, trying to make some headway in fields he was unfamiliar with. He rented a duplex within walking distance of work and each evening, after unsuccessfully attempting to call home, he would tour the local restaurants in his neighbourhood on foot, sampling from cuisines he'd never tried before.

Looking back, Alex was amazed that he hadn't put on any weight during that period. One thing he would never forget was the encroaching worry that occupied him at the beginning of the fifth of the six months he was due to be working there.

When he discovered that the home phone number no longer worked, in desperation, he wrote Joanna a letter. The weeks passed with no reply, so it came as a surprise when one of the receptionists at Miller Aviation handed him a letter addressed to him. It could only have come from one person, but he was proved wrong.

The formal dispassionate tone worded by the solicitors informed him that Joanna had made an application for divorce based on the grounds of unreasonable behaviour. At least she had saved them the embarrassment of going through a divorce because of adultery, although Alex wasn't sure if that was legally an option because technically he had been unfaithful with another man and not a woman. Alex was torn about what to do when his six-month job placement finished. Napier-Bell Engineering had kept his job open, ready for his return, but if the letter was anything to go by, he would not be welcome back at the family home.

At the time, Alex didn't realise how painfully transparent his emotions were, even though he regarded himself as a proudly repressed Englishman. Looking back, he was grateful that people had gossiped. Word got out that something was wrong and one evening he answered a knock on his duplex door and found Frank standing there.

Alex could still recall Frank's voice and that unmistakable Wyoming accent. "So, when were you thinkin' of tellin' me what's goin' on with you? And don't give me any of that English horseshit that you're fine."

After inviting Frank in, Alex tried to make him welcome, but Frank wouldn't even sit until Alex had "spilled the beans." It didn't take long for Alex to wither under Frank's glare and tell him everything, although he omitted to mention what had happened in Brad's hotel room. Afterwards, Frank didn't say a word. He slowly paced up and down, occasionally muttering under his breath until he stopped and turned to ask Alex a question.

"What do you want?" Frank asked.

It was a simple enough question, but designed to cut through all the crap. The only realistic option left for Alex was to return to England with his tail between his legs and carry on working for Napier-Bell Engineering, hoping that the courts would allow him to occasionally see Daniel. Alex then admitted to Frank that since arriving in LA, he'd thrived on being tested to the limits of his abilities, and he wanted to carry on pushing the boundaries of the research he'd been doing at Miller Aviation.

"Without my work, I'm nothing," he confessed to Frank.

It had been uttered as a dejected admission of failure and self-loathing, yet Frank gave him a sharp penetrating look before announcing that he had to go as there was somewhere he needed to be. At the front door, Frank instructed Alex to be outside his office at nine a.m. the following morning, then he'd left without another word. To say that his life changed the next day would've been a frivolous understatement. In fact Alex likened it to being reborn. Waiting for him on Frank's desk was a contract.

Frank explained that after he'd left Alex's duplex the previous evening he had made a few phone calls. It transpired that Frank knew a lot of important people. They'd assured him that because Alex possessed certain unique skills in an important area of research, this would almost certainly guarantee an extension of his visa and fast-track his application for a green card and permanent residency in the United States, if he so wanted. The contract offered him a full-time job at Miller Aviation Corps with a salary double that of Napier-Bell Engineering and also included a company car. Alex admitted, shamefaced, to an incredulous Frank, that he didn't know how to drive and by the end of the day, Frank's secretary had booked him a bunch of lessons at a local driving school, all paid for. He looked up at Frank to ask him why he was going to all this trouble and expense for someone he barely knew.

Without hesitating, Frank replied, "I've never been a gamblin' man Alex, but I know a good thing when I see it. Now it's up to you to prove that I'm right."

The guilt wasn't immediate after he'd made the decision to sign the contract then and there. *When someone throws you a life line, you tend to grab it with both hands. There's plenty of time to consider the implications afterwards.*

The first year was the worst. He considered flying straight back after Joanna had told him not to return, but for what? He doubted she would let him see Daniel, and Joanna obviously didn't want any contact with him either. Alex had called home every evening after his last conversation with her, but the phone always went unanswered. When the number was no longer recognised, he'd considered phoning Aunt Edith for news of his family, but couldn't bear the prospect of hearing her disapproving tone as she lamented his actions.

Luckily, after he'd signed the contract, things had settled down. Alex let the solicitors back in England sort everything out. He didn't contest the divorce and offered to put the house in her name whilst continuing to pay the mortgage as well as child support, in the vain hope that one day it would count for something. After that, there was no further contact until two years later, when an envelope arrived with a short note inside instructing him to stop sending letters to Daniel. There was a concession that he could continue sending him birthday and Christmas cards. A change of address had been scribbled underneath. She hadn't even signed it but he'd recognised her handwriting.

At least Aunt Edith hadn't severed all contact, which was something. Alex still wrote to her two or three times a year and she would always eventually reply, her handwriting becoming more spidery as the years passed. She had to be in her early eighties by now. The tone of her letters was as ever, formal and distant, yet because Aunt Edith had invested so much into Alex's education whilst instilling in him a hunger to succeed, Alex could always detect unspoken pride woven into her carefully worded replies whenever he sent her news of how well he was doing. Aunt Edith never mentioned Joanna or Daniel to him again and Alex suspected she was still deeply disappointed in him for the way things turned out. He hoped that she'd stayed in contact with them, but never asked her outright.

It was soon after his second year of living in Los Angeles that Alex was introduced to Juliette. Brad returned from one of his talent-scouting trips abroad accompanied by the Swiss-born woman. Although she was only visiting for a month, her brilliant mind caught Frank's eye and he made her an offer to join Alex's team that she couldn't refuse. As the only other European working there, Alex bonded with Juliette right from the start. What particularly attracted him to her was the disparaging way she spoke whenever anyone referred to Brad. It led him to suspect that Brad had been unsuccessful in using his charms to woo Juliette into bed.

His third year passed in a flurry of successful projects. The only time Alex ever came up for air back then was in the early evenings when he left Miller Aviation bound for home. With the freedom that came with finally being able to drive a car, he used to take long circuitous routes to familiarise himself with the layout of Los Angeles and to discover new restaurants where he would dine alone most nights. That third year was also a time when, yet again, without warning, everything changed. Alex still regarded Frank's illness as one of life's cruel jokes. The punch line was that Frank died, and nobody laughed.

Three years, mused Alex. *Does one-thousand-and-ninety-five-days sound longer instead? Whatever.* That was how long he'd known Frank. The man who'd saved him when his world had fallen apart. The man whose final act had been to hand Alex something so precious, enabling him to carry on the work that they were both so passionate about.

* * * *

September 1984

It was the sheer expanse of the view in front of him that Alex found so overwhelming. He couldn't remember a time when he had ever looked out over such a vast amount of land. Alex stood there transfixed, his hands resting on the railing that ran around the perimeter of the terrace. Directly below him was a huge pond surrounded by bulrushes, its mirrored surface reflecting the cotton-ball clouds above. Beyond it was a vast plain, peppered with brush and grasses that stretched off into the distance. To the west, the land disappeared, swallowed by large dense forests. The horizon was dominated by a range of mountains whose immensity and grandeur could not be ignored.

A familiar voice called out. "Room for one more?"

Alex turned around. Frank waved from the rear door of the ranch. Alex beckoned for Frank to join him. Although not as stunning as the view, Frank's ranch was impressive. It was a sprawling two-storey red-painted wooden structure that had housed many generations of his family over the years. Alex now understood why Frank preferred it here in Wyoming instead of Los Angeles. He still couldn't believe that Frank, out of the blue, had invited him to stay for a long weekend to celebrate the Labor Day holiday. It had been an even bigger surprise to discover that apart from Frank's family, he was the only guest. Alex turned back to the view. He wanted Frank to retain his dignity as he made his way unsteadily across the paved terrace. In the six months since the cancer diagnosis, Frank had lost an alarming amount of weight and also aged visibly. Now though he was unsteady on his feet and his body was frail, he would still angrily rebuff anyone who tried to assist him.

"Pretty impressive, huh?" asked Frank, as he drew level with Alex and grasped the railing for support. He gestured towards the mountains with his gnarled wooden walking stick.

"I've never seen anything like it," Alex replied.

Frank grunted and tapped Alex's leg with his stick. "Let's walk a bit." He shuffled over to a wide set of steps and together they slowly descended down to a well-worn path that circled the pond.

"You're probably still wonderin' why I invited you here," began Frank, not waiting for an answer. "Well, you know for sure how much I enjoy our time together outside of the office and this weekend is testament to that. But there was another reason, which is that I wanted to give you somethin'. I know that I don't have much time left, so I've started getting my affairs in order."

Alex glanced at Frank, whose eyes were firmly fixed on his own feet as they moved slowly along the path.

"Over the past three years, I've admired your work ethic," Frank continued. "Take that lummox Brad, for example. Somehow he's become successful mainly because of his charm and good looks. Don't get me wrong—he's no idiot, or he wouldn't be working for Miller Aviation. But people like him, they don't fool me. You, on the other hand, you quietly get on with it and come up with the actual goods, which is what I like. Plus you're already taking my company in new directions. None of my daughters were ever interested in joinin'. All they want to do is spend the profits." Frank struck out at a weed with his walking stick, clipping the head clean off. "I'll be gone soon, and my firm is too large for me to pass it over to you. Even in a buy-out, you couldn't raise anywhere near the funds needed." Frank shrugged. "I guess this is what happens when you're too successful." He laughed and broke into a hacking coughing fit. Alex moved over to help but Frank waved him away as he hawked something up into his mouth which he spat out onto the ground. "Sorry 'bout that."

Alex waited as Frank composed himself. "You were talking about what will happen to your company," prompted Alex as they walked on.

"Ah yes, of course," said Frank. "Well, the family will fall on it like vultures and pick it apart, that's for sure." He cackled briefly. "Before that happens though, I want you to have the one thing that I prize the most. There's no one shrewd enough in my family to realise just how much it's worth. So what they don't see, they won't miss."

Alex looked questioningly at Frank, who glanced back at him with a gleam in his eyes, still wearing his best movie star grin.

"Experience," Frank whispered, tapping a finger against the side of his head. "My staff. Take the best I've got, and start up your own company. They'll go with you with my blessing. Make somethin' of yourself, my boy. Become who you were meant to be. Carry on my dream and turn it into yours."

Alex stopped in his tracks and stared at Frank who was regarding him shrewdly. "Are you serious?"

Frank nodded. "Think you're up to it?"

Alex was astounded. "That's a genius idea. I don't know what to say."

"Well, yes would be a good start." Frank cackled again and reached up to drape his arm across Alex's shoulders. He steered him around so that they were both facing towards the ranch. "C'mon, let's head back. I've got a bottle of somethin' chillin' in my study that you might like. Then we can discuss things in more detail."

Alex allowed himself to be shepherded away, only half listening as Frank talked animatedly about the brand-new Marlborough Sauvignon blanc he'd recently discovered.

* * * *

May 1993

He wished he'd had another chance to visit the ranch again, even if it was just to pay his respects one last time. Frank had died a couple of months after Labor Day and the family had insisted on a private funeral. Apparently he'd been buried somewhere near the back of the ranch facing the mountains that Frank had loved all his life. Even though nine years had now passed, Alex was sure that the view from the back of the ranch hadn't changed at all. As Frank had predicted, immediately after his death, his family had sold the company. Sadly, dollars were more important to them than an old man's legacy. Alex still had nothing but admiration for Frank's foresight. Would he have had the presence of mind back then, after Frank had died, to assemble the best of his workforce and start a new company? He very much doubted it.

Thanks to people like Juliette, his new company had flourished from the outset, and three years later he'd become rich enough to buy this property. After helping himself to a glass of chilled white Sancerre, Alex took the small flight of stairs down to the cavernous, vaulted living room with its long sofas and grand fireplace. Automatic soft lighting clicked on, bathing the space with a muted glow. He drifted about the room, checking that everything was as it should be. There was no dust marring the glass top of the driftwood coffee table and the polished antique brass coal scuttle gleamed brightly. Alex admired Luis' painting hanging above the mantelpiece as he had done countless times before. Companion pieces graced the other walls of the room, gifts from Luis over the years. He smiled, remembering the look of amazement on Luis' face when he'd revealed his first art purchase. Yet another moment that had brought them closer.

Alex turned away. It was too nice an evening to sit inside, and anyway, this room was designed more for entertaining than relaxing. He folded back the glass doors that separated the lounge from the garden and stepped outside beneath a wooden pergola where he set his glass down on a small wrought-iron table. Apart from the pool lighting that suffused up through the water from below, the garden was dim. The shadowy outlines of the tall trees that lined its perimeter stood out against the darkening sky. There were hidden spotlights that Alex could've turned on, but he preferred it like this. He pulled out a wicker chair from under the table and sat, taking a moment to appreciate the heady scent coming from the jasmine that had climbed up the sides of the pergola and along the wooden beams overhead, where hundreds of white flowers now hung. Planting it had been one of the first things he'd done after moving in so that even whilst relaxing and enjoying the opulence of the house and garden, the scent would remind him of his first panicked six months in Los Angeles and everything that he had abandoned back home. He viewed it as a less painful form of self-flagellation. Alex took a sip from the glass, and let out a little murmur of appreciation at the citrus notes of the wine. There was something else there. Possibly mineral based? *Maybe the taste you'd get from licking a stone*, he mused.

Frank had introduced Alex to a few wines he'd never encountered before — something else they'd had in common. What had surprised Alex was that although Frank had been a staunch patriot, he'd held American wine in low regard and sneered at any bottle that didn't herald from Europe.

Alex still found it strange and rather miraculous that through the twists and turns of his life he had ended up here. Was it blind luck, either good or bad depending on how you looked at it, or just fate alone that had guided his steps along this path? He'd never know.

Alex picked up his wine glass and raised it to the sky in salutation. "Here's to you, Frank. By rights, that ugly award should have your name on it."

Overhead, stars pinpricked the clear dark sky, which was marred with a criss-cross of old contrails from passing planes. The wind, high above, had widened the lines and blown them crooked, their white edges now blurred and indistinct.

Alex sat back down and toyed with the rim of the wine glass and stared at the pale yellowy wine within. "Twelve years," he murmured aloud and shook his head with disbelief. Christ, he was now fifty-three years old. Where had the time gone? Alex smirked. The answer was obvious. He'd buried himself in work — as usual.

The phone rang, jarring him from his reverie. He pushed back his chair, which scraped across the terracotta tiles, and hurried inside to the kitchen. He snatched up the phone mid-ring.

"Hello?"

"Hey, it's me, how did it go?"

Alex smiled. Somehow just the sound of Luis' voice made everything all right again. "I got through it. Let's leave it at that." On the other end of the phone, Luis chuckled. "What about you though?" Alex asked. "Was the exhibition a success?"

"Mmm-hmm, there was a good turnout. A couple of magazines sent some people, so I'll have a better idea once the reviews are published."

"They'll all be singing your praises, you'll see. Did you sell any pieces?" asked Alex.

"Mmm, one or two."

Alex smiled to himself again. Luis always downplayed his success. One or two sold probably meant that every piece on display had been snapped up. "Are we still on for tomorrow? I was planning to get to yours early. Say nine a.m.? So we have the whole weekend together."

"Sounds good. I'll make croissants and we can have breakfast in the garden. Look, I'd better go, I'm still at the exhibition and I need to say goodbye to a few people. I just phoned to make sure that you actually turned up to your own award ceremony."

Alex laughed. "You know me too well. We can catch up properly tomorrow. See you in the morning."

Luis blew him an audible kiss down the phone. "Bye, Alex."

"Bye." Alex hung up and stood there for a moment.

He hated that sometimes he was too cowardly to return Luis' displays of affection. Admitting he was gay had been hard enough, but he was not yet comfortable with showing any signs of his love for Luis in public. No one at work knew except Juliette, and Luis had quickly learnt and accepted that any attempt to display closeness, such as the one time he'd tried to hold Alex's hand in a supermarket, were quickly rebuffed. Still, he was getting better and Luis was patient and understanding. After all, they'd known each other for six years now and even if their relationship had no official title, he liked the way it was going. What Alex found disconcerting was that he'd been attracted to Luis right from the start, but in a way that had never happened before. Over the years he had secretly appreciated many handsome men, but always in an abstract superficial way. They would possess the usual alluring physical attributes, such as an easy smile or pert buttocks hidden frustratingly behind an opaque veil of fabric. Something to admire briefly before he moved on. Luis, though, had displayed far more important subtleties such as his quiet air of confidence and a softly spoken extensive vocabulary, coupled with his polite demeanour which made him stand out amongst others. Being with him completed Alex in a way he didn't understand. Maybe Luis exuded a resonance, or vibration, or whatever the fuck people called it? Even in the early days whenever they were together, it was as if they were old friends who'd met up after years apart, instantly comfortable in each other's presence because time had no relevance when two people were naturally attuned to each other.

God, he was getting old. He could remember the time when the first thing that had attracted him to Brad was the bulge in his crotch. And look where that had gotten him. Alex groaned out loud. Sometimes his proclivity for introspection was wearing. Before going back outside to finish his wine, Alex flipped through the small pile of mail, most of it junk. Towards the bottom was a letter marked with an air-mail stamp. His name and address had been written by a hand he didn't recognise. Intrigued, he examined the English postmark closely. It hadn't been posted from anywhere familiar. He tore the top off the envelope. Inside were some folded pages. Alex pulled them out and opened them. He only managed to read the first two words before his vision blurred and a strangled sound — something between a moan and a sob — escaped from his mouth. Alex furiously wiped away the tears that welled in his eyes.

"It can't be," he said in disbelief as he gripped the sides of the letter with both hands, the pages creasing, and reread the opening two words over and over again.

Dear Dad...

Sign up for our newsletter and find out about all our romance book releases, eBook sales and promotions, sneak peeks and FREE romance books!

Want to see more like this?
Here's a taster for you to enjoy!

Noir Nights: A Valentine to Die For
Aver Rigsly

Excerpt

February 1954.
New York City.

"Mrs. Banks…this is going to be hard to hear."

"What exactly are you telling me, Mr. Morris?"

Ricky's head was pounding, right behind his eyes and down the back of his neck. A full-blown shit-show of a hangover. He took a last puff of his cigarette and smooshed the butt of it out in the ashtray.

"I'm sorry to say, but it's what you were afraid of."

"I knew it," she snapped, her ruby-painted lips pursed tight. "I just knew it."

"Unfortunately, I have photo evidence here of your husband, on multiple occasions, visiting, let's say…some of the less savory parts of the city, ma'am."

He reached into the top drawer of his desk, plucked out a glossy photograph and slid it across for Mrs. Banks to inspect.

"And who is she? Who is the whore?"

"Actually, there are *three* different broads here." He pulled out a couple more photos, a short stack of four-by-five gelatin silver prints that he had developed himself in his makeshift darkroom. He laid the photos out, candid shots of Mr. Banks in his snazzy Buick Roadmaster, ladies hanging in through the passenger-side window, sitting beside him in the car, *kissing* the side of Mr. Banks' thick neck — and those were just the photos that were considered decent compared to the others processing down the hall.

"I should have goddamn known. Theo is a *fucking pig* and always has been."

Ricky raised his eyebrows but kept his cool, nodding to make her feel better. That was just Mrs. Banks — that sharp tongue of hers was very unladylike, no matter how expensive her silk pantyhose and real mink coat were, or how many strands of pearls she looped over her hand-tailored housedress.

Regardless, she wasn't wrong about Mr. Banks. Ricky had spent the last week tailing Theodore Banks around the Financial District. Theo was a man who knew how to make dough. A pencil-pushing broker, Banks was the perfect example of a man whose money didn't buy happiness. His wife was half his age — a stunning doll in her own right — and Ricky had noticed the moment they'd met how well she presented herself. She was a real looker of a dame, but Theo had a wandering eye and a penchant for not keeping his prick in his pants.

It was sort of pathetic how easy it had been to track him down and snap the photos of him getting a messy blow job in the front seat of his Buick. The fella had hardly lasted more than five minutes. Ricky did not envy Mrs. Banks, the poor woman, considering what she must deal with in the marital bed.

"What the hell am I supposed to do now?" she asked, digging into her handbag and rummaging around before pulling out a sleek chrome cigarette case.

She popped the clasp and pulled out a menthol from the red velvet-lined inside. Her hands were shaking.

"Here, let me." Ricky stood and leaned over the desk, offering her a light from his silver Zippo. Her red lips wrapped around the end of the cigarette and smoke curled up as she took the first few puffs.

"Thank you," she said.

"Of course, and, Mrs. Banks? As for the…delicate predicament you find yourself in…"

"Yes?"

"As I see it, your best course of action would be to pursue a legal divorce."

"Divorce? Like hire a lawyer?"

"That would be what I would do in your position, ma'am. You've suffered long and hard from a husband who is not only an adulterer, but who has also been recklessly spending your household income on lewd, and may I add, *illegal* activities."

"Well, yes. Who knows how much money he's thrown away on those filthy prostitutes?"

"Exactly, ma'am. May I ask, Mrs. Banks, is your name also on all your husband's accounts?"

"Yes…"

"Well, I'm certain that if you ask a bank teller to show you all withdrawal statements for the past few months, you will see quite a bit of cash being removed. I could even give you the dates that all these photographs were taken, which I suspect would match the same dates of the withdrawals. On top of *that*," Ricky said, hardly feeling the pounding headache as he played his role of charming confidant, "while these photos here might be argued against and possibly dismissed by the right defender in a court of law, I have in my possession downright *illicit* photographs that would be impossible to sweep under the rug. The more proof of the wrongdoing built against the accused, the better chance the court will grant you a larger portion of your husband's estate."

"Is that so?" Her cigarette smoldered forgotten between her fingers, her hands no longer shaking.

"Yes, indeed. Between the photos I have and any bank statements showing the frivolous spending, you could make out with quite a pretty penny, Mrs. Banks. More than enough, I'd say, to keep a lady such as yourself very comfortable."

"At least until I find a second husband," she quipped. "I can't help but notice that you aren't wearing a wedding band, Mr. Morris. Are you single? Or maybe that quiet blonde girl at the door is your girlfriend?"

"You mean Liz? No, she's just my secretary and close friend. And I have never been interested in marriage. I'm a simple bachelor and I enjoy it that way."

"Such a shame," she said. "So, what do I owe you? For your services, and for those *other* photographs you mentioned. I would very much like to purchase those as well."

"In my line of work as a private investigator, I am often the bearer of bad news, and I feel terrible for your hardship, ma'am, so I'll give you a courtesy discount. It would be my honor. How about we call it…eight hundred and fifty for everything, and I'll be happy to have done business with you, Mrs. Banks."

"Do you accept traveler's checks?"

"Of course, ma'am."

"Splendid." She dug around in her handbag again, and Ricky leaned back in his chair. He lit a new cigarette, pleased with himself. Tonight, he was going to order a juicy steak dinner with all the fixings and a hefty glass of whiskey to go along with it. Jobs like these were perfect for milking desperate housewives. Show them a few pictures of their sleazy asshole husbands, and they turned to putty in his hands. Gold-diggers like Mrs. Banks were the best kind of all—all too eager to spend their husband's money.

She handed over the checks, almost nine-hundred-bucks' worth, and Ricky tucked them safely into his desk drawer.

"Much thanks indeed, ma'am."

"Thank you, Mr. Morris. I will be sure to mention your name if any of my friends need similar help."

"That's all I can ask for, ma'am. You know where to send them. My door is always open to those in need."

If they had the green for it. *Simple as that.*

About the Author

Tom Crampton lives in the Georgian city of Bath in England, with his husband Charlie, and over 60 assorted houseplants. He first started writing during the Covid pandemic. *A Different Corner* is his first novel.

Tom loves to hear from readers. You can find his contact information, website details and author profile page at https://www.firstforromance.com

ENTWINED PUBLISHING